Even be[...]
exclaim[...]

As I stepped out onto the front porch, I followed his "What in the world?" with a "Shoot and bother!"

Sticking up out of a snowbank were two unmoving legs encased in red velvet and black boots. Amos was standing a few feet from the bizarre scene with his mouth hanging open. "J–jumpin' Jehoshaphat, Ivy," he stuttered, "I think we just killed Santa Claus!"

Other mysteries by Nancy Mehl

In the Dead of Winter
Bye Bye Bertie
For Whom the Wedding Bell Tolls

There Goes Santa Claus

An Ivy Towers Mystery

Nancy Mehl

HEARTSONG
PRESENTS
MYSTERIES

Dedication:
To J.M., who taught me that "feelings buried alive never die." You've changed my life.

My thanks to:
Deputy Sheriff Robert P. (Pat) Taylor. Thank you for keeping Amos honest. Gail Martin for the use of her wonderful Christmas play. Mark F. Hansen, Ph.D., Extension Specialist Emeritus, Michigan State University. Thank you for your heart for farmers and for making me rethink my plot. Darrin W. Figgins, funeral director and embalmer for Garnand Funeral Home in Ulysses, Kansas. Donn Teske, President, Kansas Farmers Union. Travis Calvert with Plastic-Mart.com, who educated me about transfer tanks. My wonderful readers Kim Woodhouse and Faye Spieker. You're the best! My super agent, Janet Benrey, and my wonderful editors, Susan Downs and Candice Speare. Norman and Danny. You guys hold my heart. And, of course, to the One who loves me most. Thank You for being good—all the time.

ISBN 978-1-60260-289-2

Scripture taken from the HOLY BIBLE, NEW INTERNATIONAL VERSION®. NIV®. Copyright © 1973, 1978, 1984 by International Bible Society. Used by permission of Zondervan. All rights reserved.

Scripture taken from the NEW REVISED STANDARD VERSION BIBLE, copyright © 1989, Division of Christian Education of the National Council of the Churches of Christ in the United States of America. Used by permission. All rights reserved.

All of the characters and events in this book are fictitious. Any resemblance to actual persons, living or dead, or to actual events is purely coincidental.

Cover design: Kirk DouPonce, DogEared Design
Cover illustration: Jody Williams

Our mission is to publish and distribute inspirational products offering exceptional value and biblical encouragement to the masses.

Printed in the U.S.A.

1

It's not often a human being is given the chance to save a fallen angel. I pulled my late great-aunt's ceramic angel from one of the lower boughs of our Christmas tree. Then I straightened up, grabbed the side of the ladder, and tried once again to fasten the ornament to the top of the giant Scotch pine that reached almost to the ceiling in our living room. This time I was successful, and the rescued cherub safely stared down at the floor below her where she had almost plummeted to her early demise.

"Maybe you should have let me do that." Amos held the rickety ladder while I gingerly climbed down.

"I think not." I took the last step and breathed a sigh of relief. Watching Aunt Bitty's prized Christmas tree topper shatter into dust wasn't one of my Christmas wishes. "You've already broken three ornaments. You're permanently off ornament detail."

"Wasn't my fault," he grumbled. "Pal thought I was playing ball with him and knocked them out of my hand."

Our small black and white Border collie stared morosely from the couch where he'd been banished. His head hung over the side of the cushion, and his chocolate eyes were pools of abject misery. Yet every time we looked toward him, his tail would thump loudly against the fabric. He was aware that a line had been crossed but that punishment wouldn't last long. We were too tenderhearted, and he was confident in his ability to wrap us around his furry white paw. As soon as I plopped down on the couch, he scooted up next to me. When I stroked his silky head, he rolled over on his back, his tongue hanging from the side of his mouth. It was Pal's way of letting us know that a good tummy scratching would be appreciated. Of course, I complied.

From the chair across the room, Miss Skiffins, our tiny calico cat, looked disdainfully at her doggy brother who was caught up in the throes of tummy-rubbing bliss. Obviously not amused by his uncouth actions, she rested her head on her front paws, trying to look as dignified as possible. Although she treated Pal like an undisciplined sibling who embarrassed her on a regular basis, the truth was, she absolutely adored him. She loved to curl up next to him and sleep, and wherever he went, she followed.

Amos folded the ladder and leaned it against the wall. Then he sat down on the floor and plugged in the extension cord connected to the lights. The tiny white bulbs blazed forth, turning our beautifully decorated tree into something breathtaking. Even Pal lifted his head in appreciation.

"Wow," was all I could say.

Amos came over and sat down on the couch between Pal and me. "It's perfect. I'm glad you had all those ornaments—otherwise we would have had to buy those goofy round balls they sell at the five-and-dime in Hugoton."

I grabbed his hand and held it. "We're certainly not lacking decorations. Between what Bitty left and what Mom and Dad gave me before they went to China, we have more than we can use."

"Sorry I couldn't contribute." Amos let go of my hand and put his arm around me. "My parents didn't put much effort into Christmas. Most years we didn't even have a tree."

I reached up and pulled his face toward mine. "Those days are over, bub. You are now married to the queen of Christmas." I kissed him and brushed a lock of honey blond hair away from his hazel eyes. "I'm giving you some grace since this is our first Christmas together as man and wife, but next year, the tree goes up right after Thanksgiving. Not the week before Christmas."

He grinned. "Sorry again, Your Majesty. I'm trying to get all these new traditions down. I thought you were kidding about putting the tree up the day after I'd stuffed myself with turkey. I was still in a turkey coma. It turns everything your wife says into gobbler gook."

I laughed. "You mean gobbledygook?"

"I think my translation says it better." He closed his eyes and smiled. "You're a turkey master, my dear. I can still taste it."

"You can thank Aunt Bitty for that."

Bitty's turkey recipe hadn't let me down. Dinner was great, and the main course was scrumptious. The only thing missing was Bitty Flanagan herself. Although it had been a little over two years since she'd been murdered in her bookstore, I still missed her every day.

However, the wisdom she left behind was my constant companion. I tried to emulate her as much as I could, but my penchant for impatience and undue curiosity still landed me in hot water from time to time.

"Too bad your parents can't make it here for the holidays," Amos said. "I know you'll miss them."

My parents were in China, running a mission. They'd come to Winter Break for my wedding in February, but it wasn't possible for them to leave their work right now. China was experiencing a spiritual awakening. It was exciting yet challenging, because with revival came persecution. Several foreign missionaries and Christian businesspeople had recently been expelled from the country. I could only wonder if my parents would be next.

I nodded. "Yes, I will. But spending our first Christmas together as man and wife is really special. That makes up for it."

He grinned. "I hardly think we'll be lonely. How many people are coming for Christmas dinner at last count?"

"Well, there's Dewey, of course. And Isaac and Alma. Oh, and Hope Hartwell. Elmer. And Barney Shackleford. This will be his first Christmas without Dela."

"I figured he'd go to Dodge City. They both had family there."

"That's true. But most of them are Dela's, and they haven't been very nice to Barney since she died. I think they had their eyes on Dela's jewelry collection, thinking he would just hand it over. When he didn't, they turned on him. I'm glad he's happy here, and I'm thrilled he accepted my invitation for dinner. I hope we can help him make it through the day without missing Dela too much."

"I think being in the Christmas play will distract him, too. Emily told me he's taking Ferd's role."

Ferd Baumgartner, Emily's uncle, had played shepherd number three for forty years. His death in April left the part open. Barney had been happy to step in.

"Well, it's not like these folks had nowhere else to go on Christmas Day," Amos said. "Ruby puts on a huge dinner at the Redbird Café every year."

I snuggled up closer to him. "I know, but it's not the same as being with a real family at Christmas. There's something wonderful about sharing your home and table with good friends."

He kissed the top of my head. "I never experienced that until I married you. This is the first real family I've ever had."

"Speaking of family, did you call your dad?"

I could feel Amos's body stiffen. Even though his father had come for our wedding, there was still animosity between them. After spending years apart because of Aaron's drinking, repairing their relationship was proving harder than I'd imagined. They had both reached out to each other, but not with open arms. Amos still resented his dad for his abusive behavior toward him and his mother when he was a child. He was even angrier that his father had left when Amos was only nine years old. Things only got worse when Amos went to live with him as a teenager. His mother decided to leave town with her new boyfriend, and Amos got the very clear message that he would only be in the way. Feeling that he had no other option, and believing that he and I had no future because I had decided to go to college in Wichita, he headed to Oklahoma where his father lived. He'd hoped that since so much time had passed, things would be different. But his father was still drinking, and his uncontrolled temper and physical attacks finally broke whatever hope Amos held of restoring their relationship. Amos came back to Winter Break, where he felt accepted, and had been here ever since. When we got engaged, Amos decided to reach out once more to his dad because he felt that continuing to harbor resentment might interfere with his relationship with me. But even now, although Aaron had been sober for almost three years, there was still a wall that divided them.

"I called him, but he wasn't sure he could come. I guess he has something better to do."

"Nonsense," I said. "You know he's all alone in Oklahoma. Did you make certain he knew we really wanted him?"

Amos pulled away from me and stood up. "For crying out loud, Ivy, I didn't beg him to spend Christmas here. I simply told him he was welcome to come. What more did you want me to do?"

I didn't answer since I knew he wasn't really asking for a response. "Why don't I make us both a cup of hot chocolate, and we can stare at the tree for a few more minutes before we go to bed?" Amos went over and pretended to be adjusting some of the branches. I knew it was a ruse. I also knew it was time to change the subject.

I barely heard him mumble, "Okay."

I went to the kitchen, took the chocolate syrup out of the refrigerator, and squirted it into a couple of cups. I'd call Aaron myself and invite him to come for Christmas. Maybe if I paved the way, he'd feel more welcome. I was aware that he carried a lot of guilt over his past treatment of Amos and his mother, and he wasn't sure he had the right to be involved in his son's life now. My concern was that until both men could put the past behind them, neither one of them would be emotionally healthy.

After pouring in the milk, I popped both cups in the microwave. Then I called Pal and led him to the French doors in the dining room. Almost the entire wall was glass, including the doors. The view looked out over our back deck and onto Lake Winter Break, a small lake named after our town of a little more than six hundred people. Amos had raised the yellow flag on the pole next to the lake, indicating that the water was frozen enough for skating. The lights next to the lake were on and snow was drifting lazily down from the sky. It snowed a lot in Winter Break. In fact, more snowfall was reported here every year than in any other place in Kansas. It was an odd phenomenon that those who lived here took for granted.

I pushed the doors open, and Pal ran outside to do his business. It didn't take long. Staying out in the cold wasn't something he liked to do. It was probably because less than a year ago he had lived outside, abandoned by his previous owner. For whatever reason, it took less than two minutes for him to run down the steps of the deck, do his thing, and hurry back to me. I let him in and brushed the snow off his coat. He wiggled up next to my legs, his tail wagging furiously. It was as if each time he came inside the house, he celebrated being here with us. I reached down and hugged him. "I love you, you silly dog." He rewarded me with a quick lick on the cheek.

The microwave buzzed, and I retrieved our cups. After dropping a couple of big marshmallows in each one, I carried them into the living room. Pal and Miss Skiffins followed behind me as though we were some kind of small, rather silly parade.

Amos was back on the couch. I snuggled up next to him. We sipped our chocolate and stared at our first Christmas tree without saying a word. That's one of the most wonderful things about being married to the right person. Sometimes you don't have to talk. Just being together is enough. Of course, most people wouldn't believe I could spend much time without opening my mouth; I'm not known for keeping my trap shut. One of my weaknesses is a propensity for saying things I shouldn't. It had gotten me into trouble more than once. I was working on it, but realistically, a complete victory over this aspect of my personality probably wasn't going to happen anytime soon.

"Six o'clock comes pretty early, Ivy," Amos said finally. "I think it's time to head upstairs."

I picked up our cups and took them to the kitchen. After turning down the heat and flipping off all the lights except the one in the kitchen, I followed my husband and our animal friends upstairs. By the time I finished in the bathroom, Amos was already asleep, with Pal curled up at the foot of our bed and Miss Skiffins dozing in the overstuffed chair in the corner. Although she never started out on the bed, most mornings when we woke up she was cuddled next to Pal, sleeping peacefully.

I climbed under the covers, thankful for our electric blanket. I loved nestling under the covers when the night was cold and the blanket was warm and toasty. After I was settled in, I checked the alarm next to my side of the bed so I could wake Amos up in the morning when it went off. He had started wearing earplugs at night after tactfully telling me that my snoring could probably be heard by Odie Rimrucker, whose house was about half a mile down the road. I would have been offended, but I had it on pretty good authority from my ex–college roommate that she could still hear me even when she plugged headphones into her CD player and turned it up. I suspect she wasn't too unhappy to see me drop out of school and move to Winter Break. After assuring myself that the clock was set correctly, I fell asleep almost immediately.

I was dreaming that I was trying to prepare Christmas dinner for the whole town and all my shelves were bare. I was in a panic, slamming kitchen cabinet doors in frustration, when a loud noise startled me awake. I glanced at the clock. It was a little after one. I heard several thumps that sounded just like the cabinet doors in my dream, and then the sound of something being dragged made me sit up in bed. I reached over and grabbed Amos's shoulder, shaking him until he mumbled, "Wha–whatsa matter?"

"Amos," I hissed. "I think someone's on our roof. Wake up!"

He struggled to sit up. "What? What did you say?"

"Take the earplugs out of your ears!" I yelled while pointing to my own ears and making a gesture to show him what I wanted him to do.

"Oh," he said, "I forgot." He reached into his left ear and pulled out the blue foam plug. "What do you want, Ivy?" he asked, his eyes bleary. "I've got to get some sleep."

"There's someone on our roof," I said, trying to keep my voice down. Of course, if our rooftop visitor could actually hear me, shouting at Amos about his earplugs a few seconds earlier certainly would have alerted him that someone knew he was on the property.

"On our roof?" he repeated, scratching his head as if it would wake him up. "What are you talking about? No one could possibly be on our roof."

"I'm telling you, I heard it."

Amos shook his head. "I don't hear anything. You probably dreamed it." He grinned sleepily. "Or maybe it's Santa Claus coming a little early."

"Amos Parker, that's not funny. Something is definitely on our roof. Maybe someone is trying to break into the house."

"Through the roof? He'd have to be a pretty bad burglar."

Another loud thump right above our heads finally

convinced Amos that I wasn't hallucinating. He got up and grabbed his robe. Pal was in full alert, but he didn't start barking until he sensed that we were concerned about what was happening. Miss Skiffins jumped down from the bed and leaped up on the chair, annoyed that we'd disrupted her sleep. Both Amos and I went to the window. As Amos raised the window shade, there was a strange ripping sound, and something large fell past our window and down onto the driveway below. We peered down at the ground, but it was impossible to see anything. Although the high-intensity glow from our yard light was great for illuminating our property, looking directly at it could cause temporary blindness. Amos had insisted on lighting the back and front yards to deter burglars. I wasn't sure what kind of burglars would travel the bumpy and usually snow-packed dirt road to our house for a chance to steal what little we owned, but Amos was trying to protect us and arguing with him was useless. Thick shades managed to block the light at night so I could sleep. My biggest concern was that I would wake up some morning to find that a confused pilot had ended up in our yard, thinking it was a landing strip.

Amos pulled his gun out of the drawer. "Stay here, Ivy. I mean it."

As a Stevens County sheriff's deputy, he was used to giving orders. Unfortunately, I wasn't used to taking them. I waited a few seconds and then followed him down the stairs. Pal came after me. When I reached the bottom, I saw the front door wide open. The porch light highlighted the entryway. Even before I reached the door, I heard Amos exclaim loudly, "What in the world?"

As I stepped out onto the front porch, I followed his "What in the world?" with a "Shoot and bother!"

Sticking up out of a snowbank were two unmoving legs encased in red velvet and black boots. Amos was standing a few feet from the bizarre scene with his mouth hanging open. "J–jumpin' Jehoshaphat, Ivy," he stuttered, "I think we just killed Santa Claus!"

2

A very dead Santa lay spread-eagle on our driveway, blood seeping from behind his head and onto the snow that surrounded him. Sheriff Milt Hitchens stood over him. "Never seen nothin' like this before," he said in his low, gravelly voice. "Been a sheriff for a lotta years, but this is the first time I've been called out to pick up Santa Claus, alive or dead."

Amos stood next to his boss, nodding his head. If we were supposed to come up with some kind of explanation, the sheriff was going to have a long wait on his hands.

"And you say you never saw this man before?" he asked us for about the fifth or sixth time. I'd gone back upstairs and put on my robe. Over that, I'd pulled on my heavy, quilted winter coat. Even so, my teeth chattered as if they had a mind of their own.

"We—we don't know him, Sheriff," I said. It took awhile to get the words out. "And we have no idea why he was on our roof."

Hitchens lowered his head and gazed at me with narrowed eyes. "You realize this is the second time in less than a year I've stood over a dead body in your driveway?"

Amos looked alarmed. "But you know we had nothing to do with that other case. You were there when we caught the killer."

"I understand that, Deputy, but you have to admit

that you and your wife seem to attract some pretty strange goings-on. I already told you more than once that Winter Break ain't no Cabot Cove." He glowered at me. "And you ain't no Jessica Fruity Fletcher." He swung his gaze to my already distressed husband. "I think it's safe to say you know I ain't no Sheriff Tupper."

I was surprised that he even knew about Sheriff Tupper, the affable lawman from the first few seasons of the popular *Murder, She Wrote* television drama. And he was right. Personality-wise, he was definitely more like Sheriff Metzger on steroids. Metzger was a transplant from the New York City police force and the second Cabot Cove sheriff. But even the surliest streetwise New York cop couldn't hold a candle to Milt Hitchens. I wanted to point out that I was fairly certain Jessica's middle name wasn't "Fruity," but it seemed wiser to keep that comment to myself for the moment. Even in his civilian clothes and driving an old black Chevy truck instead of his usual patrol car, Hitchens was an imposing figure. I'd never seen him dressed in anything except his uniform. It was silly of me to assume he slept in it, but still, it was odd to see him looking like a regular person. Too bad it didn't have a positive impact on his personality. Even the frigid weather didn't seem to faze him. He was only wearing a thick denim shirt over a T-shirt. I guess when you're really tough, even the cold is afraid to touch you. Somehow his lack of a coat made me feel even more frozen.

I glared at him. Did he think I found this situation amusing? Hitchens had been almost civil to me after I helped him catch a murderer several months earlier, but his attitude had obviously drifted back into one of animosity. "I assure you, Sheriff, that I am not suffering from Cabot Cove Syndrome. I have no idea why people in Winter Break drop dead from mysterious causes so often. Neither do I understand why it always seems to happen around me. I find it very disturbing." I could feel myself flushing from more than the cold. Anger had a way of showing up in my face like a neon stoplight. And the color didn't go well with my dark red, curly hair. "If you don't mind, I'm going inside. It's freezing out here. If you have any more questions for me, I'd appreciate it if you'd come in the house where it's warm."

I turned and stomped through the snow to my front door. I half expected Amos or Hitchens to call me back, but no one said anything. I waved at Elmer Buskins, the owner of the only funeral home in Winter Break, who stood next to his black 1975 Cadillac hearse parked near our garage. Although the Caddy was old, it had been repainted and restored. It was an impressive vehicle, and I got the heebie-jeebies whenever I saw it. Elmer would take Santa back to his mortuary, where Dr. Lucy Barber, the only doctor serving Winter Break, would decide what would happen next. She lived in Hugoton and acted as deputy coroner in these parts. Even though the man's death appeared to be an accident, unless he was identified, she would probably decide to have him sent to the coroner's office in Wichita so he could be fingerprinted and have his DNA tested. Hopefully he would match a missing person. If not, I assumed they would have to bury him as a John Doe.

Actually, it kind of disturbed me that I understood the routine. The knowledge wasn't all firsthand, although I'd certainly had enough of that. Amos had once been called out by a local farmer who'd found a body in his wheat field. The man was never identified. Finally, he was buried anonymously without a tombstone. That case still bothered Amos. I hoped this wasn't going to end up the same way, not only for the dead man's sake, but because I wanted to know why in the world a guy would dress up like Santa Claus and climb up on my roof. What had he been thinking? And why had he picked our house? One thing I was certain about: This guy wasn't really Old Saint Nick. The beard on his chin wasn't as "white as snow." It was more like five-day stubble, and he had no "round little belly." He looked as if his last good meal had taken place a long, long time ago, and when I'd bent down to see if he was still breathing, I'd caught the strong smell of alcohol.

I stepped inside the house and wiggled out of my coat and boots. Then I went to the kitchen to make a cup of hot tea. By the time Amos opened the front door, I had two steaming cups of chamomile tea sitting on the counter. It seemed like I was always fixing something hot to drink. In Winter Break, it was more about survival than enjoyment.

Pal was lying on the kitchen floor, his head pointed toward the front door. Although he'd stopped barking, he knew something unusual was happening. When he was certain Amos and I were safe, he'd settle down. He was very protective of us. When he saw Amos, he stood up, wagging his tail so hard his whole back end vibrated.

Amos leaned down and petted him. "We're okay, boy. Everything's all right." Pal took this as the sign that he was off duty, and he bounded up the steps to the bedroom. By the time Amos and I got upstairs, he would be snoozing away at the foot of our bed.

I held out Amos's cup, and he smiled gratefully. "Sometimes it gets so cold here I swear I can't remember what it's like to feel warm."

"Didn't seem to bother Hitchens," I said. "I guess he's so tough he doesn't even need a coat."

Amos shook his head. "I'm surprised he wasn't wearing the new coat his cousin from England sent him. He works for some bank there or something. Hitchens has been crowing about that fancy jacket for weeks."

I laughed. "I can't quite imagine Hitchens with a British accent. How did a relative of his end up in England?"

He shrugged. "Who knows? He probably left to get away from the good sheriff."

"Amos! That's not nice." But I didn't say it wasn't true.

He took a sip of his tea, a frown on his face. "There may be a reason he's been even harder to get along with lately. He's being forced to retire in six months."

My mouth dropped open. "What? Hitchens isn't young, but he still seems able to do his job."

Amos shrugged. "I don't know much about it. It's all pretty hush-hush, but there have been complaints about his methods. His way of cutting corners may have finally gotten him in trouble. Of course, it's all just speculation right now."

I didn't like the way Hitchens acted most of the time. And I sure didn't enjoy being on the wrong end of his temper, but forced retirement? My previous irritation turned to compassion. I felt sorry for him. If he wasn't the sheriff, what would happen to him? He didn't seem capable of much else.

Amos glanced up at the kitchen clock. "I don't have to go in to work until noon. Thank goodness. I'm wiped out."

"Well, it's not every day a man falls off your roof."

"I hope this isn't like that movie we saw where the guy who found Santa lying dead in his front yard had to become the new Santa. I have no desire to move to the North Pole." He stared out through the back windows. "Not that it would be much different from Winter Break."

"I really don't think you should be cracking jokes," I sniffed. "I mean, a man died right in our front yard."

"It's not like it's the first time—"

"Knock it off!" I said loudly. "Hitchens is right. It's like we're a target. Why do all these people die around us?"

"Us? My life was boring and mundane until you came into it. Now people are dropping like flies."

"Amos! Stop that." I had to admit he had a point. I tried to put the morbid thoughts out of my mind. "Did you see that old letter in the dead man's pocket?"

Amos, who was in mid-sip, spit hot tea my way. "What? You went through his pockets? What were you thinking?"

I grabbed a nearby napkin and dabbed at the wet

spots on my flannel pajamas. "I was *thinking*," I said self-righteously, "that a man we don't know climbed on top of our roof for a reason we don't know. I was *thinking* that if he had any identification, it would go a long way toward telling me why I was awakened in the middle of the night and treated to the worst Christmas surprise of my life. Silly me, assuming I had the right to know why I was scared halfway out of my wits tonight!"

Amos's gritted teeth told me I hadn't managed to escape his wrath. "Ivy Towers Parker, I've told you time after time that you should never touch evidence. If Sheriff Hitchens finds out what you did—"

"The only way he'll ever find out is if you tell him. I put the letter back in his pocket. Hitchens will never even know I looked at it. I had my gloves on, so I didn't leave any fingerprints. Besides, this was an accident, not a murder. You told me to leave evidence alone at crime scenes. This is not a crime scene."

Amos leaned over and stared into my eyes. "When did you read the letter? I was with you almost the entire. . ." He shook his head. "It was when I went inside to call Hitchens." He said it more as a statement of fact than a question.

I smiled sweetly at him. "Yes. And the searchlight you installed in our front yard made it easy to read."

"Look, Ivy," he said, his voice tight with emotion, "you know I appreciate your Sherlock Holmes mind. But there are limits, and messing with evidence is one of them. Your curiosity could get me into big trouble. Hitchens got here in record time tonight. You could have been standing there with your hand in Santa's pocket when he pulled up. Even though this looks like an accident, Hitchens is sensitive about you and your interference. I don't think he wants you near anything that involves him. You surely got that impression this morning."

Now I was the one getting irritated. "Excuse me, bucko, but my *curiosity* has helped us to solve more than one murder. After we exposed Dela Shackleford's killer, you were pretty happy with all the attention you got from Hitchens and the rest of your cowboy-cop friends."

"Okay," Amos said, rubbing his hands across his face, "never call me 'bucko' again, and never, ever call members of the sheriff's department 'cowboy cops' in front of any living, breathing human being. If that got back to Hitchens. . ."

I smiled at him. "As long as you play your cards right, you'll be fine. Now wouldn't you like to know what was written on the note in Santa's pocket?"

Amos plopped down on the kitchen bar stool. "Do I have a choice?"

I sat down next to him. "Not really. It was strange, Amos. It was a letter to Santa with our address scribbled at the top. That ink looked new, but the rest of the letter appeared to be pretty old. Some of the letters had faded and the paper was torn. I could barely make it out, but it was clearly from a child, asking for a Cabbage Patch doll with red hair. The writer must have been a little girl. There was something else about her mommy and daddy. That part was hard to read because the words were faded."

"A Cabbage Patch doll? Are those things still for sale?"

I shrugged. "I don't know. I think they were really popular in the eighties. Frankly, that letter looked like it could have been written that long ago."

"Was there a signature?"

I shook my head. "I don't think so. It was pretty faint, but it looked like the little girl just wrote 'Ho Ho' at the bottom of the page. Then she drew a little red heart. I think she was trying to tell Santa that she loved him."

Amos sighed and gulped down the rest of the liquid in his cup. "So Santa Claus climbs up on our roof with a twenty-year-old letter in his pocket and falls off? I don't suppose you saw a red bag full of toys you forgot to tell me about?"

I picked up our cups and put them in the sink. "No bag. No nothing. It might be worth your while to climb on the roof when the sun comes up and see if there's anything else there that might tell us something about our nocturnal visitor."

Amos stood up and flipped off the light. "So Santa Claus, who is supposed to be pretty good walking around on rooftops, falls off and plunges to his death, and your first thought is to send me up there?" He shook his head. "And you wonder why people keep keeling over around you. I'm beginning to see the method behind your madness."

I followed him to the bottom of the stairs. "Well, who knows? Maybe you'll get to meet Santa's reindeer. I've always wanted to know if Rudolph really leads the way."

I'm not sure what he said after that, but for the sake of our peaceful home, I decided not to pursue it.

T hat's the strangest story I ever heard." Dewey
Tater, the owner of Winter Break's only grocery
store, stared at me like I had potatoes growing out of
my ears. "You sure you didn't dream this, Ivy?"

I sighed and poured myself another cup of coffee.
"I wish it were a dream. Unfortunately for the poor
man who lost his life last night, it really happened. I
can't get him out of my head—or that letter. Who was
this guy? And who is the little girl?"

Dewey and I shared breakfast together every
morning before we opened the doors of our respective
businesses. Miss Bitty's Bygone Bookstore sat right
across the street from Laban's Food-a-Rama. Dewey
had taken over the Food-a-Rama when he was only
twenty-two years old. His father passed away suddenly,
leaving Dewey and his mother without another source
of income. His mother died twelve years ago, but
Dewey stayed on. In all those years, he'd never married.
The only woman he'd ever loved was my great-aunt
Bitty, and Dewey wasn't interested in anyone else. He
was waiting patiently for the day when Bitty would
welcome him to heaven. I'd quit trying to set him up.
He'd told me more than once that he didn't want some
other woman "mucking up" his reunion.

"Uh-oh," Dewey said. "You've got that look in
your eyes again."

"What look?"

"That 'I have no intention of letting this go until I know what's going on' look."

I waved my hand at him dismissively. "I have no earthly idea what you're talking about."

"Oh, sure," he chortled. "So what happens next?" He took another sugar-free muffin from the basket I'd set on the big table in the sitting room, which was nestled comfortably in the back of my bookstore. I always made breakfast with Dewey's diabetes in mind. I'd gotten pretty good at no-sugar recipes, and I knew he really appreciated it. Changing his way of eating hadn't been easy. In fact, he only did it because he'd made a promise to Bitty before she died. And Dewey was a man of his word.

It took awhile for the store to get warm in the mornings, so we'd parked ourselves in front of the fireplace until eight thirty, when we would get ready to flip our CLOSED signs to OPEN. The flames crackled merrily along, chasing away the cold that tried to seep in through any crack it could find in the old house, which had been converted to a bookstore by my aunt. Even though she was gone, I felt her presence here every day. In a way, she was also with us in a physical sense. On the mantel over the fireplace sat a bronze urn. It was shaped like a book and on its side was a gold cross. Even though I knew she was in heaven, Aunt Bitty's mortal remains were still in her bookstore, with me.

"I don't know," I said. "After Lucy looks things over, I'm pretty sure Elmer will take the body to Wichita. Hopefully they can figure out who he is and why he died."

"I suspect falling off a roof and landing on your head would answer the 'how' question. You're certain he's not from around here?" Dewey reached for the coffee carafe. I pushed it closer to him.

"As certain as I can be. I mean, maybe I don't know all the six hundred or so people who live in Winter Break, but if he does comes from here, I've never seen him before. And Amos didn't recognize him either."

"What's your hubby think about all this?"

I shook my head. "He's as confused as I am. He checked out the roof this morning before I left to see if he could find a clue that would help us to understand what happened, but the only thing he found was a piece of red cloth stuck on the metal around the chimney. The man must have ripped his suit when he fell. Amos did figure out that he'd climbed that big tree on the east side of the house and jumped to the roof from there, but that didn't really help us much either. And as far as any tracks on the ground, it snowed so much last night, Godzilla could have marched in circles around our house and we'd have never known it."

Dewey chuckled. "I hear you. But one thing I don't understand. How did he get to your place, Ivy? Your house sits back a ways from the main road."

"I don't know. Amos is on the lookout for an abandoned car somewhere nearby. If he doesn't find it, I'm at a loss."

Dewey took a sip of coffee. "I'll bet someone in town knows something about this guy. He couldn't have simply appeared out of nowhere."

"I hope you're right. We're going to Ruby's for lunch.

Amos is going to put up some flyers asking people to contact him if they have any helpful information. He wants to be certain the man's not connected to anyone in Winter Break before they send him to Wichita."

Dewey snorted. "Why doesn't Amos just tell Bertha Pennypacker about it? That should take care of spreading the word."

"Now, Dewey," I said reprovingly, "you know that Bertha and I are finally getting along. I don't think you should be saying negative things about her. Bertha's had plenty of reasons to be. . .difficult."

Dewey laughed. "Difficult? Buttoning my shirt in the morning is *difficult*. Passing up Ruby's hot apple pie is *difficult*. Bertha Pennypacker is more than difficult—she's downright impossible. I know you think she's your friend now, but I'm telling you, you'd better watch your back. I still don't trust her."

"Why, I'm surprised at you. Doesn't the Bible tell us to believe the best about people?" I shook my head. "Bitty always looked for what she called the 'sunshine' in everyone. Did you forget to look for the sunshine in Bertha?"

Dewey leaned back in his chair and crossed his arms across his chest. Then he gazed at me beneath his thick gray eyebrows. "Yes, the Bible certainly does tell us to believe the best about people. And it also tells us to be as harmless as doves and as wise as serpents. I think you need to work on your serpent skills."

I shot him my most holier-than-thou expression. "I can't believe you're actually telling me to act like a serpent. If Bitty were here—"

"She'd tell you the same thing. Maybe in a nicer way, but she was pretty smart about people. Maybe she looked for the sunshine, but she was intelligent enough to know that sometimes it hides behind dark clouds." He looked down, his face etched in sadness. "Well, I guess she knew that most of the time. She trusted someone she shouldn't have, and she lost her life. I don't want the same thing to happen to you. There's something else going on with Delbert and Bertha, and I don't like it."

Bertha had hated me ever since I'd come to Winter Break. I wasn't sure why, but her dislike was so strong it was almost tangible. After I helped Amos figure out that her husband was stealing cows from farms around Winter Break and selling them, Delbert had gone to jail. Bertha's animosity grew even more caustic. Then last February, I'd reached out to her, even asking her to be a bridesmaid in my wedding. Things had been fine between us since then. I'd been a little nervous since Delbert was recently released, but Amos and I had run into them several times at Ruby's Redbird Café, the only restaurant in Winter Break. They'd both been friendly enough.

"Are you saying you think Bertha's going to try to kill me one of these days?" I couldn't help grinning at the idea, but Dewey's expression stayed sour.

"I want you to be careful, Ivy. I mean it. I just get this really bad feeling when I'm around those two."

I could see that he was really troubled. Although I wasn't the least bit concerned about Bertha, I didn't want him to worry. "I promise to watch my step around

Bertha and Delbert," I said gently. "Now can we finish our breakfast without any more predictions of gloom and doom?"

He nodded and reached for another muffin. "Sure seems strange not to have Amos come busting in while we're eating."

It was Amos's habit to join us every morning. First he'd drop me off at the bookstore. Then he'd run over to the small sheriff's office Stevens County kept in Winter Break. He liked to check for faxes and make any necessary phone calls. After that he'd head back here for breakfast. This morning I'd driven myself into town so he could hang around the house and relax for a while. Since the road to our place had been cleared by one of the local farmers, it hadn't been too bad. Usually in the winter Amos drove both of us, since his patrol car had special tires that helped to stabilize it on slippery roads. My car, on the other hand, seemed to have an affinity for snowdrifts. If it kept snowing today, I'd leave my car at the bookstore tonight, and Amos would drive us home.

I hoped he was getting some rest this morning. He was really wiped out after last night's Santa situation. Usually he was pretty resilient, but lately there had been quite a few thefts of diesel fuel from farms in and around Stevens County. The cost of fuel was climbing higher and higher—and there were rumors it could get even worse. Thieves who carted off several hundred gallons of fuel could clean up by selling it at a discount. The problem was that the sheriff's department hadn't been able to track down the fuel's final destination. With rising prices, it was entirely possible that farmers were buying the discounted fuel in an attempt to keep their farms profitable. Amos and the rest of the deputies had been running all over the county trying to catch the "diesel demons," but so far, they had skillfully eluded detection.

Dewey and I sat in front of the fire as long as we could. At a quarter to nine, he eased himself out of his chair, pulled on his coat, boots, and knit cap, and shuffled across the street in the snow. I carried my coffee cup over to the front window and watched him. He'd turned eighty years old in August, and I could see the effects of age catching up to him. Dewey had always been a strong, robust man. Watching him become frailer with every passing year made me sad, but I knew he wasn't the least bit concerned with his own mortality. Like my aunt, he had a strong sense of heaven in his heart. He looked forward to closing his eyes on this earth and opening them surrounded by the glory of God. I understood. I longed for that day, too. However, I knew God had something for me to do, and I had a burning desire to finish the course He'd prepared for me.

I believed strongly that Amos and I were meant to have children, but it hadn't happened yet. My best friend, Emily Taylor, already had one child and was pregnant again. I had to fight feelings of envy when I saw her rounded tummy. Amos wasn't worried, though, and chided me for getting antsy so soon. We'd only been married ten months; still, I'd really expected to conceive before now. I'd purchased a couple of pregnancy tests from the drugstore in Hugoton because I knew Winter Break would be wrapped in snow for a while and it might be difficult for me to get out of town. I'd hidden them under the sink in the upstairs bathroom just in case. Hopefully I'd have an occasion to use them. My heart longed to hold our child. It was the only blessing I felt my life was lacking.

I unlocked the front door and flipped my sign to OPEN, but only a handful of people would wander in on a day like today. Most of my business was done over the Internet. Buyers of rare books liked to shop online unless the book was extremely valuable. Then they would travel to Winter Break to see it for themselves. I not only used the Net to buy (and sell) books; I also scoured estate sales when the weather permitted. I'd found many wonderful, valuable books that way.

Even though most of my business was done through electronic means, I wouldn't have traded Miss Bitty's Bygone Bookstore for anything. It had a quality that new, modern stores couldn't begin to touch. Floor-to-ceiling oak shelves held old books with stories that could transport the reader to faraway lands—carried on the wings of the past, the present, and the future. Fantasy, mystery, history, and romance lay beneath the aged covers of books waiting for just the right person to pluck them from their perch and take a ride. The old oak grandfather clock by the stairs ticked on in its endless rhythm, and the silver bell over the door waited patiently until someone stepped inside so it could sing a song of welcome. Polished wooden floors gleamed, and the scent of lemon oil permeated the air. The bookstore was a magical place that had held me in its grasp ever since the first time I came to visit my aunt Bitty here. But until she died and left me the bookstore, I'd never imagined that it would someday be mine. Now that it was, it felt as if I'd always been here. As if the store had always known I was going to own it someday.

Although I had a loyal group of regular visitors, not many meetings were held here anymore. When I first took over the store, there were several requests to use our sitting room for various gatherings. Even though Winter Break is small, it has its share of book clubs. When the new library was established, the clubs had all moved there. Although I missed the lively groups, it was better this way. Now that I was married, I wanted to spend my evenings at home with Amos instead of keeping the store open late. Hope Hartwell, our young librarian, lived near the library and had joined each book club because of her varied and extensive literary interests.

Hope was a young woman who almost always had her nose in a book. Although she was close to Faith Baumgartner, who worked beside her as a volunteer, Hope's world didn't appear to extend much further than the front doors of the library. Several available young men had shown an interest in her, yet she had spurned them all—except for Emily's brother, Zachariah. Zach was tall, with dark, chocolate-colored eyes like his sister's. His hair was ebony, and most of the time he looked like he needed a haircut. Personally, I liked his hair a little long. He reminded me of the covers of some of the corny romance novels for sale at the drugstore in Hugoton. But the most important thing about Zach was his gentle spirit and his love for God. He worked hard on the family farm, taking over after his father died, but those close to him knew that he wanted to pastor a church someday. He currently attended the church his family had helped to build. First Mennonite Church had been started in the 1800s by German immigrants from Gutenberg. Their descendants, nearly one hundred of them, held membership at First Mennonite—except for a few, including my friend Emily. She'd married the son of the pastor of Faith Community Church and attended there. Emily told me that Zach loved his church but wanted to experience other congregations. The few times he'd visited Faith Community, he'd really enjoyed the more contemporary worship format and the free-flowing service. Even though at twenty-four he was old enough to choose his own church, loyalty to his mother kept him at First Mennonite.

The past couple of months Zach had developed an unusual passion for reading. He was frequently found at the library, asking Hope for advice about what book to read next. They had developed a friendship. I suspected that Zach was biding his time. It was probably why he was still close to Hope—he hadn't made a move yet that she could reject. But he would. I worried about it. I couldn't stand to see his heart broken. And I felt that Hope would miss out on a wonderful young man if she resisted him the way she had everyone else.

I was sitting at my desk, going over a list of books

that needed to be mailed out, trying not to think about our Santa Claus catastrophe, when the little silver bell over the door jingled. Zach Baumgartner stepped inside, grinning at me. It startled me to see him since I'd just had him on my mind.

"Hi, Ivy," he said, removing his cap. It was an endearing, chivalrous gesture. Something I didn't see much of anymore.

"Hi, yourself! What brings you here so early?"

He glanced around the bookstore, and I got the feeling he was checking to see if anyone else was with me.

"Isaac isn't in today," I offered. Isaac Holsapple was my assistant, but he only worked Monday through Wednesday.

"I—I wasn't looking for him," Zach said tentatively. "It's you I wanted to talk to."

I stood up. "How about a cup of coffee? It's still hot."

I was granted another sincere smile. He ran his hand through his thick dark hair. "That sounds wonderful. I'm chilled to the bone."

Without another word, he followed me back to the sitting room. Luckily, I had a clean cup sitting on the tray. I'd brought it downstairs for Amos out of habit. I poured the coffee and handed it to him. "Now what can I do for you, Zach?"

"I know you sell rare books on the Internet, Ivy," he said softly, looking down at his coffee cup. "But Emily told me you also have some for sale in your shop?"

I nodded. "Yes, that's true. I have quite a few. Is there a particular book you're looking for?"

Zach's fair complexion turned pink. "Uh, well. . ."

He cleared his throat and tried again. "It's a book called *Miss Jellytot's Visit*." He almost whispered the title as if he thought someone else might be listening.

I smiled and choked down a laugh. Hearing "Miss Jellytot" come out of Zach's very manly mouth was pretty funny. "Goodness. I haven't heard anyone mention Miss Jellytot for many years. I know the book. It was written by Mabel Leigh Hunt. I read it when I was young. Unfortunately, I don't have a copy, Zach."

His optimistic expression fell. "Oh. I was hoping. . . I mean, I know it's close to Christmas, but. . ."

"Hold on a minute. I said I didn't have a copy. That doesn't mean I can't find one. Come with me."

We picked up our coffee cups, and Zach followed me back to the front of the bookstore. I motioned to him to have a seat in one of the chairs sitting near my desk, and I sat down and turned on my computer. Winter Break only has dial-up service, so it takes awhile to log on. When I first moved to the tiny town, the lack of high-speed Internet service and cell phones drove me crazy. Now I was used to it. Living life at a slower pace had its advantages. Waiting for an Internet connection, however, definitely wasn't one of them.

While we waited, Zach and I chatted about Emily and her pregnancy. I was delighted to hear him talk enthusiastically about Charlie, Emily and Buddy's firstborn, who was one and a half already. Zach was obviously an involved and very dedicated uncle, and he was just as excited about the baby yet to be born. We'd just started talking about the names Emily and her husband, Buddy, had been considering, when my computer connected to the Internet.

"Give me a minute, Zach. Let's see if we can find your book." I pulled up my e-mail account and checked my bookstore list. Within a few minutes, a request for a copy of *Miss Jellytot's Visit* had gone out to several dealers who handled old and collectible books. A short time later, a response came back. A friend from Denver, Noel Spivey, informed me that he had a first edition in good shape. *It's a library copy,* he wrote. *Almost all available copies of this book are from libraries. This one has very little wear, but the original library sleeve is still in the front along with the checkout page. Is this a problem?*

"I've found one, Zach," I said, "but it's a library copy. Unfortunately, most of the copies of this book went to libraries. Is that okay, or do you want me to keep checking?"

He colored again. "No, actually, a library copy would be great. How much is it? Is there any way to get it here before Christmas?"

I typed in his questions.

You can have it if you want it, Ivy. I'll overnight it.

Zach was in front of my computer, so he couldn't see what I typed. *It's for a young man who wants to give the book to a pretty lady. Offering it to him for free won't work. He needs to feel that it cost him something.*

I waited a minute until Noel typed back. *Okay. Tell him it's $25.00—and I'll overnight it for $10.00. How does that sound?*

I knew it cost more than ten dollars to overnight packages, but I felt that thirty-five dollars was doable for Zach.

Sounds good, Noel. Thanks. Send it to me.

It's on its way, he typed back.

"Zach, my friend can sell the book to you and ship it overnight for thirty-five dollars. Is that okay with you?"

His whole body slumped with relief. "That would be great. How do I pay him?"

I smiled and logged off. "You pay me, and I'll make sure he gets it."

Zach stood up and pulled his wallet out of his back jeans pocket. He counted out thirty-five dollars and handed it to me. "Do you want a receipt?" I asked.

He shook his head. "No thanks. I appreciate your help." He slid his wallet back in his pocket. "I'll stop back tomorrow and pick it up."

I smiled at him. "This is Winter Break, Zach. Overnight means it will probably be here Monday. I'm sure you know that Alma doesn't always open the post office on Saturdays. Especially if the guy who brings the mail from Hugoton doesn't want to drive out here because the roads are bad."

"That's right," he replied, looking alarmed.

"Don't worry. The mail will be here by Monday or Tuesday, I'm sure. If Alma doesn't open the post office, I'll meet the truck myself. But she's usually pretty reliable during the week."

He reached out his hand. "Thank you very much. This means a lot to me."

I'd been hoping he would tell me who the book was for, but he hadn't, even though I was sure I knew. A discreet person would have left well enough alone, but I never claimed to be perfect. I stuck my hand out and took his. "You're welcome. I must say you don't seem like the type to be a fan of Mabel Leigh Hunt. Is this a gift?"

He dropped my fingers like they were hot potatoes, and the lovely shade of pink he'd exhibited earlier made its return.

"Well, I—I mean, I. . ."

"You don't have to tell me, Zach. You're free to come here and buy any book you want. Sorry if I was being nosy." I really did feel a little guilty. I hadn't expected him to react with so much emotion. Of course, he'd already answered my question. I knew exactly where the book was going.

He straightened up and looked around. Then he leaned in closer to the desk. I'd already told him that we were alone, but I found his caution charming. "To tell you the truth, it's for Hope Hartwell. We were talking about books the other day, and she mentioned that *Miss Jellytot's Visit* was one of her favorites as a kid. Unfortunately, she lost her copy years ago. She's always hoped to find another one."

"I see why the library edition is such a perfect fit." I smiled as reassuringly as I could. "Hope is blessed to have you for a friend. She seems to spend a lot of time alone. Amos and I have asked her out to eat several times, but she's only gone with us once. You know, she stayed with me for a while when she first came to town, and I thought we were pretty good friends. Unfortunately, I hardly ever see her. I stop by the library to visit her and Faith at least once a week, but that's about the only time we get to talk. I invite her to church almost every week, but she rarely comes."

Zach's expression grew serious. "I know. I've asked her, too, but she doesn't seem very interested. She talks about God, but I don't think she likes church much. I've wanted to ask her why, but—"

"You don't want to push her?" I interjected.

He nodded slowly. "Exactly. I feel sometimes like I'm trying to touch a wild deer. If I move too fast, she'll run away."

It was a pretty accurate comparison. Hope did remind me of a frightened animal sometimes. Her short stature, turned-up nose, and short ash blond hair made me think of pictures in a book I'd had as a child. She looked just like a pixie, and when she was relaxed and comfortable, her personality matched her appearance. She was animated and bubbly—interested in everything around her. But more than once I'd seen a guarded look cross her face, and when it did, an emotional barrier inside her slammed shut faster than a front door on a frigid Winter Break morning. After that, it took awhile to get her to open up again. Zach was playing it smart.

"I think your gift will mean a lot to her," I said. "And you're right to take it slow. People get in too big a rush sometimes. Let Hope learn to trust you. I think you'll end up becoming very good friends." Now Zach and I both knew that being Hope's "very good friend" wasn't exactly what he had in mind, but neither one of us said it.

"Thanks, Ivy," he said solemnly, handing me his coffee cup. "I certainly hope you're right." He pulled on his cap and, with a wave, walked out the door. The icy air swooped past him, and I found myself shivering. My coffee was cold, and there wasn't much left in the carafe. I was on my way to make another pot when Amos pushed the front door open.

"Any breakfast left?" He took off his heavy coat and put it on the coatrack.

"I left you some huckleberry muffins on the kitchen counter at home. Didn't you find them?"

He chuckled. "I ate those, and I'm ready for another one. Didn't you and Dewey leave anything?"

I pointed toward the sitting room. "I think there's one muffin left, but it's cold by now."

"I don't care. Every other part of me is frozen. Might as well eat frozen food, too."

I laughed. "I hardly think you'll find a huckleberry Popsicle. The basket's been sitting on the table near the fire. I was just on my way to make another pot of coffee."

Amos grinned, sprinted to the back of the shop, and grabbed the carafe. Then he hurried back and handed it to me. "Don't say I never did anything for you."

"Oh, thanks. You're my hero." I leaned over and kissed him. "Did you get enough sleep? I didn't expect to see you until around noon."

"I slept some. To be honest, I'm feeling rather guilty about this Santa Claus thing. If I hadn't been wearing those blasted earplugs, maybe I would have heard him sooner and been able to keep him from falling. I think he was surprised when I opened the window and that's why he slipped."

"Amos Parker! It's not your fault that man was on

our roof. You didn't do anything wrong, and you have every right to wear earplugs. It makes just as much sense to blame me for forcing you to use them, and I don't think it's my fault at all. Besides, maybe he really was a robber." Even though I'd said it, I didn't really believe it. What kind of burglar would dress up like Santa Claus to break into someone's house? And why not go in through a door or a window? I reached over and hugged Amos. "I'll make some more coffee, and we'll sit and talk about it. Just remember, we're having lunch at Ruby's. You need to leave some room."

"That's for sure. I think a nice Redbird Burger might be in order."

Ruby's massive one-pound burgers were legendary in the town of Winter Break. Full of cheddar cheese, chopped grilled onions, and jalapeños, they were good enough to make farmers drive in from their fields and mothers find babysitters for their children just to get a place in the Redbird Café when Ruby was frying them up. The old woman was very secretive about her recipe and often told overenthusiastic diners that she was going to "go to my grave with the very last Redbird Burger clutched in my cold, dead hand." As far as I knew, I was the only person in Winter Break, beside her family, who had the recipe. Ruby had given it to us for a wedding present, along with free Redbird Burgers for life, as a way to thank us for finding her long-lost son, Bert, and bringing him home. I'd tucked the recipe away where no one would accidentally stumble across it during a visit. I'd never tried to re-create her burger. It almost felt sacrilegious to make something that was so. . .well, *Ruby*.

"You eat one of those for lunch, and you'll fall asleep in your patrol car," I said. "I'm having egg salad."

Amos shivered dramatically. "I love Ruby's cooking, but eggs should only be lying on a plate next to a mess of bacon. They weren't created for sandwiches."

I looked up and down his slim, muscled physique. "You're going to get older one of these days, bub. You'd better start eating lighter, or you're going to be carrying around one of those Redbird Burger bellies."

Humor flashed in his almost amber-colored eyes. "Would you still love me?"

"Sure, but what if you can't fit behind the steering wheel of your car? You might have to quit working for the sheriff and join the circus."

"Well, as long as your feelings won't change. . ."

I laughed and headed up the stairs to make more coffee. The little apartment where I'd lived when I first came to Winter Break had become a storage area for books, records, and furniture I hadn't yet moved to my house. I still used the kitchen every day. I kept food here in case the weather was bad and I didn't want to drive home for lunch. I could also make a sandwich if I needed to work late.

I took the coffee out of the refrigerator and got the coffeemaker going. As it chortled in the background, I stood in the tiny kitchen and envisioned Aunt Bitty standing at the stove, making us hot chocolate while jellytots baked in the oven. There was a reason I'd immediately known about the book Zach asked about. It was one of my childhood favorites. My love for the book had led me to ask Bitty to make the cookie the book described. And she had. They were delicious. I hadn't had a jellytot since I'd been in Winter Break as a child. Maybe it was time I baked some myself. I had a big metal recipe box at home that had belonged to my aunt. Hopefully the recipe was stuffed inside it.

I ran my hand across the old Formica table that was still sitting in the kitchen. In my mind, I could see both of us chattering away like a couple of monkeys, eating cookies and talking about life. Sometimes I could almost swear I heard her talk to me. Dewey said the same thing. "She's still in my head, Ivy," he'd told me. "As well as in my heart." More than once, that voice had gently led me to a place where I was able to find God's will for my life. And that's the way it should be with people in our lives. They should always lead us to listen to the voice of the Holy Spirit—and not try to take His place. My aunt had been really good at that.

I took the creamer out of the fridge and put it on the counter in case Amos wanted some. Then I wandered back to Bitty's old bedroom. I'd moved most of her furniture to my house. Now extra books were stored here on shelves that Amos had built for me. The shelves were full, and there were piles of books sitting on the floor next to the wall. I wandered over to the closet and opened the door. The smell of Bitty's perfume still lingered. Probably because I'd knocked a bottle over and broken it when we were moving things out. The cologne had spilled across the floor and seeped under the closet door. I was actually kind of glad it had happened. It was nice to smell her fragrance. Of course, all I had to do was buy a bottle of Jean Naté. It was all she ever wore.

Her beautiful black tweed coat with its leather buttons hung on a padded hanger. Black leather gloves still poked out of the right pocket, as if waiting for their owner to return. I touched the coat's soft fabric and then stroked the silk lining. It was beautiful. Although I'd given some of Bitty's clothes away to the church for its rummage sale, I'd held on to this coat. I'd intended to wear it myself, but I hadn't been able to put it on yet—even after two years. It still didn't feel right. It was Bitty's. How could anyone else ever wear it?

I glanced up at the top shelf in the closet and saw Amy, the Precious Moments doll I'd gotten for Christmas when I was five. Her teardrop-shaped eyes stared down at me. I'd brought her with me during summer vacation when I was seven and had forgotten to take her home. About that same time I'd graduated to Barbie, and Amy had ended up here, abandoned and alone. For some reason, looking at the doll and remembering the childish handwriting on the note in the late Santa's pocket got to me. I started to cry, and by the time Amos found me, I was bawling my eyes out, clutching that silly doll. Although I couldn't admit it to my husband, I knew my desire for a baby had a lot to do with my minor emotional breakdown. I mumbled something about feeling bad for our nocturnal visitor and for the little girl who probably never got the doll she wanted.

"For goodness' sake, Ivy," Amos said gently, sitting down on the floor next to me. "I feel bad for the guy, too, but there's nothing we can do for him now. And as far as the letter—that little girl is probably your age by now. I'm sure she's over it. Besides," he said, putting his arm around me, "how do you know she didn't get the doll? Maybe she did."

"M–maybe," I sniffed, "but what if she didn't? What if no one ever saw her letter? W–what if. . ." A thought popped into my head. I turned around and looked up into Amos's concerned face. "I feel so stupid," I said. "I should have realized. . ." I wiggled away from him and jumped to my feet.

"Whoa. Wait a minute." Amos grabbed the edge of a nearby chair and pulled himself up. "What are you thinking?"

I leaned over and kissed him. "It's so clear. I should have realized it sooner. I guess I was so focused on the dead guy I didn't think it through."

Amos made one of those exasperated sounds he makes frequently around me. It was a cross between a sigh and a grunt. "What in the world are you talking about? I don't see—"

"The doll." I stared down at the tear stained doll I'd been holding in my arms. "Why would this guy climb up on a roof dressed like Santa with a letter from a child in his pocket?"

"Hmm. I don't know," Amos said in a low voice. "Because he was nuts? Because he was drunk? He smelled like he'd taken a bath in booze."

"Yeah, I noticed that, too, but he had to be there for a reason, Amos."

My handsome husband looked at me blankly.

"He was trying to deliver that doll. It's got to still

be there—at the house."

Amos shook his head. "I didn't see anything this morning."

I grabbed his arm. "But you were trying to find out how Santa got up on our roof. You weren't looking for a bag or a doll. If it fell off the roof when Santa took a tumble, the snow would have covered it up by this morning. We've got to go home and look."

"Okay," Amos said reluctantly, "but it will have to be after I get back this evening. You wait for me. I don't want you driving your car unless I follow you."

I stamped my food with impatience. "But it will be dark by then. It will be so much harder to see."

He stepped back and frowned at me. "I don't care, Ivy. You wait for me. It's still snowing out there. I don't want you to get stuck." He put his hand under my chin. "You have to promise me you'll wait, okay?"

"Okay. Okay," I said irritably. "I'll wait for you. Try not to be too late, though. And bring your flashlight."

"I will. And, Ivy?"

"Yes?" I said, anticipating another lecture about not going home without him.

"Could you please quit calling the dead guy Santa? It's making me feel funny."

"What would you like me to call him? Chuck?"

"That would be better. From now on, let's call him Chuck until we find out his real name."

Amos's serious expression made me want to giggle, but I choked it down. A man's death wasn't a laughing matter.

The smell of fresh-brewed coffee and a final

gurgling sound made it clear that the coffee was ready. Amos followed me to the kitchen, where I filled the carafe. He carried it downstairs while I followed behind, still clutching Amy. I couldn't seem to put her down. Somehow I had to find out who the little girl in the letter was and how Santa, I mean *Chuck*, was related to her. And as silly as it sounded, I had to know if she ever got her red-haired Cabbage Patch doll.

4

A little before noon, we headed over to Ruby's Redbird Café for lunch. As soon as we walked in the door, it was obvious Ruby and Bert were cooking Redbird Burgers. The aroma was unmistakable. The smell of fried onions and jalapeños filled the room, and it looked as though every seat in the restaurant was filled. Usually you could at least find a stool at the old lunch counter, but there wasn't an empty one to be had. For a moment I thought we might be out of luck, but then I heard someone call my name. Pastor Ephraim Taylor and his wife, Bev, sat at a booth in the back of the café. He waved us over.

"Why don't you sit with us?" he said after we waded past several tables. "We're almost done." Bev got up and slid in next to her husband, leaving the other side of the booth empty.

"Thanks," Amos said gratefully. "I was beginning to think we'd have to eat standing up."

"No problem," Pastor Taylor said with a smile. "This will give us a chance to visit a little. I have something I want to ask Ivy."

Amos and I scooted in. The remnants of Redbird Burgers were on each of the Taylors' plates. Pastor Taylor had obviously given up—defeated by the huge hamburger. Bev was still working at it. She stabbed another piece with her fork. Using silverware wasn't unusual. The monstrous pile of meat with cheddar cheese inside and out and fried onions dripping off the top wasn't meant for timid eaters. Sometimes employing a knife and fork was a hungry customer's only hope.

Pastor Taylor leaned forward as if to keep whatever he was saying private. At Ruby's, you could probably shout out your business standing on top of one of the tables and no one would pay any attention. Ruby's was the place where gossip reigned supreme. Unless you were the prime target, your conversation was ignored for spicier fare. Turns out, Pastor Taylor's caution was well advised.

"So the story is circulating around town that you two killed Santa Claus. I'd love to hear more about that."

"I swear," Amos said gruffly, "there's no need for a local paper. News travels faster in Winter Break than anywhere else in the world."

Pastor Taylor grinned. "Well, news may be faster somewhere else, but we have a few residents who've taken it upon themselves to announce everyone else's business as quickly as is humanly possible."

He was too spiritual to mention any names, but I knew who the town busybodies were. A quick look around the café exposed several possibilities.

"Before you draw any conclusions," Bev said, "Sheriff Hitchens stopped by for breakfast this morning. He's the bigmouth who got everyone riled up."

"Now, Bev," Pastor Taylor said, shaking his gray head, "we don't really want to call the sheriff a 'bigmouth,' do we?"

Bev winked one of her large green eyes at me where her husband couldn't see it. "No, I guess not, Ephraim. I'm sorry."

I stifled a giggle. Bev was a wonderful support to her husband, but their personalities were certainly different. She liked to "tell it like it is," while he went out of his way to be as benevolent as possible toward everyone.

"Hi, folks! Whatcha havin'?" Bonnie Bird stepped up to the table to take our order. She and Bert had only been married a few months, but it was obvious that marriage agreed with them. If their perpetual smiles were any indication, things were going very well. She held her notepad out in front of her stained uniform, waiting for our order.

"Now, Bonnie, you don't really need to ask me, do you?" Amos said with a smile.

She shook her head and laughed. "Already wrote you down for a burger. Just waitin' on you, Ivy."

I opened my mouth, intending to say, "Egg salad," but my unreliable lips formed the words "Redbird Burger."

Bonnie waved her pen at Amos. "You're a bad influence on our girl, Deputy Parker."

Amos waggled his finger back at her. "Now you know better than that. Ivy thinks for herself. I take no responsibility for her frailties."

"Okay, you two," I interjected. "Time to change the subject. I've given in to my fleshly desires, and I admit it. Now bring me my burger!"

As everyone laughed, I noticed Bubba Weber sitting

a couple of tables away from us. He was sitting with Marvin and Edith Baumgartner. Next to Edith sat Sister Crystal Edgewater. Sister Crystal was an odd woman who had lately begun to have "words from the Lord." She'd interrupted several church services with her strange ramblings. Finally, Pastor Taylor mandated that further words would have to be delivered to him before they were announced to the congregation. Now I'd heard my share of "words," and most of them bore witness with my spirit, but Sister Crystal, as she asked to be called, was a different matter. Most of the time, I couldn't figure out what she was talking about. I had faith that whatever God had to say was going to make sense and agree with the Bible. But Sister Crystal Ball, as a few members of our congregation had nicknamed her. . . Well, let's just say that her lines of communication seemed to need some flushing with a strong drain cleaner.

Marvin and Edith were in awe of Sister Crystal, so I wasn't surprised to see them with her, but I was a bit dismayed to see Bubba in their midst. Bubba was a simple, innocent soul who kept bees and sold honey in Winter Break and nearby Hugoton. When he looked my way, I waved. He wiggled his fingers at me and flashed an enthusiastic smile. The rest of his group smiled halfheartedly and went back to their conversation. I wondered if they were munching on something besides Redbird Burgers. Amos and I were most probably the main course.

"Did you hear what I said, Ivy?"

Pastor Taylor's voice broke through my musings.

I turned my head to find everyone at the table staring at me. "I–I'm sorry. I was thinking about something else."

Bev looked over at the table where the Baumgartners and Sister Crystal were sitting with Bubba. "Some people have nothing better to do than talk about other people." She turned back to smile kindly at me. "Of course, Santa Claus falling off one's roof does make for an intriguing discussion. I can't really blame our citizens for being fascinated."

Knowing the Taylors were curious, Amos launched into a brief description of the event.

"Poor man," Bev said when he finished. "What in the world was he doing up there?"

"You just asked the sixty-four-thousand-dollar question," I said. "I'm determined to find out. If it was important enough to risk his life for, it's important enough for me to try to understand it." I wanted to add that I had every intention of making the man's final delivery. If I could find the doll and figure out whom he was trying to give it to, maybe I could complete the last mission of his life. But I wasn't ready to admit my plan out loud.

Pastor Taylor reached over and patted my hand. "You have a compassionate heart, Ivy. And a very inquisitive nature. I think that's why you're able to help so many people. Most of us would feel bad for this man and walk away. But you always go the extra mile. I think you have a yearning for justice. It's a gift from God."

Without warning my eyes teared up. "Everyone else says I stick my nose where it doesn't belong. You and

Amos are the only ones who've ever seen my nosiness as a gift."

Bev smiled at me. "I think a few folks in this town are a little afraid of someone who has been so instrumental in bringing several criminals to justice, Ivy. They think you have some kind of power to see inside their minds, but of course, that's just silly. I can't tell you how much I admire you. Since you've come to town, several bad people have been called to account for their evil deeds." She blushed. "Goodness. That sounds very melodramatic, but you know what I mean, don't you, dear?"

A tear ran down my cheek before I could wipe it away. "Yes," I whispered, "I know exactly what you mean. Thank you for saying it." I gazed back toward the table where Edith Baumgartner sat, giving me the hairy eyeball. "I'm afraid most people don't see things the way you do. This Santa Claus story is certainly going to add fuel to the fire."

"Well," Pastor Taylor said, "you may not want to hear this, but I have to agree with my wife. Having Santa Claus fall off your roof isn't an everyday occurrence, now, is it?"

"No, it certainly isn't," Amos said. "But I've begun to realize that being married to Ivy means my life will never be boring."

I slapped his arm. "Being married to me? I had nothing to do with that man sliding off our roof."

"I know that. Quit hitting me. It seems that you— you attract unusual things."

I sighed. "You sound just like Hitchens. You think

I have Cabot Cove Syndrome, too."

Amos shook his head vigorously. "No way," he said, imitating the sheriff's gravelly voice. "You ain't no Jessica Fruity Fletcher."

Bev and Pastor Taylor guffawed at Amos's dead-on impersonation of our quirky sheriff. I couldn't help but join in. Just as everyone began to settle down, Bonnie arrived with our burgers. The aroma drew my attention away from the conversation. Ruby and Bert topped the massive burgers with two slices of thick, sharp cheddar cheese. It always went on after the burgers came off the grill. It was the warmth of the meat and the hot, grilled onions piled on top that melted the cheese. Between the buns and the burger was a slice of tomato, a lettuce leaf, some sweet pickle relish, and a generous dab of mustard.

Although Ruby did allow her customers to ask for spicy mustard if they preferred, everyone knew never to request ketchup on a Redbird Burger. Ruby had suspended Redbird Burger privileges only once that I knew of. A traveling salesman pushing tractor parts had stopped in at the diner after being told about Ruby's heavenly hamburgers by some of his customers. There was a ketchup dispenser on a nearby table that had been used on a pile of Ruby's homemade french fries. Those were one of the few things she allowed ketchup to touch. Before anyone could stop him, he pulled off his bun and squirted the red stuff all over it. I was told that all conversation in the diner stopped. When the man went to pay his bill, he was informed in no uncertain terms that he had eaten his last Redbird

Burger. He never came back.

Amos and I bowed our heads, and he said a brief prayer. It was a necessary form of protection before devouring the humongous slab of beef. I cut my burger in half. The cheddar cheese in the middle gurgled out and ran down the side. "You said you wanted to ask me a question. Was there something else on your mind besides our strange encounter last night?"

Pastor Taylor bobbed his head up and down. "I almost forgot. I wanted to talk to you about the Christmas play."

Faith Community's annual Christmas Eve play was a long-standing Winter Break tradition. Almost everyone, even the members of First Mennonite Church, gathered at Faith Community on Christmas Eve. In fact, several of the roles were played by members of First Mennonite. The re-creation of the birth of Jesus was resplendent with angels and farm animals. The plum roles of Mary and Joseph were sought after as if they would propel the chosen actor and actress to fame and stardom. Of course, this wasn't true except in the case of Harriet Weatherwax, who in the 1960s went on to play the role of Stella in *A Streetcar Named Desire* in a production by the Liberal Playhouse Group. Supposedly, her performance was show-stopping. Not long after that, she left Winter Break for Hollywood. It is still whispered among the citizens of Winter Break that going from the role of Mary to Stella sent Harriet on a downward spiral that resulted in her ending up as a go-go dancer. However, I had it on pretty good authority from Ruby Bird that Harriet moved to

Omaha to live with her sister, where she got married and is now a grandmother several times over, as well as a pillar in her church. Of course, that story isn't as interesting as the go-go dancer angle.

"What about the play?" I asked the question and then took a big bite of my burger. That way I could chew while Pastor Taylor talked. Planning was everything.

He pushed the remainder of his burger around on his plate and sighed. "Did you hear that Sarah Johnson quit as director?"

I stopped chewing and tried to swallow everything in my mouth so I could respond. That resulted in a brief moment of choking. Amos began pounding on my back, which was much more painful than the momentary discomfort that came from a lack of oxygen. Finally, I was able to choke out, "Stop beating me!" After getting the remaining burger down my throat, I took a drink of water. "Sarah Johnson has directed that play for the past twenty years. What happened?" My voice came out sounding like someone had their hands around my neck and was choking the life out of me. Pastor Taylor looked perplexed.

"She asked why Sarah quit," Amos said, interpreting for me. I made an inner vow not to try to talk with my mouth full again. My mother's admonition all those years ago turned out to be a wise one after all.

"Oh," Pastor Taylor said, concern for my well-being still obvious in his expression. "Her daughter in Wichita is expecting. The baby isn't due until the end of January, but her doctor said they might do a Caesarean by the weekend because of complications.

She left to be with her."

I looked at him blankly, still not seeing what this had to do with me.

"She doesn't understand why you're telling her this," Amos said helpfully.

"Okay, that's enough," I said crossly. "I haven't lost the power of speech. Why are you telling me this, Pastor?"

He and Bev quickly exchanged glances. Uh-oh. I had a feeling I wasn't going to like his answer.

"You are so creative, Ivy," my soon-to-be ex-pastor said, smiling. "Could you see your way clear to step in for Sarah?" Adding another incentive, he said, "There just isn't anyone else."

"I—I—I—" I suddenly wished I was choking again. It would explain my inability to form a coherent sentence. "Pastor," I finally spit out, "selling books doesn't qualify me to direct a play." Of course, my two years of drama classes in high school may have had some bearing on my ability to fill in at the last moment, but I had no intention of sharing that. Once again, my soon-to-be-ex-husband jumped in to help me out.

"Ivy took drama in high school," he said proudly. "She directed several plays, didn't you, honey?"

The icy stare I sent his way stopped him in mid-bite. "Yes, I did. Thank you for bringing that up, *dear*. But it's been a long time. Why don't you do it, Bev?" I said with a guilty smile. As if she didn't have enough to do.

She shook her head. "I would if I could, Ivy, but

it just doesn't work. I tried to help Sarah one year, and there were all kinds of problems. Any direction I gave caused hurt feelings. There were charges of favoritism. We almost lost one of our ushers because I told him that he needed to bow when he presented the baby Jesus with his gift of frankincense. When he bent down, his turban fell off and his toupee followed. It was rather embarrassing."

"You do know that the wise men actually arrived a couple of years after Jesus was born, right?" I said.

"Yes," Pastor Taylor said. "We also know that Jesus was probably born in April. The play wasn't originally written with the wise men included. Mariah Pettibone, Alma's mother, added them in the late seventies, but now everyone is used to them. If we ever tried to kick them out, there would be a revolt in Winter Break that would equal the summer when Ruby declared she wasn't making any more Redbird Burgers." He shuddered. "I can't go through that again."

"There really isn't anyone else?"

The Taylors shook their heads in unison, the same rather pitiful look etched on both their faces. "I certainly can't do it, Ivy," Pastor said. "I'm already playing the prophet. I just don't have any extra time, and I'd run into the same problem Bev had if I tried to direct."

"I'll help around the house so you'll have more time," Amos said cautiously. Obviously he was getting a little more careful with his offers of assistance. Smart man.

I knew when I was licked. "Okay, okay. What do I do next?"

Pastor Taylor's smile almost split his face in two. "Oh, thank you, Ivy. God will bless you back. When you give, it is given back to you, pressed down, shaken together—"

"Yeah, yeah," I said, interrupting him. "Thanks. Now when's the next rehearsal?"

"Tonight at seven. I'll meet you at the church, and I'll let everyone know about the changes. There'll be a copy of the script waiting for you. And if it's any consolation, most of the characters have played their parts for years. I think this play could go on without a director since everyone is so acquainted with it. The only new cast members besides Barney Shackleford are Joseph and Mary. Zach Baumgartner is playing Joseph because Buddy Taylor didn't think he should spend too much time away from Emily, and Faith Baumgartner is playing Mary." He lowered his voice and looked a little uncomfortable. "Unfortunately, Maybelle Pennypacker, who usually plays Mary, had to withdraw because she sprained her foot. I need to warn you that Bertha wanted to take her place."

Amos's mouth dropped open. "Bertha Pennypacker thought she could play the role of Mary? I mean—I'm not saying—I mean—"

I stopped him before he tripped over his tongue and his head landed in his plate. "Bertha wouldn't make a good Mary. She's too old, too big, and, well, too. . ." I wanted to say "coarse," but it didn't sound right.

Pastor Taylor nodded. "Yes, she's 'too' a lot of things. Sarah didn't want to hurt her feelings, but she knew it wouldn't have been a good match. Even though, as Bertha pointed out, she has black hair like Mary."

At some point in her life, Bertha had decided that she was supposed to have jet-black hair. And she was so wrong. It looked ludicrous on her, but no one had the heart to tell her so. The cheap home perms she gave herself only turned her overly dyed hair to frizz. There was no way to say it nicely; Bertha Pennypacker was not an attractive lady.

"So how did Sarah get her to back off?"

Pastor Taylor and his wife exchanged side-glances. "You know Bertha makes a lot of her own clothes, right?" Bev said.

I certainly did. Unfortunately, it was painfully obvious. Either Bertha was under the impression she was a child, or she thought she actually looked good in lace, bows, and bright, flowery dresses. And she was wrong about that, too.

"Sarah told her we really needed her more in the wardrobe department and asked her if she would help Inez Baumgartner make and repair all the costumes. That seemed to satisfy Bertha. Then she asked Faith to take the part of Mary."

"So Bertha will be helping with costumes? How does Inez feel about that?" I was distressed to hear the squeak in my voice. I'd just spent the morning defending Bertha to Dewey. The idea of working with her concerned me, though. Bertha wore her feelings on her sleeve and could get offended very easily. I hoped Inez, Emily's mother, would be able to keep her happy.

"You know Inez," Bev replied. "She said she

was happy for the help and would welcome Bertha's involvement."

"That sounds like Inez. I'm sure it will work out fine," I said with more conviction than I felt.

The Taylors appeared to take this as a sign that they should evacuate the premises immediately before I changed my mind. After thanking me again, they both ran toward the front door as if the devil himself were chasing them.

Amos scooted out of our side of the booth and slid into the other side. We preferred sitting that way because we liked to be able to face each other. However, I was pretty sure the expression on my face wasn't something he was going to enjoy seeing.

He ignored the warning. "Are you sure you know what you're doing?" he asked, his eyebrows knitted together with concern for me.

I almost tossed the rest of my Redbird Burger at him. But he probably would have liked that. "Are you kidding me?" I hissed. "You practically threw me at them! Why didn't you consider the ramifications a little sooner?"

He picked up his burger. "It sounded like something you could do." Then he took a big bite as if it would protect him somehow. It didn't.

"You should have allowed me to make this decision on my own. Your little cheerleader 'rah-rahs' didn't help me."

After swallowing, he approached the subject a different way. "Look, Ivy," he said defensively, "I think this will be a good chance for you to get involved a little more in the church. All we do is sit in the pew every Sunday. We haven't really volunteered to help out in any of the ministry outreaches."

"That's because I've been trying to get the bookstore on its feet, and you've been chasing bad guys all over the county."

I hoped bringing up his current problem would help us to change the subject for a while. I needed a distraction so I could adjust my attitude. Amos was right about giving some time and effort at church. I'd been thinking about it for a while. But directing the Christmas play hadn't made it onto my list of possibilities. A small voice inside my head brought up the idea that there was a slight chance this was where God wanted me to be—even if I didn't see it yet. I was mulling that over in my mind, but I wanted to wait awhile for the idea to ferment before I embraced it. Being upset was a lot easier.

Thankfully, my attempt at changing the subject succeeded. Amos sighed and shook his head. "Got a report about another farmer's diesel fuel being pilfered the night before last. There's no rhyme or reason to the pattern. We always seem to be in the wrong place at the wrong time."

"I understand that diesel fuel prices have risen, but I don't understand what the thief is doing with all of it."

"Thieves," Amos said, correcting me. "There's got to be more than one person involved. No single individual could pull this off."

"Okay, *thieves*. My point is, who in the world needs hundreds of gallons of diesel fuel?"

Amos sighed. "Farmers who use it to fuel their farm equipment. Of course, there's not a huge call for it in the winter, but come spring, without enough fuel, their farms could come to a standstill."

I thought for a moment. "Who would have a vehicle large enough to steal that much fuel in the first place?"

Amos, who had used my brief pause to take another bite of his burger, held his finger up, signifying that he needed some time to properly chew and swallow. After my experience, I respected his decision. I used his chewing time to take another bite myself.

"That's an excellent point," he said finally. "It would have to be someone with a truck that could hold a pretty large transfer tank."

I shrugged my shoulders, using the charades form of communication.

"Another farmer," he said, answering my unspoken question. "Either it's a farmer—or someone who works with diesel fuel. But we haven't had one lead that's checked out." Amos stared down at his half-eaten burger with a frown. "Unfortunately, trying to eliminate all the farmers in the area is going to be a Herculean job. I suggested that we investigate everyone who has had fuel stolen just in case someone is trying to avoid suspicion by playing a victim, but Hitchens thought it would be a waste of time. He says the real thief won't do anything that will bring him across our radar screen."

I reached across the table and grabbed his hand. "Well, I think your idea has real merit. Maybe you should be the sheriff of Stevens County after Hitchens retires."

Amos snorted. "Fat chance of that. I'm too low on the totem pole to get a chance at the job. The undersheriff will probably get it."

"The Bible says that promotion comes from God," I said.

"It would certainly take an act of God for me to get elected."

"Well, maybe you'll be a sheriff somewhere else. Stevens County doesn't have the only sheriff's department in Kansas."

Amos nodded, but I was pretty sure he was thinking the same thing I was. We had no desire to leave Winter Break. Not only was the town our home, but we now lived in our dream house. I'd fallen in love with the cornflower blue, Queen Anne–style Victorian house with its large wraparound porch, turrets, and balconies the very first time I saw it when I was a little girl. Amos loved it as much as I did. The owners, Marion and Cecil Biddle, who had moved to Florida, sold it to us for much less than it was worth because they believed that the house was supposed to be ours. I couldn't imagine walking away from it—or from Winter Break.

Amos finished his burger, but I had to leave some of mine. I knew if I finished it, I'd feel miserable the rest of the afternoon and would probably fall asleep at my desk. Amos waved at Bonnie, who came over after dropping burgers off at another table.

"Bonnie," Amos said when she stepped up next to us, "I've got some flyers I'd like to post around the café and on the windows. Can you ask Ruby to step out here a minute so I can ask her if it's okay?"

The truth was, since he worked for the sheriff's department, he could have insisted that the flyers go up. But it was always better to approach Ruby with a request rather than an order. She didn't take kindly to being told what to do.

"Why don't you bring them up to the cash register, and I'll ask her to come out and take a look at them," Bonnie said. The folder with the flyers Amos had made at home and copied at the office was sitting on the table. When he opened the folder and pulled them out, Bonnie took one and stared at it. "Be better if you had a picture of the guy," she said. "This description doesn't say much."

"I agree," Amos said. "But I'm not sure how to distribute a picture of a corpse, especially with a large head wound. A drawing that shows how he looked when he was alive might work, but the only person on our staff who draws worth a lick is Big Marge, and she won't get near a dead body."

Bonnie hesitated for a moment. "You know," she said slowly, "I used to be a pretty fair sketch artist. In fact, I won a couple of awards in school. I still draw a little, but I suppose the—the body is already on its way to the coroner's office?"

"No, he's still at Elmer's. Will be until Lucy gets here to check him over. I guess she plans on coming tomorrow." He touched Bonnie's arm. "I hate to ask this, but would you consider giving this a shot? I could redo the flyers and add your sketch."

She grimaced. "I want to help, Amos. I'm just not

sure how I'll react. I've never done anything like this before."

"Could you give it a try? If it's too difficult, we'll forget it. But if you can do it, it sure might help us to figure out who this guy is. Someone in Winter Break should know him. I can't imagine he'd pick this small town unless there was some kind of connection."

"Okay, I guess I can try." Bonnie glanced at her watch. "How about four o'clock? Things will wind down here by then. I could run over to Elmer's for a few minutes."

"That would be wonderful," Amos said gratefully. "I'll meet you at four. In the meantime, I'd still like to post what I've got. Just in case."

After telling us again to wait at the cash register for Ruby, Bonnie left. Amos handed me the folder and took a box of metal tacks out of his inside coat pocket. "Will you help me put some of these up on the walls?" He took some tape from his other pocket. "I'll take the front window and the bathroom."

"I guess, but if Bonnie decides she can draw the picture you want, we'll have to do this all over again."

"It's worth it if we can find this guy's family. I think they have a right to know he's dead."

"You're right," I said, grabbing my purse and pulling out some money for Bonnie's tip.

We waited for a couple of minutes at the cash register for Ruby to come out of the kitchen. While we stood there, we were inundated with questions from residents who wanted to know if we'd really killed Santa Claus. I knew they were trying to be funny, but Winter

Break kids were out of school for Christmas vacation, and two of them sat nearby. I was afraid they'd hear the jokes and be devastated. I finally hushed Newton and Marybelle Widdle, who wanted to know if we planned on delivering all the Christmas presents ourselves this year. Everyone had pretty much settled down when Ruby Bird hit the metal doors that led to the kitchen with both hands and yelled out, "So I hear you two dropped ol' Saint Nick off your roof and broke his neck!"

One look at the wide eyes of Jake and Mindy Miller and their parents, Bill and Marie, told me that life was going to be difficult in Winter Break for a while.

5

Amos dropped me off at the bookstore and headed to Hugoton. He intended to tell the sheriff about Bonnie and come back early to meet her at Buskin's Funeral Home. On Fridays, I send out books to people who have purchased them from me. I had quite a lot of books going out, so I busied myself with getting boxes and mailers ready to take to Alma at the post office. Although it wasn't his regular workday, Isaac Holsapple, my assistant, came over at about one thirty to help me. As we were sorting through books, I told him about agreeing to direct the church play.

"Do you think that's wise, Miss Ivy?" The thick lenses in his large round spectacles made his eyes appear huge. He looked like a surprised owl.

I carefully wrapped a first edition of *The Silver Trumpet* by Owen Barfield in bubble wrap and placed it in one of the boxes. "I don't know. I want to get more involved at church, and Pastor Taylor could really use the help." I shrugged and picked up another book. "Besides, what can go wrong with a play about the birth of Christ? We're all brothers and sisters in the Spirit."

Isaac shook his head. "I've never been involved in the play before, but I am in the choir. Down through the years, we've certainly seen our share of problems."

I glanced over at him. He sat on the floor in front of an empty box, a pile of books next to him. His thin body, long stringy hair, and oversized nose reminded me of an anorexic troll. But the funny thing about Isaac was that when he smiled, there was something beautiful in him that transcended his outward appearance. Over the past two years he had become more than my assistant. He was my dear and trusted friend. He still insisted on calling me *Miss* Ivy. It was an old habit that began when I was a child. He called my aunt *Miss* Bitty out of respect for her as his employer, and because I was her niece, the custom had passed to me. Now that he worked for me, he continued the practice. It bothered me at first, but now I accepted it as part of his personality. I'd tried to make a joke out of it once by calling him *Mr.* Isaac. His reaction wasn't positive. In fact, he seemed offended. I never did it again.

"Hopefully this year will go smoothly," I said. "I'm praying for that."

"If I can do anything to help you, please don't hesitate to ask. Alma and I know the songs, so we have some extra time."

"Thank you. I appreciate that. How are things going with you two?"

Isaac stopped and stared at the book in his hand. "Quite well, actually. I care for her very deeply."

I stopped what I was doing. "Are you thinking about *popping the question?*"

He gazed up at me, his eyes even bigger than before. "I don't know. I've thought about it, but with my past history. . ."

When Isaac was young, he'd caused a car crash that

took the life of Bitty's fiancé, Robert. After the accident, Isaac's life had spiraled out of control. Eventually his wife divorced him and took his son. He never heard from them again. Bitty found out about his situation and went to the rescue, letting him know not only that she forgave him, but that God had forgiven him, too. Then she offered him a job. He'd been at the bookstore ever since.

"Isaac," I said as gently as I could, "you're a different person now. You deserve to find love. Why don't you ask God what *He* wants? If He tells you to go for it, maybe you could trust Him, even if you don't trust yourself."

He smiled and nodded. "Wise words, Miss Ivy. Thank you. I will consider them carefully."

"And as far as your offer of assistance with the play, maybe you could take over as director? That would be a great help."

He laughed. "I'm dreadfully sorry, but I don't want to steal your glory. I'm sure you understand."

"Oh, big help you are."

He laughed again, and we got back to work. It took us a couple of hours to get everything ready to go. Isaac offered to take the packages to the post office. With more snow on the way, there was no telling when they'd actually go out, but at this point, the best we could do was get them to Alma and hope for the best. Besides, I was certain Isaac and Alma would welcome the chance to see each other.

After he left, I kept working. There were a few books I'd been looking for to sell to interested buyers. I spent some time searching the Internet to see if I could find worthwhile copies within my price range.

A little after four, Miriam Tuttle, a widow who had been left with quite a bit of debt when her husband died, stopped by with two shopping bags full of books she hoped I'd be willing to buy. Her grandson, Benjie, helped her carry them inside the store. Benjie's parents had deserted him as a baby. Miriam had no idea where his father was, but Mary Beth, Miriam's daughter, was in rehab again in Kansas City. I'd lost count of how many times Mary Beth had broken her promise to stay clean and sober. Yet Miriam had faith that someday she'd get her daughter back and Benjie's mother would return to him.

The church was helping Miriam get back on her feet. Several people, including Barney Shackleford, had paid off some old farm loans and were helping to make the monthly mortgage payments. Dewey had forgiven a fairly substantial account at the store. The church was doing exactly what it was supposed to do—take care of widows and orphans. And Faith Community wasn't the only church reaching out to Miriam and Benjie. First Mennonite had committed to helping Miriam get her crop ready in the spring. I had no idea what would happen down the road. I guessed that at some point, Miriam would probably sell her farm, but there was no doubt that she and Benjie would be taken care of by the Winter Break Christian community.

"I—I hope there's something here you can use," Miriam said softly as eight-year-old Benjie lifted the two bags up onto my desk. I couldn't help but notice her thin cloth coat. There were patches upon patches trying to hold it together. And her hands were chapped and red. No one in Winter Break went outside in the winter without gloves. Miriam obviously didn't have any, yet Benjie sported a heavy, quilted coat with a hood, insulated gloves, and snow boots that looked brand new. I was certain Miriam had put her grandson's needs above her own.

I lifted the books out of the bags and quickly checked them over. Although all the books were old, the first group I viewed didn't contain anything valuable. However, at the bottom of the second bag was an old Fannie Farmer cookbook that was worth about seventy dollars. I looked at Miriam, who was staring at me with hopeful expectation. She was holding Benjie's hand, her thin fingers wrapped tightly around his. It was entirely possible that my decision would determine what kind of Christmas they would have this year. I smiled. "Why, Miriam, what a treasure you have here. Would you accept two hundred and fifty for these books?"

Her pale blue eyes filled with tears, and her tremulous smile was worth more than all the money I had in the bank. She nodded quickly. Benjie's big, dark eyes widened with joy. He grinned and hugged his grandmother. "I told you those old books were worth something, Grandma," he said. Then he straightened up and stuck out his chin. "She doesn't know much about books," he told me solemnly. "I had to talk her into bringing them to you."

"You have a good eye, Benjie," I said with a smile. "Maybe you could help me out here sometimes. An hour or so after school would be great. I could give you, say, twenty dollars a week?"

His eyes widened. "That would be really neat." He looked up at Miriam. "Is it okay, Grandma?"

Miriam wiped a tear from her cheek. "As long as your homework is done, I think that would be wonderful." She gave me a grateful smile. "Thank you, Ivy. You're so kind—"

"Oh, shoot and bother," I said, interrupting her. "He'll be a real asset. Benjie, if you'll drop by after Christmas, we'll get a schedule set up. But as your grandmother says, you have to have your homework out of the way first. In fact, if you want to, you could bring it with you and study in the sitting room before you start your work."

"Okay," he said with a grin. "I really like it here."

I reached over and ruffled his dark hair. "I do, too, Benjie." I pulled out my checkbook and wrote Miriam a check. When I handed it to her, she grabbed onto my hand and held it for a few seconds.

"God bless you, Ivy," she said. "I don't know how to thank you."

"You don't need to. I think I got the best deal." I was telling the truth, but my reward wasn't monetary. It was something worth much more. Before I lost my nerve, I choked out my next words. "You know what, Miriam, now that I think about it, there is something you could do for me."

The old woman looked surprised. "Anything, dear."

"Would you please take a gander at Bitty's old coat? I don't want to throw it out. If I could find someone who was able to wear it—well, it would mean a lot to me."

"I'd be happy to take a look at it," she said uncertainly. "We were about the same size."

"That's why I thought of you. If you'll wait just a minute, I'll go upstairs and get it."

All the way up the stairs, my legs felt like they weighed a thousand pounds. I didn't want to give Bitty's coat away. What was I doing? I went into her room and opened the closet door. The beautiful coat hung there in front of me. I stared at it while I searched desperately for a way to tell Miriam I'd changed my mind. Suddenly Bitty's voice drifted through my thoughts.

"Why, Ivy. Don't you know that there's nothing on this earth we can truly give away? God will always find a way to bless you back for what you do for others. You can't possibly outgive Him. Besides, you know where your real treasure is, don't you?"

I wiped away the tear that trickled down my cheek and grabbed the coat with the gloves still in the pocket. And on a hook near the coat was Bitty's black wool hat. It looked great with the coat. I plucked it from the hook and headed down the stairs. My legs felt much lighter coming down than they had going up.

Miriam gasped when she saw the coat. "Oh my," she said, her voice trembling. "I remember it now. I always thought it was the most beautiful coat I'd ever seen."

I smiled. "I'm so glad. If you can give it a home, it would mean more to me than I can express. Why don't you try it on?"

Miriam slid out of the green wool coat she was

wearing and put her arms inside the black tweed. Although I already knew it would fit her, she looked thrilled when she buttoned the front buttons.

"My goodness," I said. "It looks like it was made for you, Miriam. I can hardly believe it."

"I—I don't know what to say." Tears spilled down the old woman's wrinkled cheeks. "Are you sure you want to give this to me? I mean, it was Bitty's, and it's so nice. . . ."

"Don't be silly," I said, handing her the hat and pulling the gloves out of the pocket. "These go with it. I'm so happy to find someone who can get some use out of it."

I picked up the old coat and held it out to her. She started to take it, but Benjie reached out and pulled her hand away. "You need to throw that old thing away, Grandma," he insisted. "I told you it wasn't any good." He looked up at me. "Can you throw it in the trash, Ivy? It's so bad no one else will wear it. Grandma's mended it so many times there's nowhere else to sew."

I looked at Miriam. "What would you like me to do?"

She gazed down at her new coat and stroked the soft fabric. "I think I'd like you to throw it away if you don't mind." A smile lit up her face. "Yes, I think that's what I would like you to do. Would it be too much trouble?"

"No," I said gently. "It would be a distinct pleasure."

As they headed toward the door, Benjie turned around and grinned at me. "Mindy Miller told me that you and Amos killed Santa Claus, but I know you didn't do it." His beatific smile didn't quench the sick feeling in my stomach. Obviously the story about Chuck's final moments had spread like wildfire throughout Winter Break. Amos and I were going to have to do something about the situation before parents began banning us from contact with their children.

"Hush, Benjie," Miriam scolded. "I told you that man wasn't Santa Claus."

"I know that, Grandma," he responded patiently. "I know Santa is still at the North Pole. That's what I told Mindy. She tried to tell me that Santa couldn't bring me a BMX bike like the one in the window in Hugoton because he's dead." He pulled at his grandmother's sleeve. "But he's not, and I'm sure he's going to bring me that bike. You just watch." He waved at me and pulled Miriam toward the door. "Bye, Ivy!"

I waved good-bye, but as they walked out, I wondered about that bike comment. The look on Miriam's face displayed doubt that she was going to be able to fulfill his request from Santa. Maybe old Saint Nick was going to need a little more help.

I busied myself the rest of the afternoon with paperwork, but my mind kept wandering back to Miriam and Benjie. I'd never talked to Amos about how we would handle Santa Claus when we had children, but my intention was to do it exactly the way my parents had. They'd made it clear from the beginning that Santa Claus wasn't a real person. I'd also been informed that it wasn't my job to set other children straight—that it was up to their parents to decide what they were told. I'd kept the secret, but I'd been tempted a couple of times to blurt out the truth.

In the second grade, Debbie Dunagan told me that I was so bad Santa would never bring me anything. And in third grade, Mrs. Hess, my teacher, informed the entire class that I could expect a large lump of coal in my stocking because I drew a picture of her with a witch's hat and a big, long nose that sported a huge, hairy wart. I was able to keep my mouth shut, but only because I felt quite superior to the other poor, misled children who believed Santa Claus to be authentic.

A few years ago, I'd asked my mother exactly why they'd never given in to the whole Santa Claus myth. "Ivy," my mother had said seriously, "it was because when we really thought about it, we were afraid if we weren't honest about the existence of Santa Claus, you might not believe us when we talked to you about God. And we couldn't take that chance." She'd sighed and hugged me. "And we've never been sorry about that decision. You've always known that God was real. That's all we ever wanted."

A little after five thirty, Amos opened the front door. "Hey, Bonnie drew a pretty good picture of Chuck. I already made up new flyers and took them over to Ruby's. Hopefully we'll finally get some answers."

"I hope you're right." I closed my account books and locked them in my desk. Then I stood up and stretched. I was stiff from sitting so long.

"Hitchens wasn't in the office, so I had to leave him a message about the new flyers. But I'm sure he'll be pleased." He briskly rubbed his arms with his gloved hands. "I hope play practice doesn't last too long tonight. I'm chilled to the bone. I want to go home, watch some football, and sit in front of the fire."

I smiled as he took off his coat and hat and hung them up on the rack by the door. "We've got a fire right here. Why don't you sit in front of that, and I'll make us a couple of sandwiches."

"Sounds good. I don't suppose you have a football we can toss around?"

"Sorry. I'm afraid you'll have to get your fix this weekend."

"Okay," he grumbled. "But I have a feeling watching play practice tonight isn't going to be as exciting as watching the Colts."

Amos had become a huge fan of Tony Dungy and the Indianapolis Colts. Tony was a great coach and an even greater Christian. Amos deeply respected him. "I'm sure the play will be very exciting. Even if no one goes for a scream pass."

Amos raised an eyebrow and stared at me. "A *scream* pass? Do you mean a *screen* pass?"

"*Screen* pass. Sorry. Did I just offend your football sensibilities?"

He folded his arms and leaned against the stairs. "I don't know how to answer that, because I don't know what football sensibilities are, but I am intrigued by your use of the term *scream pass*. Were you under the impression that at some point in the game the players would actually scream? How did you imagine that would work? Maybe it would confuse the other team and they'd drop the ball?"

"Oh, for goodness' sake, let it go," I mumbled. "You take sports way too seriously." I scooted my chair in and turned off my desk lamp.

"Well," he said, giving me an odd look, "at least I don't take it so seriously I feel the need to scream about it."

"Do you want a sandwich or not?" I could feel my face getting hot. I probably looked like a beet with red hair. Not an attractive sight.

"I'll help you carry everything downstairs." He grabbed me as I walked by and pulled me close. "Sometimes you're really cute, you know that?"

Before I could answer, he kissed me. I almost forgot why I was irritated with him. Almost. When he pulled back, I smiled up at him. "You're cute, too. But if you don't stop making fun of me, I may kick Elmer Buskins out of the play and make you play the part of the Roman soldier."

He laughed. "Sorry, but our yearly play wouldn't be the same without his opening line: 'Hear ye, *thitithenth* of Galilee.'"

I slapped him on the arm and pushed him away. "Quit making fun of Elmer. He can't help it if he has a speech impediment."

"Hey, I'm just glad they moved him from being a shepherd. When he said, 'You thood be a theep,' everyone thought he was telling the other shepherds they should be *sheep*. It was pretty confusing."

"I have to admit that the line between *a sheep* and *asleep* is pretty thin when it comes out of Elmer's mouth." I shook my finger at him, but I couldn't keep a smile off my face. "Let's quit talking about poor Elmer and get our dinner ready."

We went upstairs and I made two large corned beef and Swiss cheese sandwiches with spicy mustard. After Pal had come to live with us, I'd had to go home every day at noon to let him out. I'd started eating lunch at home and had quit keeping much food in the little kitchen above the bookstore. But since Amos installed a doggy door, I'd restocked Bitty's old fridge and the kitchen shelves to provide for lunches and emergency dinners—like tonight. At first I'd been afraid that Miss Skiffins would try to get out the small door that led to the back patio at home, but she had no use for it. She'd hated the outside ever since the time she'd gotten out once accidentally. It was actually Pal who'd brought her home, and I was pretty sure he wasn't willing to repeat the performance. He kept a close watch on her, so I didn't worry about it.

We carried our sandwiches downstairs, ate, and sat in front of the fire in the sitting room until it was time to head over to the church.

"So what's your plan?" Amos asked as we put on our coats. "Are you going to get really involved tonight or just let everyone run through the play so you can see what needs to be done?"

I held out my arms and let Amos help me into my heavy coat. "I have no idea," I said. "I assume this thing will go smoothly. I mean, most of the performers have been playing the same role for years."

"Yes, but your Mary and Joseph are new. And one of your shepherds. You'll probably have to help them."

"Well, maybe, but I'm sure they've been practicing. Besides, there aren't that many lines. Most of the play seems to be spent chasing errant sheep who try to run off the stage."

Amos opened the door, and we stepped out into a frigid night with snow falling rather furiously. Not the least bit unusual for Winter Break.

"At least they don't try to put one of Newton Widdle's cows next to the manger anymore. Every time the audience clapped, the poor cow would—"

"I remember what the cow would do," I said, interrupting him. "Let's not bring that up."

Amos laughed. "I can still recall the smell—"

"Oh, hush," I said, trying not to giggle. At the time, it hadn't been funny to the actors onstage, but I had to admit that it was pretty humorous to those of us who watched from the audience. I opened the car door and slid inside, quickly slamming the door behind me. Unfortunately, the interior wasn't much warmer than the exterior.

When we pulled into the church parking lot, there were already quite a few cars. Besides the actors and the people who worked behind the scene, play practices usually drew a respectable crowd. Isaac told me that Sally Redfield, who owns Sally's Sew 'n' Such, would bring her knitting, and Dewey would sit in the back and eventually fall asleep. Most practices were accompanied by the sound of Dewey's snoring.

We parked as close as we could and then held on to each other as we navigated the icy parking lot. Living in Winter Break meant you needed heavy boots with good traction. We were all pretty practiced at traversing the snow and ice.

When we stepped inside the church, there was a rush of warm air that felt so good, it made me shiver. But we kept our coats on. It usually took awhile to warm up.

A few people were standing near the stage. The rest were scattered around the sanctuary. Through the sound of intense discussion, I heard Bertha Penny-packer's shrill voice ring out. "Well, I like her, but I think there's something strange going on there. I guess we just have to hope we all live through this play." The comment was followed by her loud, brash laugh.

I heard someone else say, "Shhhh." All eyes turned toward us. Was Bertha's comment directed at me?

I walked up to the group and looked around. Elmer Buskins was sitting off to the side, away from the main group. He and his employee, Billy Mumfree, were deep into their own conversation. Elmer and I were good friends. I knew he would never take part in a gossip session about me. Marybelle and Newton Widdle were standing next to Bertha. The embarrassed looks on their faces revealed exactly whom they'd been talking about. Maynard Comstock, a church deacon, and the man whose toupee had come off with his turban, sat in the front row. He looked guilty, but I knew he wasn't an instigator. Maynard was a follower. Bubba sat next to him and smiled up at me. He probably didn't have a clue that Bertha's comment was inappropriate.

Several others who had roles in the play were in a group that sat several rows back from the front. They were carrying on an animated conversation with Pastor Taylor. I was convinced that they were oblivious to

Bertha and her pack.

I smiled at Bertha and said hi. Pretending I hadn't heard her was going to be difficult, but I didn't have much choice if I wanted to keep the play going smoothly.

Amos stood next to me, and he looked angry. I grabbed his arm. "Thanks, honey," I said as sweetly as I could, "but I can take it from here. Why don't you sit down and relax." I squeezed his forearm when I said the word "relax." He got the message and walked away, shooting Bertha a frosty look.

"Could I have everyone's attention?" I asked loudly. Elmer and Billy turned and stared at me, and all conversation ceased in the sanctuary. "Could you all move up close to the stage so I won't have to yell?" Bertha and the Widdles sat down on the front row next to Maynard and Bubba. The rest of the people began moving in. The doors at the back of the sanctuary opened, and several other cast members wandered inside. Billy got up and went to a side door on the right side of the room. He stuck his head inside and said something and then went back to his seat. Almost immediately the door swung open and the choir filed out. They'd probably been practicing in the community room. Gail Martin, the beautiful young woman who served as the worship leader at Faith Community, ushered them in. The choir and their leader gathered to my right and waited. I said a quick, silent prayer for guidance. Something I should have done before I actually stood in front of the cast. Aunt Bitty's voice rose up from inside me. "Pray before you get in trouble, Ivy," she used to say. "Asking God to keep the gate closed is a lot easier than asking Him to help you chase down all the cows after they've already left the barn." Well, it was possible at least a few of the cows were running wild. I needed to round them up and slam that gate shut before the situation got out of hand.

I took a deep breath and plastered a smile on my face. "As you all probably know, Sarah Johnson has had to leave town to be with her daughter. I've been asked to fill in as director." I widened my smile, flashed my pearly whites, and hoped that shreds of corned beef weren't stuck between my teeth. "Now I know you guys don't really need a director, because you've got this play down cold, but I'm here to help you in any way I can." I could tell by a couple of quick smiles and relaxed shoulders that my announcement was a welcome one. Pastor Taylor gave me a wink of encouragement that made me feel better, too. "I'm really looking forward to seeing your wonderful play, so let's run through it, okay?"

Inez Baumgartner raised her hand. "We have a small problem," she said softly. "We've lost our Mary."

My stomach turned over. This didn't sound like a small problem to me. "Where did we lose her?" I asked, hoping this was a temporary situation and Mary would turn up shortly.

Inez cleared her throat and raised one eyebrow. "I don't mean we actually *lost* her. I know where she is, but Faith has the flu. She told us to go on without her."

This certainly wasn't what I wanted to hear. First

Maybelle, now Faith. What was it about Mary? I forced myself to keep my eyes from drifting toward Bertha. Was she going to volunteer again?

Inez may have been thinking the same thing, because before anyone had a chance to comment, she interjected, "But we've found a replacement."

As if on cue, the sanctuary doors opened and Hope came walking down the aisle. "Sorry I'm late," she said with a small smile.

I heard a sharp intake of breath that I was certain came from Bertha. I sent another prayer heavenward, but this time it was one of thanksgiving. I glanced quickly at Inez, certain she would be able to interpret the hopeful and extremely relieved look on my face. She nodded, and my stomach settled down.

"Glad to have you, Hope," I said as she slid into the second pew. "Thanks for filling in." To be honest, I was a little surprised. Hope's lack of participation in church had led me to believe she wasn't very interested in spiritual things. I remembered what Zach had said, though, about Hope talking about God. Maybe the play was safe—a way to honor God at Christmas yet not actually be a part of the church. Whatever the reason, I was thrilled she was here. I wondered if she knew who was playing Joseph. This could prove to be very interesting.

"I think we should run through the whole thing once and see where we are," I said, addressing the entire group. "Let's get onstage and try it, okay?"

As the actors and the choir headed toward the platform, I grabbed Hope's arm. "Do you need to use the script? You can read your part until you memorize it."

She smiled. "Thanks, but Inez gave me a copy of the script a couple days ago. I've been going over it. I think I've got it down." She hesitated for a moment before saying, "You know, Christmas isn't my favorite time of the year for quite a few reasons. Usually I wouldn't do this under any circumstances, but when Inez told me there wasn't anyone else, I decided that perhaps it was time to give Christmas another chance." She gazed at me with shiny eyes. "I'm hoping this will be good for me."

I saw Zach coming up from behind her. He patted her lightly on the shoulder. "I'm sure it will be, Hope. I know we're blessed to have you. Forgive me if I'm interrupting," he said to me in his deep, gentle voice. "I just wanted to tell Hope that I'm looking forward to working with her."

Hope jumped at his touch, and she looked surprised to see him. I found it odd since Faith knew that Zach was in the play, and Hope was her friend. I looked over at Inez, who was sitting on the front pew, sewing a robe. She wouldn't return my gaze, but the overly innocent look on her face gave her away. I was pretty sure Faith wasn't that sick and that she and her aunt Inez were playing matchmaker. I just hoped their ploy wouldn't blow up in everyone's face.

"Let's get onstage," I said, trying to distract Hope and get her focused on something besides Zach. As my actors found their spots and the choir climbed up on the risers behind them, Gail took her place in front of them. Although Bev usually played the piano during our services, she'd stepped aside for the pianist from

First Mennonite. Bea Baumgartner was a lovely woman whom everyone loved. Called "Aunt Bea" by those who knew her, she reminded me a lot of Aunt Bitty. She was also a dead ringer for Bea Taylor from the *Andy Griffith Show*. She wasn't as good on the piano as Bev, but no one cared because they all adored her so much. I guess it was an example of "love covering over a multitude of sins," or in this case, a few wrong notes.

I started to walk closer to the stage when I felt someone tug on my sleeve. It was Bertha. "I know you heard what I said, Ivy, even though you acted like you didn't. Sometimes I open my big, stupid mouth when I shouldn't." Her red-rimmed eyes filled with tears. "Can you forgive me—again?"

I wanted to slap her, but instead I hugged her. "Of course, Bertha. Let's just make this play the best one ever, okay?"

I stepped back and she nodded several times. "Okay. I'll do what I can. And thank you. I can't figure out why you're so nice to me."

"I guess it's because God is so nice to us."

That seemed to satisfy her, and she squeezed her large body into the seat next to Inez, who smiled her approval at me.

I walked up closer to the stage, where everyone stood watching their new director, who was wondering why in the world she'd thought she could do this. "Okay, let me see you run through the entire thing. I won't stop or interrupt you. I want to see where we are." I looked back at Byron Bettner, who ran the sound system and the lights. "Don't worry about the lights tonight, Byron.

Just check the sound, okay?"

He nodded, and I sat down. "Okay, Gail. Get us started."

Gail lifted her arms, and Aunt Bea began playing the introduction to "O Little Town of Bethlehem." The choir sang four verses of the beautiful carol. By the time they sang the last line, "O come to us, abide with us, our Lord Emmanuel," I was tearing up.

As soon as the final strains died, Pastor Taylor came walking in from stage right and took his place in the middle of the stage. His deep voice boomed out, saying his part with confidence. He was cast perfectly as the prophet.

"The people walking in darkness have seen a great light; on those living in the land of the shadow of death a light has dawned. You have enlarged the nation and increased their joy; they rejoice before you as people rejoice at the harvest, as men rejoice when dividing the plunder. For to us a child is born, to us a son is given, and the government will be on his shoulders. And he will be called Wonderful Counselor, Mighty God, Everlasting Father, Prince of Peace." He began to descend from the platform and walk down the center aisle of the church, looking to the right and then the left as if talking to the people seated in the pews. "His authority shall grow continually, and there shall be endless peace for the throne of David and his kingdom. He will establish and uphold it with justice and with righteousness from this time onward and forevermore. The zeal of the Lord of hosts will do this." Then he exited the back of the church.

When the door closed behind him, the choir began to sing "O Holy Night." I was trying to envision them in their robes, with the lights shining down from above. I'd seen this play several times when I was a child visiting Aunt Bitty at Christmas, and twice since I'd moved to Winter Break. Every time, I'd felt the presence of the Lord. I realized that volunteering to fill in for Sarah meant that for the very first time, I actually had a part in this wonderful experience. I was humbled and grateful, and I felt bad for complaining about it.

After the song ended, Elmer Buskins entered from stage left. He held his hands up as if reading a scroll, and another Christmas tradition unfolded in front of me. "Hear ye, thitithenth of Galilee. Hear the decwee of Thether Auguthtuth." Elmer stepped down from the platform and also began walking toward the back of the church. "All thitithenth mutht wethithur for the purputh of taxathun. Wegithtwathun mutht be done in the thity of your lineage. Thith hath been decweed."

No one really paid attention to Elmer's speech impediment anymore. We were used to it. If anyone else ever played the part of the soldier, it wouldn't seem right somehow.

Zach and Hope came walking slowly together to the middle of the stage. Zach had his arm around her, supposedly supporting his pregnant wife. Hope seemed stiff and uncomfortable as she delivered her lines, and I worried that being this close to Zach was going to hurt any chance of deepening their relationship. I tried to concentrate on the rest of the play, but my concern for Hope and my curiosity as to why she was so fearful of getting close to people kept interrupting my thoughts.

I tried to shift my concentration to Bubba, who was playing one of the three shepherds. He was supposed to fall to his knees when confronted by an angel who had come to announce the good news that the Messiah had been born. However, the bad news was that Bubba's knees made loud cracking sounds when he attempted to kneel, and I wasn't certain he was going to be able to get up again. I was wondering if he would consider exchanging places with Billy Mumfree, who stood nearby on two younger knees, when someone slid into the pew next to me. I turned my head to find Sister Crystal peering into my face, her steely blue eyes locked onto mine. "I must talk to you a minute," she whispered. "I have a word for you."

I was skeptical that God would interrupt the play with a special telegram for me, but I could always hope He wanted to tell me how to save Bubba's knees without hurting his ego. I stuck my index finger up in the international sign that meant, *Can this wait until the next song from the choir?* Sister Crystal seemed to understand and nodded her head. I refocused my attention on the stage. Billy was helping Bubba to his feet while he was trying to say, "Let us go to Bethlehem and see this thing that has taken place—that the Lord has made known to us." It took a little while, but eventually the shepherds exited stage right, and Gail raised her arms and began to lead the choir in "Hark! the Herald Angels Sing."

I motioned to Sister Crystal that we should go out to the foyer. She slid out and I followed her. Amos raised his eyebrows as we passed him and pointed toward the foyer. I shook my head. I knew he would come with me if I wanted him to, but I felt that I could handle Crystal alone.

"What can I do for you, Sister Crystal?" I asked when the sanctuary doors closed behind us.

"I feel impressed to share a scripture with you," she said. Her tightly permed gray curls shook along with the rest of her. "It is this," she said, her voice taking on an appropriately spiritual tone. "My righteousness draws near speedily, my salvation is on the way, and my arm will bring justice to the nations. The islands will look to me and wait in hope for my arm."

She stepped back and looked at me with expectation. I wasn't sure exactly what I was supposed to do, so I just smiled and nodded like I understood exactly what she meant. With that, she turned on her heel and walked out the front door. I stood there for a moment trying to make some sense out of her words. I finally decided it must be an off day for "words from the Lord" and headed back into the sanctuary. There were no islands in Kansas, and although I definitely wanted justice for Chuck, I couldn't see how that would affect "the nations." Amos looked over at me again, and I shrugged my shoulders. I'd have to tell him about my odd meeting later, after rehearsal.

I took my seat just as the choir reached the last note. Mary and Joseph had returned to the stage. As the singing died away, the shepherds returned. I was distressed to see Bubba limping slightly.

The play progressed without further injury, and once we'd run all the way through, I asked everyone to take a seat while we talked about various problems and concerns. Several people voiced their apprehension about the state of the old costumes, especially the angels' robes and the shepherds' tunics. The old white sheets they'd been made from had seen better days. Billy Mumfree kept asking why his sheet had a yellow stain in the middle, but no one was able to come up with an acceptable answer. Inez told the group that if she could find some good white sheets, she and Bertha would work hard to make new costumes before the play Wednesday night.

Pastor Taylor actually found a tactful way to suggest that Bubba and Billy change parts. The pastor was gentle and caring, and did it in a way that protected Bubba's pride. I was happy he'd taken the reins in that situation. It was more evidence that his pastor's anointing was definitely God-given.

About nine thirty we dismissed, and people started to file out. I spent some time going over my notes. When I was finished, I grabbed my purse and started toward Amos, who was still sitting in his same seat in the back of the sanctuary. Although every time I'd looked back at him he'd appeared to be focusing on the play, I was pretty sure he'd dozed off several times. Trying to chase down the fuel thieves had caused many late nights, since they usually struck after dark. But before I got halfway down the aisle, I heard someone call my name.

Hope stood behind me with a frown on her face. "Ivy, could I talk to you for a minute?" I thought she'd left, and I wondered if she'd been waiting for me all this time.

I came back to where she waited and motioned to the pew next to us. Hope scooted in and I sat down beside her.

"You were wonderful tonight," I said. "Of course, I doubt Mary had short blond hair, but we can fix that."

Hope looked down at her hands, which were in her lap. "Thanks, Ivy, but I'm not sure I can do this. Could you find someone else?"

I reached over and put my hand on top of hers. "Won't you tell me what's bothering you? I know something's wrong, but I don't know what it is."

She looked up at me, her large blue eyes full of pain. "As I told you, I—I'm not a Christmas person," she said softly. "This was an experiment for me, but I think it's no use."

"Can you tell me why you feel this way?" I asked gently. "I'm not being nosy, Hope. You're my friend, and I care about you. Maybe sharing with someone else will help."

Her bottom lip quivered, and she hesitated a moment. Then she took a deep breath. "You know I lived with my grandmother until her death, but you probably don't know why."

"I heard that you'd lost your parents when you were young."

She sighed, and her body trembled. "Yes, I guess

you could say I lost them. They were drunks. My mother died from liver disease when I was four. My father stayed for a few years after that, but when I was six, I woke up on Christmas morning to an empty apartment. He was gone, and I never saw him again. A couple of years later, my grandmother found out that he'd died."

A tear splashed down on my hand, but I left it covering hers.

"That Christmas I woke up expecting a visit from Santa Claus and found out that I was alone." She laughed, but there wasn't any joy in it. The sound hurt me inside. "So you can see why I don't really get much out of this particular holiday."

I was quiet for a moment while I prayed for the right words. "I'm so sorry that happened to you. I hate to see you suffer forever for something that wasn't your fault. What about other Christmases? Didn't you celebrate with your grandmother?"

"We didn't pay much attention to them," she said. "Grandma didn't have much money, so we basically treated it like any other day. About the only thing she ever gave me were books. She would buy them for a few cents at a local used bookstore or at yard sales and then give them to me on Christmas Day. They helped me get through some tough years. I think that's why I love books so much."

"Look, Christmas isn't really about Santa Claus, or presents, or even family, although all those things can be an important part." I squeezed her hand. "It's about love and forgiveness. It's about a Father who won't *ever* leave you or forsake you, Hope, on Christmas or any other day of your life. Maybe the problem is that Christmas for you has been focused on the wrong things. Perhaps if you gave it another chance by approaching it a different way, things could change."

She shrugged. "You might be right. I don't really want to be like this. I'm not happy, and I'm sure I'm no fun to be around."

"Don't be silly," I said, smiling at her. "Everyone loves you. In Winter Break, you're family. And that even includes the people who get on our nerves—just like real family members."

This time her laugh was genuine. "You mean like Bertha Pennypacker?"

I sighed. "Yes, just like Bertha. She's a pill, isn't she?"

"Yes. Yes, she is. You're great with her."

I grinned. "Trust me. I have to rely on the fruit of the Spirit. To be honest, sometimes I'd rather just throw it at her and bop her on the noggin."

We laughed together, and I felt a real connection happen. I wanted to talk about Zach, but I felt a hesitation in my spirit. It wasn't time for that yet. My natural inclination was to jump into anything that bothered me and try to fix it. I was learning that God has a special timing for most things, and if I wanted to succeed, I needed to listen to that inner voice. Maybe I was growing up a little.

"Ivy's right, Hope," a man's voice said. I jumped involuntarily. It was Amos. He'd sat down on the pew behind us, and I hadn't even noticed. "Christmas at my house was pretty much ignored, too. My father used it as an excuse to get drunk and beat up my mother. I hated any holiday that kept him from going to work. Christmas was the worst. But we can't live in the past. I don't want Christmas to be defined by what other people did or didn't do." He reached over and held out his hand. I took it. "With God's help, Ivy and I are going to enjoy our lives the way God intended us to. And I will *not* allow the ghosts of the past to steal that from either one of us." His voice cracked with emotion, and he squeezed my hand.

Tears sprang into my eyes, and Hope wiped her eyes. "God will make everything new if you let Him," Amos continued. "I've been thinking about a couple of verses in Isaiah that say, 'Forget the former things; do not dwell on the past. See, I am doing a new thing! Now it springs up; do you not perceive it? I am making a way in the desert and streams in the wasteland.' " He cleared his throat and struggled to keep his voice steady. "I'm ready to get out of the wasteland and walk into the life I know I can have with Ivy. Maybe it's time for you to make the same decision."

My watery eyes had turned into streams. I'd never heard Amos speak so eloquently. His words were anointed.

"Is this a private crying session, or can anyone join in?" Pastor Taylor stood next to our pew, a look of concern on his face.

Amos stood up and scooted out of his pew. "I think I'm done," he said, shaking his head. "There's only so much emotion a man can stand before he starts worrying about giving in to his feminine side."

Pastor Taylor laughed heartily. "I don't think that's your feminine side at all, Amos. I think that's what happens when the Holy Spirit pushes past your stubborn, he-man side."

I got up and stood beside my husband. "You're still a he-man to me," I said, playfully batting him on the arm. "In fact, you've just gone up a couple of notches on the he-man scale. And here I didn't think you could get any higher." I said it teasingly, but deep down I meant it. A real man is a godly man. It takes strength to allow the Lord to show us our weaknesses so He can make us stronger. Being perfected isn't for the fainthearted. I ought to know.

"Pastor Taylor," Hope said in a quiet voice, "I know you counsel people. Could I possibly meet with you?"

"Of course. When would you like to get together?"

She hesitated, and I felt Amos tugging on my sleeve. I reached over and squeezed Hope's shoulder. "We've got to get going. Do you need a ride back to Sarah's?"

She shook her head. "Thanks, but I'll walk. I want to talk to Pastor Taylor for a few minutes right now if it's all right with him."

"It's more than all right," he said. "Bev's in my office, which means the coffeepot's on. Why don't we go back there and talk?"

I turned and smiled at my husband. "Let's get going, he-man of mine." I waved at Hope and Pastor Taylor. "We'll see you both at Sunday night's rehearsal."

They said good-bye, and as Amos and I headed for the back of the sanctuary, they exited through the side door that led to the pastor's office. We were almost to the double doors when they were pushed open and Newton Widdle rushed in, breathless and red-faced.

"Amos, I've been hit. When we got home, there were tire tracks leading back to my storage tank. I checked it, and most of my fuel is gone."

Before Amos could say anything, Pastor Taylor came jogging into the sanctuary. "Maynard Comstock just called. Someone's made off with some of his diesel fuel."

"Pastor, I need to use your phone," Amos said. He turned to me. "Stay here while I call Hitchens."

As he ran toward Pastor Taylor, he hollered at Newton to wait for him.

This was the first time the thieves had hit Winter Break. I wondered how many other farms had been struck tonight. Our town had been violated, and it felt personal somehow. Newton walked down the aisle and sat down next to me. I didn't worry about whether or not he'd been gossiping about me. All that mattered was that we were family, and we'd been attacked.

6

It was after midnight when Amos got home. I'd fallen asleep in the living room with the TV on. Before Amos woke me up, I was dreaming that I'd lost Amy, my Precious Moments doll, in the snow. She was calling for me, and I couldn't find her. I kept trying to dig through drifts that just got deeper and deeper. Right before I opened my eyes, I felt as if I were drowning under the weight of the snow.

"Ivy, wake up. I'm back," Amos said softly, shaking my shoulder.

I reached up for him, and he sat down on the couch, wrapping his arms around me. Pal was curled up on the other side of us. He raised his head to look at Amos, his tail thumping out his joy that Amos was back where he belonged.

"Hey, boy," Amos said. "You been taking care of Ivy?"

The collie opened his mouth in what looked like a smile. He seemed to know when I was upset and would stay by my side until I felt better. I loved all his sweet doggy traits, but his concern for my well-being probably meant the most to me.

After a while, Amos pulled away and leaned against the back cushion. "Did Odie drive you home?"

I swung my legs off the couch and sat up. "Yes. He was happy to do it."

"Remind me to thank him, will you?"

"I will. So what happened?"

He sighed. "Newton and Maynard weren't the only victims. After he heard about the thefts, Mort Benniker checked his tank. Over four hundred gallons was missing."

I sat up and stared at him. "Mort and Edna are in the choir."

"I know. Everyone who was robbed was at the church tonight. It could be a coincidence, but I doubt it."

"That means whoever took the fuel knew who wouldn't be home. Could the thieves be local?"

Amos ran his hand through his hair. "I've been wondering the same thing, but Hitchens doesn't buy it. All the other thefts have been in other parts of this county or in nearby counties. He thinks it was just our turn."

"This reminds me of the time all those cows were stolen. You don't think Delbert's at it again, do you?"

Amos grunted. "We're really operating on the same wavelength. The identical thought occurred to me, but I saw him in the parking lot of the church when we left. He was there to pick up Bertha. I wondered where he was before that, so I called Bert. Sure enough, Delbert was at Ruby's up until the time he left to go to the church. He'd been there ever since he dropped Bertha off."

"I suppose we're being judgmental by jumping to conclusions. I mean, just because Delbert was behind the cow thefts doesn't mean he's involved in this."

Amos blew air slowly out through his pursed lips. "I don't know if we're being unfair or not. I mean, if a dog steals chickens once, and more chickens disappear, does that make it wrong to suspect the dog?"

I slapped him lightly on the arm. "Oh, Amos. Delbert Pennypacker's not a dog. My goodness."

Amos pulled me a little closer. "I wasn't calling him a dog. I was just trying to make a point."

I wiggled around so I could see his face. "I don't care what Hitchens says. Someone from Winter Break has to be involved, at least with what happened tonight. How in the world would anyone from outside this town know when those three farmers were not at home? I mean, even their wives were with them. No one's that lucky. And besides, don't most farmers keep their fuel tanks near their house or barn?"

"Usually closer to their barns, but what's your point?"

"Even if only one person was home, they would probably see someone messing around their tank."

"Yes." Amos drew his answer out slowly. "The thieves would have to be certain no one at all was on the property. And it's unlikely they could gain that kind of knowledge by simply watching from the outside. Around here, strangers are pretty visible. You're right. Someone in Winter Break is probably involved. At the very least, they're acting as an accomplice."

"That's what I'm saying. How much fuel was stolen?"

"Over seven-hundred gallons from what we can tell."

I shook my head. "You really think there are that many farmers interested in buying stolen fuel? I mean, even with the high prices, I find that rather hard to believe."

Amos stretched out his legs and planted his feet

on the coffee table. Usually I'd tell him to get his size twelves off my furniture, but tonight I kept my mouth shut. It didn't seem important.

"Hitchens is the one sold on the farmer angle."

"Do you think he's wrong?"

"Okay, this might sound goofy, but I know lots of farmers. In my job, I'd say over half of the people I work with own farms. And almost every farm family I've ever met is full of hardworking, honest, good people. There's a strong ethical center in these folks. I have a hard time believing there's a band of rogue farmers buying black-market diesel fuel."

I hadn't met as many farmers as Amos, but the ones I knew, who lived and worked around Winter Break, were exactly the kind of people Amos described. "It doesn't sound silly, Amos. I understand it completely. You think someone else is involved? Someone who is acting like a—a broker? What would he do with the fuel? Could he resell it to farmers without them knowing about it?"

"Not unless he's a distributor. There's red dye added to diesel fuel that's for farm use. If anyone except a distributor tried to sell it, the farmer would know the second he saw the red dye that something was wrong."

"Could it be a crooked distributor?"

Amos sighed. "It's possible, but if that's it, we haven't found them yet."

I contemplated the idea for a minute. "Since the distributors know when the fuel is delivered, they would also know who to hit next."

"But they wouldn't have a clue when the farmers

weren't home. That's one of the reasons that possibility hit a dead end."

"Okay, so what do you think the thieves are doing with the stolen fuel?"

He shrugged his shoulders, making my head bounce. "Selling it to someone. Maybe for commercial over-the-road use. It's been a big problem throughout the country. That's my guess."

"But what about the red dye? Wouldn't the people buying it know it was only supposed to be used for farms?"

He nodded. "If a truck is stopped and their tank is tested, the red dye will prove that the fuel is being misused. Unfortunately, those tests are hardly ever done. Until the government really cracks down, there's definitely a market for low-cost diesel fuel, red or not. A lot of truckers are desperate for it." He tugged on my arm. "Hey, I can barely keep my eyes open. Can we go to bed? I've got to get some shut-eye in case I have to work tomorrow."

"I thought you had tomorrow off." I couldn't keep the disappointment out of my voice. I had some of his day already mapped out.

"We'll have to see. We might need to do a little more investigation. We did get some pictures of tire tracks from Maynard's place. Unfortunately, it started snowing again, so we couldn't take pictures at Mort's or Newton's."

"Maybe the pictures will help you find out who's behind this."

"That would be great, but I doubt they'll do any

good. Almost all the tires on trucks look the same in this part of the state. It's pretty difficult to match tire tracks anyway, especially if you don't already have a suspect in mind. And if the thieves live anywhere in our area, they either bought their tires at Johnson's in Hugoton or at Gully's Tire Shop in Liberal. If they're newer tires, almost everyone with a pickup truck could be a suspect."

"You think the thief is using a pickup truck?"

"With a fuel tank in the back. It's the only thing that makes sense. And before you ask, almost every farmer in the state has a transfer tank that can be put in the back of his truck. That's how he gets fuel from his storage tank to his farm equipment." He ruffled my hair. "Now can we *please* go to bed? I'm about to stretch out on this couch and deny you the comfort of my warm body."

I laughed. "I couldn't stand that. Let's go."

He stood up and pulled me to my feet. Then he wrapped his arms around me and kissed me soundly. "Now get going before I forget how tired I am."

"Promises, promises," I purred. I turned off the TV and rounded up the animals. Before Amos reached the bottom of the stairs, I said, "I want to look for that doll tomorrow. If you don't get called in to work, will you help me?"

He turned around and frowned at me. "I doubt seriously there's anything out there, Ivy. Why are you so sure we'll find something?"

"I don't know. I just have a feeling."

Amos shook his head, but I saw him smile.

"Another one of your feelings, huh? Okay. I'll help if I can. Now upstairs, woman!"

I flipped off the lights and turned down the heat. By the time I reached the stairs, Amos was already in the bedroom, but Pal sat near the bottom step, waiting for me. Before I reached him, he lowered his head and started to cough. I waited until he finished before I knelt down next to him.

"What's the matter, boy? I hope you haven't been licking Miss Skiffins again. Dogs shouldn't have hair balls." I cupped his furry face in my hands. "You have the perfect name, you know it? You really are a pal." I was rewarded with a wet, sloppy kiss. As it turned out, that was the only kiss I would be receiving the rest of the night. Amos was sawing logs by the time I crawled into bed. It only took a few minutes for me to drift off, as well. However, I was awakened a couple of times to the sound of Pal coughing. Each time I checked him, he settled back down. I decided we'd take him to the vet on Monday if he wasn't better.

When I woke up, the bed was empty. I was afraid Amos had already gone to work. Usually he let me know before he left. I was feeling a little sorry for myself when my nose picked up the aroma of coffee and bacon.

I grabbed my robe and slippers and padded down the stairs to the kitchen. My handsome husband stood in front of the stove. I peeked over his shoulder and saw a cheese omelet bubbling in one pan and bacon crackling in another.

"What's this?" I asked. "Did your chef gene kick in again?"

Every once in a while, Amos liked to cook, and I liked to encourage him. Although I enjoyed serving him a nice dinner, sometimes I wasn't crazy about the actual steps it took to achieve the desired results—especially when I was tired from a long, busy day at the bookstore. If I could be granted the *I Dream of Jeannie* trait so I could simply cross my arms and blink for a quick, tasty outcome, I'd like cooking a lot better.

"Hitchens called early to say I didn't have to come in today. Our suspicions were correct. The tires were like almost every other tire around here. Nothing distinctive to go on." He bowed deeply, flourishing my dish towel in front of him. "Have a seat, m'lady. Your banquet is prepared."

I laughed and sat down at the breakfast bar. "To what do I owe this honor, m'lord? I thinketh thou hast losteth thy mindeth."

"Now you sound just like Elmer," he said with a grin. He cut the omelet with the spatula and scooped half of it onto a plate. Then he picked up a few pieces of bacon from the paper towel–covered plate where they were cooling. He poured me a cup of coffee, scooped the rest of the omelet up, and plopped it on his plate. After grabbing some bacon, he sat down on the stool next to me.

I reached over and took his hand as he prayed over our food. Then I stuck a forkful of eggs and melted cheese in my mouth. It was delicious. Amos was a pretty good cook. He'd had to learn to take care of himself from an early age because he'd never been able to count on his parents for anything. Since I'd come to Winter

Break, I'd begun to hear more about his childhood. It came in dabs and dribbles. I couldn't push him—he had to let it out at his own speed. I'd been surprised to hear him share as much as he had with Hope. But he had a compassionate heart. Hearing her pain had given him the incentive to reveal his own.

Although many of his stories hurt me, there was one I would never forget. Before his parents moved to Winter Break, the family lived in Chicago. Thankfully, through a neighbor lady, Amos found God when he was only six years old. The elderly woman took him to church a few times, but a stroke left her too infirm to drive. The church had a bus that would come by to get him, but his parents were usually so hungover on Sunday mornings, they wouldn't wake him up in time to catch his ride. At six years old, Amos would dress himself in his church clothes on Saturday night and lie down on top of his bed so that when the bus blew its horn, he could wake up, grab his little Bible, and run outside before he was left behind. It broke my heart to think that a little boy was driven to do something like that because there was no one in his life he could trust.

When Amos was nine, his father left. In desperation, his mother came to Winter Break to live in an old house given to her by an aunt and uncle who had moved to Abilene. That's when I first met him. At least moving here solved his church problem. Pastor Taylor and his wife bought Amos an alarm clock. They also picked him up every time the weather was bad and he couldn't walk to church. Things got better for him because of the love he received from all the people at church. Of course, things got bad again for a couple of years while he was in Oklahoma with Aaron, but at least he was able to find his way back to Winter Break—and back to the love and acceptance he so badly needed. I thanked God every day that we had both found our way home—and that we were together.

"You're quiet this morning," Amos said, breaking my reverie.

"Sorry," I said with a smile. "I was just thinking about how blessed we are, and how nice it is to wake up to a nice hot breakfast on a cold, cold morning."

He grunted. "It's cold, all right. Thermometer says it's only four degrees out there." He raised one eyebrow and looked at me with suspicion. "And you still want me to go out and dig through the snow for some doll you imagine is buried who-knows-where?"

I batted my eyelashes at him. "You got it, bucko."

"Don't call me bucko. And could I just add an addendum to that remark about being blessed?"

"No, you can't. And Pal and I will be out there helping you."

"Oh, great. I'm counting on assistance from a dog that hates being outside and a wife who has never managed to stand out in the cold for more than ten minutes without whining about it. I think I'll pass. You two can stay in here where it's warm."

"I do not whine," I said. "You're imagining things."

Amos stabbed toward me with his fork. "There. There it is. That's your whiney voice. You use it whenever you want something from me."

"Does it work?"

"Yes," he grumbled, taking another bite. After he swallowed, he frowned at me. "I'll go out and look around, but when I can't feel my toes anymore, I'm coming in. You keep the coffee hot. I may need to pour it over my entire body."

I grabbed a piece of bacon and held it up with an air of triumph. "I win again, sucka."

He laughed and grabbed the bacon from my hand, stuffing it in his mouth before I could retrieve it. Pal, who had been hovering beneath our stools hoping we'd drop a piece of food, barked happily. Unfortunately, his barking caused more coughing.

"He's been coughing all morning," Amos said. "I'm starting to get concerned about him. Maybe we need to take him to the vet. Do dogs get colds?"

"I don't know. Lucy's supposed to be in town today. She's got to look at Chuck and decide whether or not to send him to Wichita. Maybe she could come by and look at Pal."

Amos leaned over and rubbed Pal behind the ears. "I think that might be a good idea."

"On Saturdays, she always stops in to see Sally Redfield and Dewey so she can check up on their diabetes," I said. "I'll call Dewey and tell him to have her call us."

Although Lucy wasn't a veterinarian, she was an animal lover and didn't mind being consulted about the various pets and farm animals in Winter Break. I was pretty certain Pal's problem was minor and could wait until we saw the vet, but it wouldn't hurt to be cautious.

We finished eating, and I began rinsing off the dishes and putting them in the dishwasher. Although Amos was a good cook, he wasn't good at cleaning up after himself in the kitchen. I'd been told by more than one harried wife, including Emily, that this was par for the course with men. It didn't upset me this morning, however. I was getting the better part of the deal. Rooting around in the snow didn't sound the least bit appealing.

I'd just started the dishwasher when Amos came around the corner. He was dressed in his snow boots, his heavy insulated coat, his gloves, and his woolen face mask. Pal was eyeing him suspiciously, and I couldn't help but laugh. "I'd ask if you have your thermal underwear on, but at this point I'd say that's a given."

He said something, but it was mumbled from underneath the face mask and I couldn't understand it.

"Easy for you to say. I almost feel like putting my hands up and giving you all my money." He didn't laugh, but I could see his eyes crinkle around the edges. "Go, Amos. Hunt. Search. When you come back, I'll give you a nice hot cup of coffee."

He muttered something else, but I was fairly certain it wasn't complimentary, so I just pointed toward the front door. He turned, his big boots clomping on the floor. Pal followed behind him, but when Amos opened the door and the frigid air pushed its way in, Pal turned around and ran for the stairs. He was on his way back to bed, and I didn't blame him. Amos shot me one more look designed to make me feel guilty, but I just smiled. I was convinced there was something out there. Something that Chuck gave his life for. I was pretty certain it was a red-haired Cabbage Patch doll. If we did find it, I wondered if we would have to turn it over to the sheriff. Since Chuck had just fallen off the roof, why would the doll be important? Milt Hitchens was a strange bird. Sometimes he followed the rules as if he'd written the book, and other times, his procedures were sloppy—as if he were flying by the seat of his pants. It was impossible to predict his reaction in advance.

I went upstairs, took a quick hot shower, and then dressed in jeans and a sweatshirt. I was kind of a sweatshirt nut. Living in Winter Break, sweatshirts were more for protection than for looks, but I still liked fun designs and colors. I picked one of my favorites. It was pink with a picture of a yellow baby chicken, and declared the wearer as a "Jesus Chick." Usually I didn't wear pink. With red hair, sometimes it doesn't look right. But I loved this one, and somehow it seemed to work for me.

I checked on Pal, who was sleeping on the bed, dead to the world. He looked peaceful, but his breathing was a little labored. When I got downstairs, Amos was still outside. It had been almost thirty minutes, longer than he should be exposed to the elements, no matter how many pieces of clothing he had on. I was just about to tell him to come inside when the French doors in the dining room swung open and he walked in. He was holding a large green trash bag. Without saying a word, he carried it over to the kitchen counter and opened it. The plastic was frozen and crackled when it moved. Amos stuck his gloved hand down inside the bag and pulled out a Cabbage Patch doll with red hair in ponytails, her arms stretched out wide as if she were waiting for a hug.

I smiled triumphantly. "I told you so," I said to my semi-frozen husband. "Chuck was trying to deliver this doll to some little girl he thought lived here."

I reached over and picked her up. She was extremely cold to the touch but didn't look the worse for wear. She wore a little flowered outfit with lace down the front, and a white sweater with matching booties. Pinned to her sweater was a pink paper package with green lettering that read BIRTH CERTIFICATE AND ADOPTION PAPERS. The envelope was obviously old and timeworn, but except for one torn strip, it looked like it had never been opened. Through a cellophane window, the name of the doll was printed. OPAL NELL.

"I think this doll is pretty old," I said, "but it doesn't look like it's ever been played with."

Amos pulled his wool face mask off. His skin was bright red under it. "I think there's something else in here," he said, staring into the bag. He put his gloved hand inside and pulled out the remnants of a box. It was obviously the box the doll had been in, but it was in bad shape and there wasn't any cellophane covering the front of it. "I think the weight of the snow and my digging it out may have popped the doll out of its box." He tried to carefully reconstruct the box, but it was too far gone to save.

I picked up a piece of it. "It says 1985 here." I stared at Amos and shook my head. "My goodness.

This doll is almost twenty-five years old."

He laughed. "That makes her just a little bit older than you. You two could be sisters."

I hoped my face wasn't quite that round, and my hair was curly while hers was straight and braided. But she actually had a dimple in her right cheek—just like me. And we both had red hair. I suddenly felt very protective of Opal Nell. I stuck my tongue out at my comedian husband. "Very funny. But doesn't it strike you as odd that Chuck was trying to deliver a doll this old to a little girl whose letter also looked pretty ancient? It's as if Chuck was in some kind of time warp or something."

Amos looked at me with amusement. "A time warp? So we're in some kind of *Twilight Zone* episode or something?"

I grinned at him. "I don't think we're in the Twilight Zone. But I think we're smack dab in the middle of a mystery. And I also think we have to try to get this doll to the person it's supposed to go to. Before Christmas."

Amos was pulling off his gloves and coat. "Before Christmas? That's in five days, Ivy. How are we going to figure out who some obviously drunk man was trying to deliver a twenty-five-year-old doll to in five days? We have no idea who the man was or who the child is. For all we know, Chuck was drunk out of his mind and none of this means anything."

I went around the breakfast bar and poured him a cup of hot coffee. "That doesn't make sense, Amos. This man, whoever he was, either hung on to this doll for twenty-five years or went out of his way to buy it. He also bought a Santa Claus suit, dressed up in it, traveled to Winter Break—one of the smallest towns in Kansas—and in the middle of winter, in a snowstorm, he climbed up on our roof!" Without meaning to, I'd begun to raise my voice with each progressive point. "That's ridiculous! We've got to figure this out. I think it's really important."

He came over and put his arms around me. "I know it's important to you," he said gently, "but this may be a mystery even you can't solve. We have absolutely nothing to go on."

"Well, we know that he picked this house. But why?"

He let go of me. "Twenty-five years ago, Marion and Cecil lived here. We can call them to see if they have any ideas. But I doubt seriously that Chuck knew the Biddles at all."

"But they do have a daughter. Mary was living in the house twenty-five years ago. Of course, she would have been a baby. She couldn't have written this letter, and if she'd wanted a doll, Cecil and Marion would have gotten it for her. I remember her dolls. She had gobs of them."

"So what do you want me to do?"

I sighed. "Let's call them anyway. I'm out of ideas. Ask them if there was ever a little girl who lived in this house besides Mary."

"Okay, but why don't you add some of that great mocha cream you bought in Hugoton to my coffee? That's my price for bothering Marion and Cecil on a Saturday with the strangest story they're liable to hear in their whole lives."

"You've got a deal," I said with a smile. "Now go!"

Amos started for the phone but then stopped and frowned at me. "By the way, what in the world has Pal been eating?"

I shook my head. "Same old stuff. Why?"

"I found some of his little leftovers out on the snow. They were bright green—almost neon." He chuckled. "Quite a startling sight against the white snow."

"I have no idea what could have caused it. The only thing I can think of would be the Christmas cookies I made. I used some food coloring in the icing. Did you give that dog a cookie?"

"Of course not. You're the one who's always giving him scraps."

"Well, I wouldn't give him a cookie with icing on it. It wouldn't be good for him."

Amos shrugged. "I have no idea how he got hold of one, but you'd better watch where you put them. I think he might be outsmarting you."

Amos grabbed the cordless phone from the wall and took it into the living room so he could warm up by the fire. I checked the large platter of cookies on the counter. They were still covered with plastic wrap. I'd put a plate on the coffee table for Amos and me the night I baked them. Maybe Pal grabbed one when we weren't looking. Maybe his coughing had something to do with eating a cookie. I couldn't see how, but if he was sensitive to them—perhaps even allergic—it might make sense. I made a mental note to tell Lucy about his possible cookie caper.

I got the cream out of the refrigerator and added it to Amos's cup. Then I put the cup in the microwave, ready to heat up. After starting the dishwasher, I went into the living room. Amos had already hung up his coat and taken off his snow boots. He was sitting on the couch, holding the phone.

"So you don't have any idea who the guy might be?" he was saying. After a few moments, he said, "I can definitely fax you a picture. It's a rough sketch, but it's pretty accurate." He listened for a while then said, "Thanks, Cecil. No, I think we're safe. I'm thinking this guy just picked the wrong house. We may never know exactly what happened." He was quiet for a few seconds. "Yeah, thanks. You, too. We're hosting Christmas dinner here this year." Silence, then a big smile. Amos looked at me. "Yes, I'm really looking forward to it. Maybe someday you can come here and stay with us for a while. We'd love to have you." Amos nodded his head while he listened as if Cecil could see him. Then he laughed. "That would be great. You let us know, okay? Bye, Cecil." Amos hung up the phone, still smiling. "I think Cecil and Marion could be talked into coming for a visit this summer. Cecil wondered if we'd be interested in hosting a barbeque like he and Marion used to."

"Oh, that would be wonderful. I really hope they come."

Amos chuckled. "I think they would have been here already, but they wanted to make sure we had lots of alone time after the wedding. I guess after a year, they figure we can control ourselves now."

"Oh, great. Does that mean the honeymoon is over?" I teased.

"Not for me," he said, jumping up from the couch and heading toward me.

I squealed and ran into the kitchen, taking his cup out of the microwave and holding it out in front of me. "If you attack me, your special coffee is going down the sink. You've been warned."

"Coffee schmoffee," Amos said with a wicked grin. "I can make more anytime."

"You're incorrigible," I said, laughing. "Now sit down and behave yourself."

"I'll be good for now, but after I drink this coffee, all bets are off," he teased, plunking himself down on the stool in front of the counter.

"Thank you. I consider myself fully warned. Now tell me what Cecil had to say."

"He has absolutely no idea who the guy might be. And Mary never wanted a Cabbage Patch doll. She was into Barbie." He smiled. "I could have asked him if any of their three boys might have asked Santa for a doll, but I didn't think it was appropriate."

Marion and Cecil's sons wouldn't have been caught dead playing with a doll. They had been good boys but extremely rambunctious. They'd given Mary a lot of good-natured grief growing up.

"You're going to send a copy of Bonnie's sketch to Cecil?" I asked.

"I don't think it will do any good, but it can't hurt either."

I handed him his coffee. "It's hot. Be careful."

Amos blew on the coffee to cool it down. When the phone rang, he set the cup down. "Maybe Cecil remembered something." He got up and grabbed the phone.

I heard him say hello, and then he was quiet for a while. Finally, he thanked whoever it was and hung up the phone. He walked back into the kitchen with a puzzled look on his face.

"Is something wrong?" I asked. "Was that Cecil?"

Amos shook his head slowly. "No. It was Elmer. He thought we might want to know that he found something when he was preparing Chuck's body in case he has to take it to Wichita."

I handed him his coffee cup again, but he ignored it. "What did he say? Is it something important?"

He stared at me strangely. "I guess you could say that. Elmer thinks Chuck may have been shot."

I set his coffee down on the counter with a thump. "Shot? When? Didn't he die from falling off the roof?"

"I have no idea, but if he didn't, we may have a murder on our hands."

7

Amos's coffee got cold while he called Hitchens, and I poured it out. When he came back, he looked around on the counter. "Where's my coffee?"

"Sorry. I figured you'd go running out of here with guns blazing. Aren't you and Hitchens going to saddle up and send out the posse?"

He sat down on the bar stool. "First of all, we don't have a posse, and to answer your question, no. I can keep my gun holstered. Hitchens said we need to wait for Lucy. Elmer wasn't sure if what he saw was really a bullet hole, and he can't mess with the body because he could destroy important evidence. We won't know anything for certain until Lucy takes a look."

I started to say something when the phone rang again.

"Man, what now?" Amos grumbled. "Could you make some more coffee, but try not to throw it out this time? I'm determined to drink it sometime this morning."

"I'll do my part if you'll do yours."

As he went back to answer the phone, I started a new pot. I hoped Hitchens wasn't calling back to say he'd changed his mind about having Amos work today. He was on the phone a lot longer this time. By the time he got back, the coffee was ready, and I'd started rummaging through the refrigerator for lunch ideas.

I shoved his coffee cup toward him. "It's hot and it's got your mocha cream in it." I thought he'd be happy, but he just stared at his cup. I walked around the counter and sat down. "What now? You're not going to tell me that Chuck really is Santa Claus, are you?"

"No." He took a quick sip of his coffee. It was too hot to do anything else. "That was Hitchens again. He wants me to take down the flyers and back off trying to find out any more about Chuck. If he really was shot, the case will be turned over to the KBI. Hitchens doesn't want to step on their *toes*, although that wasn't the word he used."

"Take down the flyers? But we can't be certain he was actually shot until Lucy examines him. Why take the flyers down now?"

Amos sighed. "I don't know. I guess it's because we've gotten in trouble before for interfering with Bureau procedures. Hitchens doesn't want to see it happen again. Besides, he thinks we need to focus on the diesel thefts, not some dead drunk. His words—not mine."

Hitchens had a love-hate relationship with the Kansas Bureau of Investigation. He disliked them, and they ignored him. That was about the worst thing you could do to Milt Hitchens. He demanded respect, even when he didn't deserve it.

I watched Amos carefully sip his coffee. He looked as happy about this turn of events as I was. "I feel like we're abandoning Chuck, and I really want to help him. Especially if someone killed him. Besides, if the little girl who wrote the letter is his daughter, she has no idea her father is dead. She deserves to know. We can't just walk away from this."

"Unless someone recognizes him from one of our

flyers pretty quickly, I'm afraid it's out of our hands."

"Chuck died in our front yard, Amos. His death will always be personal."

He shook his head but didn't say anything. He was caught between a rock and a hard place. And Hitchens was the unmovable object he was backed up against.

"When do we have to take them down?" I asked, staring at Opal Nell, who sat next to me on the breakfast bar, her arms extended, waiting for someone to hug her.

Amos smiled slowly. "Hitchens didn't say *when* we had to take them down. Today's my day off. I'll do it on Monday."

I grinned at him. "You're kind of devious, Mr. Parker. You know that?"

He raised his cup as if toasting me. "Right back atcha, Mrs. Parker."

"You know," I said, picking up the red-haired doll, "even though you're not allowed to actively investigate Chuck's case, there's no reason I can't try to dig up a little information about this young lady."

"Except that if Chuck actually was shot, she becomes evidence in a murder investigation. We talked about this, Ivy."

"But we don't know that Chuck was actually murdered yet, so there is no investigation." I stared into the doll's blue eyes.

"Ivy. . ."

"Amos, there is *no* investigation," I insisted. "I can't possibly be tampering with evidence if there isn't a case. And besides, I'm not going to hurt the doll. She will still be in one piece."

"Even if I agreed with you, that doll can't tell you anything. It's just a toy."

I set Opal back on the counter. "Maybe. Maybe not. You know, either Chuck held on to her for a long, long time, or he bought her recently."

Amos got up off his stool and walked around the breakfast bar to the coffeemaker. He picked up the pot and poured himself another cup. "You think you can find out where he got it? It could have been anywhere. How could you possibly track something like that?"

"There's only one way I can search all over the world in just a few minutes."

"The Internet." Amos frowned at me. "I don't know. Chuck didn't look like someone who knew how to use a computer, let alone own one. Besides, he could have gotten her almost anywhere."

"Well, I guess I'll know in a few minutes if you're right." I glanced at the wall clock in the kitchen. "What time are we leaving?" I hadn't decided whether to open the store today, but although I doubted Zach's book would be at the post office, I felt like I needed to check. And I knew Amos wanted to fax Chuck's picture to Cecil.

"After I shower and change," he said. "Do me a favor, okay? Until we see where this is going, be careful where you touch the doll. Stay away from any spot that could have fingerprints."

"Shoot and bother, Amos. You make it sound like this is the crime of the century."

He sighed. "Just do it, Ivy. I mean it." He shook

his finger at me and then left to go upstairs.

I picked Opal up by her sweater, careful to keep my fingers off her plastic skin, and headed toward the corner in the dining room where my computer sat on a small antique writing desk that had been in Aunt Bitty's bedroom. I opened the top of the computer and turned it on. Then I waited. Although I didn't miss much in Wichita, I really wished Winter Break had DSL.

While I cooled my heels, I stared at the tapestry that hung on the wall over my desk. Painted years ago by Marion and left in the house when they moved to Florida, it depicted one of the skating parties she and Cecil used to host. Amos and I skated hand in hand on the frozen pond while Aunt Bitty watched from one of the wooden benches Cecil had built and put up around the lake. They were great for lacing up skates, but many older people loved to just sit and watch the children having fun. Aunt Bitty waved at me from one of the benches. She held a book in her other hand. Emily sat next to Bitty, and Buddy Taylor stood in front of her, offering her a cup of hot chocolate. Although there was no earthly way Marion could have known that Emily and Buddy would be married someday, or that Amos and I would end up together, the tapestry was almost prophetic in its content. Even to the small black and white Border collie lying next to my aunt's feet. Amos and I didn't talk about it much, but we had stared at the tapestry for years, and we'd never noticed the collie—until Pal came to live with us. There was Dewey standing next to Bitty, his hand on her shoulder, looking down at her while she looked toward me. The look on his face was so tender and loving. How had Marion known so long ago that they would fall in love someday? I was contemplating some of the other painted figures when my computer made a sound that signaled a connection had finally been achieved.

I pulled up Google and typed in "Opal Nell" and "Cabbage Patch doll." Only one link came up. It was an old eBay listing. I scrolled down the page, and there she was, Opal Nell. There was a picture of her sitting inside her box and two more of her next to it. The bidding for Opal had gone to twenty-two dollars. The winning bid had been placed by *ginam2357*. There was no way to find out who the buyer was, but I was able to see some of the stores he had purchased items from. The list seemed to consist primarily of costume jewelry, CDs, and items from the Health and Beauty category. The doll appeared to be an unusual purchase. All in all, *ginam2357* sounded female. I suspected that her name was Gina and her last name started with an *M*. That didn't really line up with our friend Chuck. Maybe there was someone else who knew him and had information about his rooftop rendezvous.

I found a link that allowed me to "ask the seller a question" and clicked the cyber button. A message box appeared, and I carefully typed in my reasons for asking for contact information for *ginam2357*. Since I already had an eBay account, having found it a good source for buying books, I clicked on the little box that promised to send a copy of my message to my e-mail account. Then I pressed SEND and watched my virtual note disappear into the vast void of the Internet. I had no idea how long it would take for me to get a response. In the meantime, I spent some time checking my e-mail until Amos came downstairs after taking his shower. He let Pal out and waited for him to come in before telling me he was ready to go. I turned off my computer and closed the lid.

"How about lunch at Ruby's?" he asked.

"You know what?" I said, smiling at him. "I'm not going to be hungry for quite some time after that great breakfast. Why don't we just come back here, and I'll make pork roast soup for dinner?" Pork roast soup was one of Aunt Bitty's best recipes, in my opinion. Amos loved it. "We'll have to stop by Dewey's for ingredients, but it's still early in the day. As long as we get back soon, I still have plenty of time to make it." It took awhile for the pork roast to cook, but it was well worth waiting for.

Amos smiled. "You've got a deal. I'll even pass up Ruby's for your pork roast soup."

As I put on my coat and slid my feet into my snow boots, I realized that Bitty's soup had become *my* soup in his mind. In a way, it made me sad. But I was certain Bitty would love to know that her recipe had become mine. She had always put a lot of importance on passing down family traditions.

It took us about twice as long as it usually did to reach downtown Winter Break. Yesterday's heavy snow had covered the back roads again. When we finally got into town, it was obvious Milton Baumgartner and his sons had already plowed Main Street. It was in pretty good shape. Amos dropped me off at the post office and then drove a few doors down to his office.

I was happy to see the light on in the post office. That meant Alma was in. When I pushed the door open, I found Isaac standing next to the counter with a big smile on his face. "Why, Miss Ivy. Good to see you. I wasn't certain if you would venture out today or not."

"I wasn't sure either. Right now, I think I'd rather be curled up in front of the fire."

He nodded. "I know what you mean. Alma and I are on our way over to Ruby's. She's making chili today. A bowl of her chili is the next best thing to a warm fire."

He was right about that. Ruby had never met a chili pepper she didn't like. Chili was the one thing she made that didn't tempt me. It had burned my mouth and upset my stomach for the last time. But Amos loved it, and so did many Winter Break residents.

"I won't keep you, then," I said. "Alma, will there be a mail delivery today?"

She shook her head. "Sorry, Ivy. Gus called to say he didn't want to risk it. I guess the roads are pretty bad all the way to the highway."

So much for "neither sleet nor snow nor gloom of night."

"Are you waiting for something special?"

"Yes, a book from Denver."

"Is it from Mr. Spivey?" Isaac asked. At one time, he hadn't liked Noel much, but in the last couple of years, his opinion had improved. Noel had helped me get the bookstore back on its feet. Thanks to him, I was selling a lot of rare books all across the country.

I nodded. "It's a Christmas gift, and I want to make certain it gets here on time. Noel overnighted it."

"Then it should definitely be here on Monday," Alma said. "Milton promised to spend Monday morning making sure the road was passable. I'll keep an eye out for your package."

I thanked her and wished them luck with Ruby's chili. Then I went across the road to the bookstore. As I walked toward the steps, I noticed a red Jeep Cherokee driving slowly down the street. It didn't look familiar, but it wasn't as if I knew every single car owned by Winter Break residents. I turned around and climbed slowly up the stairs, holding on to the wrought iron handrail Amos had installed so that I wouldn't tumble down the icy steps and injure myself. It came in pretty handy for my elderly customers, too. I was just about to slide my key into the door when I heard someone call out. The driver of the Jeep was trying to get my attention. The woman behind the wheel pulled up in front of the bookstore and waved at me. I didn't recognize her, but I came back down the steps and approached the driver's side window.

"I'm sorry to bother you," she said, "but I'm looking for someone." She was probably in her early fifties, with salt-and-pepper hair. Her kind eyes were framed by laugh wrinkles.

"Someone who lives in Winter Break?" My breath was visible in the frigid temperature, almost making it difficult to see her.

"No." She hesitated for a moment. I wanted to tell her I was freezing and that speaking quickly was more a matter of life and death in Winter Break than just a convenience. But her next words made me forget how cold I was.

"This is going to sound really strange," she said slowly. "But I'm looking for a man who may have come to Winter Break." She paused again. "Please don't laugh at me, but I think he was dressed like Santa Claus."

8

It only took a few minutes for me to turn up the heat and start a fire in the sitting room. I ran upstairs, quickly made a pot of tea, and brought it down with a couple of cups. When I carried the tray to the sitting room, the woman was seated in Bitty's rocking chair, gazing into the fire. I put the tray on the table next to her and poured the tea.

"Sugar or cream?"

She shook her head. "No. Nothing, thank you."

I handed her one of the cups and added a splash of cream to the other.

"So you say you've seen him?" she asked as I lowered myself into the overstuffed chair directly across from her.

"Yes, but before I tell you about it, could you tell me how you know him?" I didn't want to blurt out that he was dead before I knew who the woman was. If she was close to Chuck, the news could be devastating. The situation required a little finesse.

"My name is Gina Mallory. I don't really know Charles well at all. I met him at the Boots and Beer Lounge in Liberal where I work."

The hair on the back of my neck stood up. "His name is Charles?" I almost said *was* Charles but caught myself at the last second. Chuck was a nickname for Charles. Surely Amos and I hadn't actually guessed the guy's real name.

"Yes, but I only know his first name. He—he didn't talk a lot about himself. Mostly about his daughter."

The thought crossed my mind that maybe I should wait for Amos before going any further, but since he wasn't really officially investigating Chuck's death, I decided to forge ahead. "Gina," I said as gently as I could, "a man dressed like Santa Claus died here Thursday night. I wonder if it could be Charles."

Her eyes filled with tears. "Oh dear. That poor man. I knew he didn't have long, but I didn't expect it to happen so soon."

I set my cup down on the little table. "I'm sorry. You said he didn't have long. What do you mean?"

She took a tissue from her purse and dabbed at her eyes. "He—he had liver problems. From drinking. He was an alcoholic. I—I didn't want to serve him, but as I said, I only work at Boots and Beer. I wasn't allowed to cut anyone off without the owner's permission, and frankly, Butch doesn't care if people leave his place loaded to the gills."

Before I had a chance to say anything else, the front door opened and Amos came in. I was glad he wasn't wearing his uniform. I didn't want to intimidate Gina before we could get some information about Chuck. I mean Charles.

"Excuse me for just a minute." I hurried to the front of the store and quietly explained to Amos whom I was talking to. Then I asked him to go back to the office and fetch a copy of Chuck's flyer. After he left, I went back to Gina. She was still wiping tears from her face.

"I'm sorry," I said, taking my seat again. "You seem very upset, but you said you didn't know Charles very well."

"That's right. But his story really got to me. That's why I came here—to make sure everything worked out for him."

"Could you share with me what he told you? Why he came to Winter Break?"

She looked unsure. Maybe she was wondering if she was still bound to keep the confidences of a dead man.

"Gina, Charles fell off *my* roof. I really want to know why. I'm sure you can understand why this is personal."

Her eyes widened. "Your roof? Who are you?"

"I—I'm not sure what you mean. I didn't know Charles, if that's what you're asking. In fact, no one in town seems to know him."

She looked confused. "But he's your father, isn't he?"

Of all the things I was expecting to hear, that wasn't on the list. "My father? No. No, he wasn't."

"But—but he had to be."

If I didn't have a copy of my birth certificate, I might have gone to the phone and asked my parents to prove we were really related. Actually, it would answer a lot of questions I'd had down through the years, but alas, I had no doubt we were biologically connected. If they wouldn't lie to me about Santa Claus, I was pretty sure they would have mentioned that I was adopted. Besides, there were pictures of my father with curly red hair before it turned white. If you'd put him in a dress when he was four, we could have been twins. Of course, the idea of seeing my father in a dress was a rather disturbing thought.

"I'm positive we weren't related. What made you think we were?"

"Charles said he had to deliver a gift to his daughter before he died. Something he owed her." She shook her head. "At first I thought he was talking about a child, but after a while I began to wonder if she was a grown woman. He never made that clear." She sighed. "It's hard to separate the past from the present listening to someone who's had too much to drink. They tend to blend the two together. Charles was one of the saddest men I've ever met. And believe me, when you serve drinks, you hear all kinds of things."

"Did he mention his daughter's name? Did he say he was certain she lived in Winter Break?"

"He called his daughter 'Ho Ho.' " She smiled a little. "I think it was a nickname. And yes, he was certain she lived here."

I remembered the letter in Chuck's, I mean Charles's, pocket. It was signed "Ho Ho" at the bottom. I'd thought it was a reference to Santa Claus, but now I knew it was either his daughter's name or her nickname. For her sake, I hoped it wasn't her given name.

"How did Charles get to Winter Break?" I asked. "We haven't found any abandoned vehicles, and no one here seems to know him."

Gina took another sip from her cup and then set it back down. I noticed that her hand trembled slightly. "Thursday night he came in dressed like Santa Claus.

I'd helped him purchase a doll on eBay the week before, and it had come in the mail that day. It was one of those Cabbage Patch dolls. He said it had to be from 1985, and it had to have red hair." She shook her head. "He never told me why. He put the doll in a trash bag and told me he needed to come here so he could deliver it to his daughter. Then he asked if I could drive him to Winter Break after work."

"Did you?"

"I couldn't. My car hasn't been running. I was scrambling to find a way home myself. I know he asked around some, but I was busy and didn't notice if he'd found a ride or not. Then at closing time he came up to the bar and told me he'd found transportation. He thanked me for all my help." She looked at me with glistening eyes. "He was staying in a run-down motel across the street, so I assumed after he was finished delivering his gift, he'd come back. But he didn't, and I got worried." She sighed. "Now I wish I would have just borrowed Butch's car that night and taken him myself. Maybe he would still be alive."

Just then, the front door opened and Amos stepped in, carrying a sheet of paper in his hand. "Gina, do you have any idea who drove Charles here?" I asked.

"Not a clue. We were really busy Thursday night. And there were some people I didn't know. Sometimes people from surrounding small towns come to Boots and Beer for dinner and drinks. We had quite a few customers that night that I didn't recognize."

Amos walked up behind us and handed me a flyer. I took it and showed it to Gina. "Is this Charles?"

She nodded. "Yes, that's him."

"Gina, this is my husband, Amos. He's a deputy sheriff, and I think he'd like to talk to you for a little bit. Is that okay?"

She looked back and forth between us. "I—I don't understand. If Charles fell off your roof, it was an accident. Why would the sheriff's department be interested?"

"It's possible that he didn't just fall," Amos said quietly. "He may have been helped."

Gina's eyebrows arched in surprise. "But—but who would kill Charles? He was a nice man. There wouldn't be any reason. . ."

"It's entirely possible that his death was an accident," I said. "Whether it was or not, we certainly need to find his daughter and let her know her father is dead."

She considered this for a moment and then nodded her head, seemingly resigned to sharing her story. I quickly relayed to Amos what Gina had told me so far. Then I gave up my seat and took the teapot upstairs for a refill. This was definitely a two-pot situation. While I waited for the kettle to whistle, I went over Gina's story in my mind. Chuck—I mean Charles—was dying and he wanted to deliver a present to his child. But his daughter couldn't possibly still be a child. I thought back to the letter. It was obviously written a long time ago. And he'd insisted that the doll had to be made in 1985. My guess was that Charles was trying to make up for something that happened when his daughter was young. A doll like that would probably be for a girl between four and seven years old. And since 1985 was more than twenty years ago, that would make his daughter somewhere in her late twenties.

I also turned over the nickname Ho Ho in my mind. Why would anyone call their child Ho Ho? Was it a Christmas reference?

The high-pitched whistle of the teakettle made me jump. I poured the water into the pot and let the tea steep for a couple of minutes. I was brewing a special tea I'd ordered through the Internet. It was a holiday chai mix with a hint of gingerbread. The musky aroma filled the little kitchen while I leaned against the counter and wondered what to do next.

Maybe Charles's daughter really did live in Winter Break. In a drunken stupor, he'd just picked the wrong house. Not that a sober man would have attempted climbing up on a roof in the middle of winter anyway. In his state, it was entirely plausible he'd confused the address. Maybe his daughter actually lived somewhere near us. Except Amos and I lived a couple of miles out of town on the back roads and there were only a few homes anywhere close. Nearest to us was Odie Rimrucker, who was divorced and lived alone, and Milton and Mavis Baumgartner. They had no daughters, and Mavis certainly wasn't in her twenties. I mentally ran through everyone I could think of while I waited on the tea. But no one in her late twenties came up as a possibility. Either I knew their fathers, or, as with Faith and Hope, their fathers were dead. I couldn't come up with anyone whose father was actually *missing*. Of course, it was possible that Charles was a biological father and some of the young women I was thinking of were being raised by stepfathers. I didn't know the past history of everyone who called Winter Break home. By the time the tea was ready, I wasn't any closer to figuring out who Ho Ho was than I'd been before.

When I carried the teapot into the sitting room, Amos was writing down what Gina was telling him about Charles getting a ride from someone the night he died.

"If you would write up a list of everyone you can remember from that night, that would be helpful," Amos was saying. "And give me a description of the people you didn't recognize. If I can find out who drove him here, it could answer some questions."

Gina gratefully held out her cup, and I poured some more tea. "It might take me awhile. I'm afraid I don't have much time right now. I'm supposed to get in to work by four, and it's after two. Besides, I'm using Butch's car. He almost refused to let me borrow it because of the bad roads."

"Okay," Amos said. "Do you work tomorrow?"

"We open for dinner at six. I can write up your list tomorrow before work. Do you want me to mail it to you?"

Amos shook his head. "I want it as soon as possible. Why don't I come by and pick it up tomorrow night? It might be good for me to get a look at some of your customers. Maybe a few of the folks you didn't recognize on Thursday night will be there."

Gina gave Amos the address to Boots and Beer, and while he wrote down the directions, she finished her tea. After he had what he needed, she stood to go.

I felt impressed to hug her. "Thank you for caring enough to come here looking for Charles. Most people wouldn't have taken the time."

When I pulled back, I saw tears in her eyes. "I hope it will help him. I would like to know that his last wish was granted." She stared down at the floor. "I really can't believe someone might have killed him. He was so harmless. I hope you're wrong about that."

"Listen, Gina," Amos said, his tone low and serious, "I need you to understand that this case isn't being actively investigated right now since we're not sure if he was actually murdered. When I come to see you Sunday night, it's as a private citizen, not as a representative of the sheriff's department. Do you still want to help me?"

She hesitated a moment before answering. "Yes. Maybe I let Charles down Thursday night, but I'd like to help him now if I can." She started to walk away, but then she stopped. "What about the doll? Did you find it?"

"Yes, we did," I said. "It's at my house. If there's any way possible, we're going to try to get it to his daughter. You have my word."

She smiled. "Thank you. That would be wonderful. I—I'd like to see a happy ending once in a while. You don't hear many good stories when you work in the kind of place I do."

I promised to contact her if we found Charles's daughter, and then she left. I felt a great sadness emanating from her. I planned to add her name to my prayer list. It seemed to me that alcohol had victims on both sides of the bar. I sat down in Bitty's rocking chair. Amos was going over his notes.

"Amos, if Hitchens told you to leave this alone, won't he be upset if he finds out you went to Liberal?"

Amos looked up at me, his eyes narrowed and his mouth a thin line. I knew that look. "I'm not investigating. Gina came to us. Besides, I'm not going to Liberal officially."

"I want answers just as much as you do. For Charles, for Gina, and for Charles's daughter, but I have to wonder if going to Liberal is pushing things too far. Hitchens can be very unreasonable."

Amos shook his head. "Look, I'm not sure what Hitchens wants or doesn't want, but this could be important. If Chuck—er, Charles *was* shot, whoever drove him here could be responsible. I'm going to gather this information, but I'm not going to do anything with it. If I find out something important, I'll turn it over to Hitchens and he can hold it for the KBI. If anything pans out, he'll look good to them. If I don't find anything, Hitchens will never have to know." He sighed. "I can't just leave this alone and let evidence slide. We might not get another chance. Even if the only thing we find out is the identity of Charles's daughter, it will be worth it."

"I agree. I just don't want you on Hitchens's bad side. You could lose your job."

Amos chuckled. "You mean there's a good side?" He thumbed through his notes. "So we know his name is Charles. And he thought he was delivering a doll to his daughter."

I frowned at him. "What do you mean he *thought*

he was delivering a doll to his daughter? Don't you believe him?"

"You don't understand, Ivy, because your parents aren't alcoholics. Sometimes my dad would get these crazy ideas about things. They had no basis in reality. One time he was convinced that I had a brother who was killed in Viet Nam. That went on for three days."

I reached over and took his hand. "You're right—I probably don't understand. But this man moved to Liberal from somewhere else, rented a motel room, found a Santa Claus costume, and bought a doll from eBay. And what about the letter in his pocket? I don't think this was an alcoholic delusion. I think it was real."

He stared into the fire for a moment. "You might be right. Sometimes I tend to see everything through my own experiences. Charles wasn't my father." He shook his head and looked at me. "You know, maybe I *should* just leave this alone. Maybe he was just a drunk who fell off a roof. End of story."

"Amos! How can you say that? This man died in *our* front yard after falling from *our* roof. We *have* to figure this out. And I don't think God considers him to be *just another drunk*. Jesus gave His life for everyone, including alcoholics, you know."

"Wait a minute. I thought you were the one who was worried about Hitchens."

"I *am* concerned, but I'm like you. I don't want to walk away from this, and I know you don't either. You'll just have to stay off Hitchens's radar." I squeezed his hand. "Besides, I don't want half the people in town thinking we killed Santa Claus. No one needs that kind of reputation."

Amos smiled. "You're right about that. People are already wondering if we're serial killers."

"Let's prove them wrong, okay?" I let go of his hand and poured myself another cup of tea. "You know, Amos," I said softly, "even though Chuck. . .Charles wanted to quit drinking, he couldn't. He died with alcohol on his breath in a desperate attempt to make up for his past failures. I think it takes real strength to change your life and walk away from addiction."

"You're referring to my dad."

I nodded. "Jesus forgave every sin. That includes your father's. I know you're afraid to let him in again, and you're right. He doesn't deserve it. But no one really deserves God's love, do they?"

He stood up, his expression blank. "I can't talk about this right now. I want to run over to the funeral home and see if Lucy's had a chance to look at Chuck's, I mean Charles's, body."

"You know, trying to call him Charles now seems wrong. He's still Chuck to me. Can we keep that name?"

Amos shrugged. "Doesn't matter what we call him. He's dead."

I stood up and carried my cup into the main room. "You'd better phone Elmer first. He's not normally at work on Saturdays unless he has a service, and we have no idea what time Lucy plans to meet him there."

Amos followed me to my desk, where I handed him the phone. He punched in some numbers and waited. "Elmer," he said, "I was just checking to see if I could come over and. . . I'm sorry. I didn't bring my walkie-talkie with me. We're over at the bookstore—" He was quiet for a few moments, listening to whatever Elmer was saying. Suddenly his jaw dropped. "What? Are you kidding me? But how—" Using his free hand, he rubbed his forehead like he had a headache. "Okay. Okay, I'll be right there. Don't touch anything." He slammed the phone down. "You won't believe this," he said, staring at me in wonder. "Chuck is missing."

9

Amos and I stood in the empty back room of Buskin's Funeral Home. The metal table where Chuck had last rested was empty. All Elmer, Amos, and I could do was stare at it. I felt like if we focused hard enough, Chuck would suddenly reappear. I mean, how far could he have gone? And who would want a dead Chuck?

"You just noticed he was missing?" Amos asked.

Elmer nodded but kept his gaze directed toward the table. "He was here last night when I left. I notified the coroner's office yesterday that I might be bringing him in. What am I going to tell them now?"

Amos shook his head. "I called the sheriff before I came. He said he'd take care of it. I wish I knew just how he was planning to explain this."

"Was he upset?" I asked, trying to tear my eyes away from the empty table.

"Well, let's just say I thought my father had uttered every curse word known to man. I was wrong." Amos stepped away from the table and directed his attention to Elmer. "You said the back door was open when you came in?"

Elmer met his gaze, his eyes a little glazed. "Yes. But I could have forgotten to lock it. Billy and I both tend to forget about it sometimes. We don't expect anyone to break in here. I mean, what could a thief possibly take?"

"A body?" I offered helpfully. Elmer shot me a look that told me he wasn't in a humorous frame of mind at the moment.

"Did Lucy get a chance to look at him before he—he disappeared?" Amos asked.

Elmer shook his head. "She called to say she would be here later this afternoon. I guess I should let her know she doesn't need to bother."

Amos looked carefully around the room for any kind of clue to Chuck's abduction, but it was as clean as a whistle. "How would someone have removed him?" he asked Elmer. "I mean, you can't just throw a body over your shoulder and walk out, can you?"

"Obviously you can."

"What about his personal effects?" I asked.

"They were in a bag next to the body. It's gone, too," Elmer said. "Everything is gone. It's as if the poor man never existed."

That meant the letter was also missing. I felt sad about that and hoped it would turn up—along with Chuck. "Amos, why would anyone steal Chuck's body?" I asked. "It doesn't make sense."

"Chuck?" Elmer said. "His name was Chuck?"

"No," I said. "His name was Charles, but we call him Chuck."

Elmer nodded as if he understood, but I could tell from the look on his face that he had no idea why we'd given a nickname to a dead man.

"There isn't any reason," Amos said solemnly, "unless the thief was trying to keep someone from discovering that Chuck had been shot."

"But we don't know that for sure, do we?" I asked, looking at Elmer.

Elmer shook his head. "I only said it was possible. If I'd been able to clean him up, I could have been more certain." He hesitated for a moment. "There was another wound near the main area of head trauma. It *might* have been a bullet hole. I can't be sure, but if I hadn't been suspicious, I wouldn't have called you."

Amos blew out his breath slowly. "So it's possible we're never going to know what really happened here. I don't like that."

"What now?" I asked Amos. "Surely this will get the KBI's attention."

He shrugged. "Hitchens says their hands are full with some kind of bomb threat in Hutchinson. He doesn't think they're going to care too much about some intoxicated homeless guy."

I knew he was only repeating what Hitchens had told him, but I suddenly felt defensive. "He wasn't homeless."

"You know what I mean," he said sharply.

Amos didn't get snappy very often. He was as upset about Chuck as I was. I looked at my watch. "Do we still have time to get to the store before we go home, or should we just eat at Ruby's?"

Amos sighed. "We might as well go. I don't think there's much more I can do here. I don't see anything out of place. There aren't any usable tire tracks, and I can't take fingerprints because Hitchens told me not to." He looked at Elmer. "I need you to keep this to yourself. Don't tell anyone."

"Billy will know the body is missing," he said. "And I'll have to tell Dr. Barber."

Amos nodded. "Okay, but tell them it needs to be kept quiet for now—at least until I know what the sheriff wants to do about it."

"All right, Amos." Elmer looked rather forlorn. I was pretty sure this was the first time he'd ever lost a body.

With an admonition to let him know if anything else unusual happened, Amos said good-bye to Elmer and we left. We drove to Dewey's store, where Amos called the sheriff to update him while I shopped. I could tell from Amos's side of the conversation that Hitchens wasn't happy.

I bought my groceries and visited a few minutes with Dewey. Then we headed home. Pal was always excited to see us when we came in the front door. It was as if he hadn't had the pleasure of our company for weeks and couldn't understand why we didn't drop everything and spend every second catching up. Amos rolled around on the floor with him while I got the soup started. After a few minutes, Pal began coughing so badly that Amos got up and made him lie down and rest.

"Did you ask Dewey about Lucy?" he asked me. I could tell he was getting concerned.

"She hadn't shown up yet, but he expected her anytime. He said he'd tell her to call us."

"Good. Pal doesn't seem to be getting any better."

I tried not to worry while I worked on our dinner. Aunt Bitty's pork roast soup was easy to make, but it took awhile. I filled my large kettle halfway full of water, trimmed the Boston butt roast I bought from Dewey, and set it in the water. Then I cut the green beans into bite size pieces and added them along with several small slices of raw bacon. I liked using fresh green beans better, but Dewey carried a frozen brand that worked just as well. After adding salt and pepper, I left it to bubble lightly on the stove until the roast became tender and started falling off the bone. When the pork was ready, all I had to do was remove the bone, pull the roast apart into smaller chunks, and add some potatoes. Once the potatoes were soft, the soup was ready. There wasn't anything better to warm the body and comfort the soul on a frozen winter evening. Bitty had won the soup competition at the county fair so many times with her recipe, she finally quit entering so someone else could have a chance.

I was wiping down the counter when I heard a knock on the front door. "Can you get it?" I hollered to Amos.

"On my way," he called back.

I washed my hands and walked into the living room to find Lucy stepping through the front door. She greeted both of us. "Just got a very disturbing call from Elmer," she said, taking off her parka and handing it to Amos. "Not very often I'm called out to see a body that disappears."

"Tell me about it," Amos said, hanging up her coat. "I have no idea where it is or who took it."

Lucy chuckled. "Surely you two don't intend to let this go? You guys are the closest thing to Sherlock

Holmes and Dr. Watson we have in Winter Break."

Amos gestured toward the couch, where Lucy plopped down next to Pal. "You know," he grumbled, "people say that a lot, but they're never very clear on just who Sherlock is. I have a pretty good hunch they see me as the bumbling sidekick."

Lucy grinned at me and winked. "Why, Amos, I'm sure no one thinks that."

I smiled at her. When I'd first come to Winter Break, Lucy and I hadn't gotten along very well. Lucy and Amos had dated briefly, and Lucy had seen me as an intruder. But now we were good friends. I appreciated her as a person and as a competent and caring doctor.

At that moment, Pal began to cough rather violently.

"Dewey told me you were concerned about our friend here." She turned her attention to the obviously distressed dog. "How long has he been doing this?"

"It's been a couple of days now," I said. "But today it's gotten worse."

She knelt down beside Pal and put her face near his. Then she slung her long black hair over her shoulder and stared into his face. "Ivy, do you have a paper towel handy?"

Her expression scared me. I turned and hurried into the kitchen, tore a paper towel off the roll I kept next to the sink, and jogged back into the living room. I handed it to her.

"Look at this," she said, wiping it across Pal's nose. She held out the towel so we could see the bright red streak that discolored it.

"Is—is that bl–blood?" I couldn't keep my voice from shaking.

Lucy patted Pal and then ran her hands all over his body. When she pressed on his stomach, he yelped.

"Lucy, what's wrong?" Amos asked.

She patted Pal once more and then stood to her feet. "I'm not a vet, but I have a suspicion. Have you noticed any strange stools?"

While Amos told her about the bright green droppings he'd found outside earlier in the day, I whispered a prayer for Pal's protection.

Lucy stared at the floor and shook her head. "I'm afraid he's been poisoned."

"He—he may have gotten into my Christmas cookies," I said. "They have green food coloring. Would that do it?"

She shook her head. "No, Ivy. This isn't from sugar cookies. Do you two keep rat poison on the property?"

"No," Amos said. "We've never needed it."

"Somehow Pal has gotten into rat poison. That's the reason his stool is bright green. He's coughing because there's blood in his lungs."

Pal looked at me with big, sad eyes, as if apologizing for being sick. I started to cry.

Lucy came over and put her arms around me. "Don't go over the edge yet. If you just saw the green stool, that means we caught it early. I have a friend who went through this very same thing and her dog is fine. There's a shot that works as an antidote. Why don't you let me use your phone? I'll call the vet in Hugoton and have him meet me. He'll determine for sure if that's what's wrong, and if it is, we'll get Pal into treatment right away. He's got a good chance for recovery."

While Lucy made her call, Amos got down on the floor next to Pal and petted him. His face was tight with worry.

When Lucy hung up the phone, she said, "I got Dr. Wigglesworth. He's going to meet us at his office." Lucy took her coat from the rack and pulled it on. "Do you want me to take him? It's no problem."

"I'll go with you," Amos said. "You stay here, Ivy. I'll call you as soon as I find out something."

I wanted to protest, but I had soup on the stove, and I wasn't good in situations like this. I did better when I could get some alone time with God. Praying and trusting Him was the only thing that was going to keep me from sheer panic.

Amos put on his coat and then came over and wrapped his arms around me. "I believe God gave Pal to us as a gift, Ivy. He won't allow anything bad to happen to him."

"I know you're right," I said, my voice breaking. "I just love him so much."

He put his hands on my face and looked into my eyes. "God loves him even more. Let's trust Him, okay?"

I nodded, tears sliding down my face.

Amos knelt down next to Pal and gently picked him up. He walked toward the front door where Lucy stood waiting. Pal looked back at me, his big brown eyes bright and questioning. I knew he didn't understand what was happening.

"You need to find out where that poison is," Lucy said to me. "We don't want him getting into it again. And keep an eye on Miss Skiffins. If she shows any unusual signs, we'll need to get her tested."

I nodded as they closed the door. I heard the engine in Lucy's SUV start up and the tires crunch on the snow as they drove away. I stood there for a while staring at the front door. There wasn't any way for me to follow Lucy's instructions. I knew there wasn't any rat poison in the house or in any of our outbuildings. We would have found it long ago. And since the weather had turned cold and snowy, Pal couldn't have wandered very far from the house. A disturbing thought snaked its way into my thoughts. Was it possible someone had purposely poisoned him?

10

I spent the next few hours catching up on the laundry and doing housework while I waited to hear from Amos. I also spent the time praying for Pal. A peace settled over me, along with an assurance that God was watching over our little friend. But the idea that someone might have poisoned him kept circling through my mind. Why would anyone want to hurt a defenseless animal? It didn't make sense to me.

Miss Skiffins followed me from room to room, waiting at the doorways for me to finish whatever I was doing. Since Pal had come to live with us, this was only the second time he'd been away from her. The first time was when we took him to the vet to get his shots and make sure he was healthy. She obviously missed her friend and kept looking at me as if I should give her an explanation. I picked her up several times and petted her, telling her everything would be all right. Although she couldn't understand the words, I hoped my assurances meant something to her. She'd had enough loss in her little life. I knew she still missed Bitty.

Finally, the phone rang and I ran to answer it. It was Amos.

"Pal's doing okay, Ivy," was the first thing out of his mouth. "Dr. Wigglesworth says it's definitely rat poison, but he expects Pal to recover completely. He's had his shot, and we'll have to give him some follow-up pills. The doctor wants to keep him here at least overnight for observation. We can pick him up tomorrow or Monday."

Tears of joy filled my eyes. "Oh, Amos. Can't you bring him home tonight? He'll be so afraid without us. What if he thinks we're going to abandon him like his last owner? I don't want to leave him there."

"Hold on a minute." Amos put his hand over the receiver and said something to someone else. After a few back-and-forth comments, he said, "Dr. Wigglesworth really thinks it's best if Pal remains here. He wants to be certain the antidote is working. Would you feel better if I stayed here? There's a very comfy couch in the waiting room, and the doctor says I can keep Pal with me."

I wiped a tear from my cheek. "That would be great. I'll miss you, but I don't think either one of us could bear it if we left Pal there alone."

"Okay. Boy, you keep saying you want children, but I feel like we already have some."

I laughed. "You should see Miss Skiffins. She's worried about her brother. She'll be really happy when he comes home."

Amos grunted. "I get the feeling she'll be happier to see him than she will be to see me. Guess I know my place around that house."

"Well, I for one will be thrilled to see you."

"Gee, thanks. At least someone wants me." He paused, and I could hear a female voice in the background. "Ivy, Lucy will come by in the morning after Dr. Wigglesworth has checked Pal. If everything is okay, she'll drive me back. Better not plan on my getting home in time for church, though. It's started to snow again. If the roads are bad in the morning, I don't want you driving to church by yourself. Why don't you call Odie again? I know he'd be happy to swing by and pick you up."

"Okay, I will. Hope you get some sleep."

"Me, too. See you tomorrow. I love you."

"Ditto."

I hung up the phone and then spent a few minutes just thanking God for His goodness. When I checked on the soup, I discovered it was ready for the final step. I cut up the potatoes into bite-size chunks and added them to the mixture. While I waited for the potatoes to get soft, I called Odie. He said he would be happy to pick me up in the morning.

It only took about thirty minutes for the soup to finish cooking. I ladled some of it into a bowl and sat down at the dining room table in front of the French doors. The snow was so heavy it was difficult to see the lights on the lake. I kept thinking about Pal, wondering if someone really had tried to poison him. It was difficult to accept, but we'd been all over this property. If there was old rat poison here, left by the Biddles, we would have found it long ago. Maybe someone had thrown something out of their car, not realizing it was poisonous. But that didn't make any sense. How could you not know you had rat poison? And why would anyone toss it out where animals could get into it? Besides, Pal was smart. He wouldn't just eat poison. Someone would have had to put it into something—like a piece of meat. Or Pal's favorite food—peanut butter.

I finished my soup and was thinking about getting a little more, but my stomach had been upset almost all day. No wonder. It was a miracle I had any appetite at all. What a Christmas this was shaping up to be. I put the soup away, rinsed my bowl, and put it in the dishwasher. Then I made a cup of hot chocolate and sat down on the couch. Miss Skiffins, abandoning her usual standoffish attitude, curled up on my lap. As I stroked her, I dozed off. I was awakened by the phone that I'd placed next to me. I fumbled for it, not sure at first if it was the phone or my alarm clock.

"Seven hundred gallons, Ivy," Amos said. "Seven hundred gallons."

My sleepy brain somehow translated this information as a request for seven hundred gallons of pork roast soup. It would take me forever to make that much. A feeling of panic started to overrun me until I realized Amos couldn't possibly be talking about soup.

"I've been sitting here thinking, Ivy," he continued, oblivious to my consternation. "The other night we counted around seven hundred gallons of diesel fuel that was missing."

"Y–yes, that's what you said." The fog was clearing somewhat, although I was still struggling to latch onto what he was talking about. A topic introduction would have been helpful.

"Seven hundred gallons of missing fuel. It doesn't make sense. I realized it while I was sitting here staring at Pal. I should have seen it in the first place, but there was so much going on, my mind just couldn't process it."

"You should have seen what?"

"Even though we couldn't find anything distinctive about the tire tracks, they were definitely from a pickup truck."

"So what?" I knew I sounded grumpy, but the idea of having to cook for almost a thousand people, even though it was short-lived, had made me a little irritable.

"About the biggest transfer tank anyone could put on their truck and still move is around five hundred gallons. It's extremely doubtful that one truck with one tank could pick up seven hundred gallons of fuel in one night. Either there's more than one pickup. . ."

"Or it didn't all happen on one night."

"Right."

"But that still doesn't tell you who did it. You still don't have any clear clues."

"Everything we learn puts us closer to the truth," he said. "I know for certain that Newton and Maynard were hit the night of the play because we went out to their places. Newton had tire tracks and Maynard's gate was open. He'd been out there himself in the afternoon. He knew exactly how much fuel he should have had, and there wasn't much left."

"And your point is?"

"And my point is," he said, "that Mort only said he *found out* some fuel was missing. Either there was another truck, or his fuel wasn't stolen on the same night. I'm going to call him and see if I can narrow down the time of his theft. Can you look up his number for me?"

"Hold on a minute." I lifted Miss Skiffins from my

lap and set her down on the couch next to me. Then I went into the kitchen to get the Winter Break phone book. I found Mort's number, wrote it down on a piece of paper, and carried it with me back to the phone. While I was writing, something occurred to me.

"Amos," I said when I picked up the receiver, "if it turns out that Mort's fuel wasn't stolen the same night, it proves the thieves struck twice. It also means there are twice as many chances that someone saw something."

"That's what I was thinking. You know, Mort did mention he was out of town for a day or two, visiting his wife's mother. If that's when his fuel was stolen, it definitely points to someone in Winter Break. No one else would know about that."

I read the number to him then glanced at the clock. "It's almost nine thirty. Are you going to call him now?"

"Yes. I don't think he'd go to bed this early."

I chuckled. "You'd be surprised. That expression about 'getting up with the chickens' is truer than I ever imagined. I called Milton Baumgartner once at eight thirty in the evening and woke him up."

"I'm still going to take my chances with Mort. He's a pretty easygoing guy."

A thought popped into my head. "If Mort did go out of town for a couple of days, wouldn't he have made arrangements with someone to watch his pigs?"

Amos paused. "I think you're right. They'd still have to be fed and cared for. If it looks like he was hit while he was gone, I'll ask him who he left in charge."

"Let me know what you find out, okay? How's Pal doing?"

"He's doing great. But I think he's wondering why in the world we're here instead of at home. Did you figure out where he got the poison?"

"No. We never bought any, and we've been through every nook and cranny in this place. We would have found it if Cecil and Marion had left some behind."

He was quiet for a moment. "You know, Rosemary Maxwell lived there for a while, but Cecil came out and updated the house and property before you moved in. If she'd had some, he would have found it. Why don't you call him and ask him about it? If there was rat poison on the premises, he'd probably remember it. I think he was pretty careful with stuff like that because of all the kids who used to hang out there."

"I will. You know, now that you bring it up, I wonder if Rosemary could have been connected to Chuck somehow." I couldn't believe I'd completely forgotten about Marion and Cecil's one renter who'd lived in my house before I moved in. She was in prison for murder, and I was trying hard to forget she'd ever existed.

"I don't think there's any chance of that at all," he said. "First of all, she was hiding from the authorities, so she wouldn't have broadcast her location to anyone. Secondly, if I remember right, she had no children and she'd killed her husband. That doesn't leave much room for Chuck in her life, does it? And she was older than Chuck anyway. She couldn't have been his daughter— or his wife."

Amos told me he loved me and said good-bye. It dawned on me as soon as I put the phone down that with all the things that had happened in the last few days, I'd forgotten to call Amos's dad. I looked up the number in Oklahoma and he answered on the second ring.

"Aaron?" I said. "It's Ivy."

"Oh, Ivy. How good to hear from you. How are you?"

"I'm fine. I'm calling to ask you to spend Christmas with us. We really want you."

After a few seconds of silence, he said, "I would love to, but I'm really not sure Amos wants me there. This is your first Christmas as a married couple, and I don't want to mess it up. I think it would be better if we put it off at least a year."

I thought of Chuck. Sometimes putting things off can be a terrible mistake. "Aaron, I think you need to come this year. I really do. Amos needs you more than you realize. Please reconsider. I know it's a little scary. . . ."

Aaron grunted. "*Scary* isn't the word for it. I know God has forgiven me. I'm trying to forget the past and press on to the future like the Bible says—but every time I'm around Amos, I feel guilty and condemned. Now don't get me wrong—I realize I'm totally responsible for the failures of the past. The thing I'm not sure about is how long I can keep paying for them."

"I understand that; I really do. But I truly believe we still have an opportunity to be a real family. Please come. I think it's important."

He was quiet while he considered it. "Okay," he said finally, "but I don't think I should stay with you. I'll get a motel room in Hugoton. That way if I need to beat a hasty retreat, I can do it easily."

I wanted to protest, but I understood his reasoning. He promised to be in town on Christmas Eve—in time to go to the play. Then he would stay Christmas Day and drive back to Oklahoma that night. It wasn't much, but it was something. I settled for it gratefully.

I'd just put the phone down when it rang again. It was Amos.

"Mort was out of town for just one night, Ivy," he said as soon as I answered. "All of the thefts have been at night, so I'm assuming it happened then. He did notice that the snow wasn't disturbed when he checked his tank on Friday after hearing about the other burglaries. We're pretty sure it happened Thursday night. Oh, and he didn't ask anyone to check on the pigs because he wasn't planning to be gone long enough to worry about it."

"Did you say Thursday night? But that's the night. . ."

"Chuck fell off our roof. Strange, huh?"

"Very strange," I agreed. "But I don't see how it could be connected."

"Right now, I don't either." I heard him yawn. "To be honest, I'm so tired I can't think anymore about this. Think I'll try to catch a little shut-eye."

"Amos, how do the farmers in Winter Break get their fuel?"

"It's delivered by Poole and Sons Distributors in Liberal. They bring it once a month by tanker truck."

"So it's really not difficult to tell who's getting fuel or when they got it. All anyone has to know is the day the tanker comes."

"That's right." Amos yawned again. Louder this time.

"When do you think you'll be home?" I asked.

"Dr. Wigglesworth said he would be here around nine in the morning. If everything looks okay, Lucy said she'll drive me home after that."

"You know, I'm not sure I like you being out of town with your old girlfriend. You remember you're married, bub."

Amos laughed heartily. "You have nothing to worry about. I'm too afraid of you to do anything that would get me in trouble."

"Good. I've got you just where I want you."

"Yes, you certainly do," he said softly. "If I get home early enough, I'll drop Pal off at the house and come to the church."

"Good, but tell Lucy not to drive too fast. It's snowing to beat the band right now."

Amos grunted. "I'm so used to snow, I'm more concerned about remembering how to drive when the roads are clear."

"Give Pal a kiss for me. I'll see you both tomorrow."

"How 'bout we shake hands? I'm not much of a doggy kisser."

"Okay. But tell him I love him."

"I think I can handle that."

"Good night, Amos. I love you," I said.

"Ditto."

I hung up the phone and looked around the living room. This was the very first night we'd been apart since we'd gotten married. It felt odd to go to bed without him. Thankfully, I was so tired I fell asleep as soon as I climbed under the covers.

My eyes flew open around two in the morning after a disturbing dream in which Sister Crystal shook her finger at me and yelled, "It's the arm! The arm will bring justice to the nations. Go to the island!" After lying in bed for a while, wondering why I'd had such a silly dream, I finally went back to sleep.

I woke up a few hours later and rolled over on Miss Skiffins, who screeched her unhappiness with me so loudly I jumped out of bed and fell over my own shoes, which were sitting next to the bed. I pulled myself up and gave her the evil eye. At least my version of the evil eye. Then I felt so guilty I chased her down, picked her up, and apologized until she batted me in the face with her paw. All in all, my morning had started out with a bang.

I found my slippers, moved my shoes to the closet where they should have been, and clomped down the stairs. One look outside told me that it had snowed most of the night.

I made some breakfast and then called Odie to make sure he was still going to church. He acted surprised that I'd even think to question him about it. Even though I'd been in Winter Break for a couple of years, I was still getting used to the relaxed attitude about snow that permeated the residents. They were used to it. It was no big deal. I, on the other hand, felt it was a problem when I looked outside and could no longer see the steps that led to our back deck.

I ate breakfast, showered, and dressed, then waited

in the living room for Odie's car horn. When I was a kid, Odie Rimrucker was the town drunk. But many years ago, he'd found his way back to sobriety. In fact, it was my Aunt Bitty who had helped him with his journey. I think his gratefulness to her made him particularly solicitous toward me. I thought about all the people around me who had been affected by alcohol. Amos told me once that his father had been involved with other drugs, as well, when he was in Oklahoma. But in Winter Break, the drug of choice was alcohol, and it was only available through Hiram Ledbetter, who freely sold Ledbetter's Life-Preserving Liniment. Dewey had the only store in town, but he refused to sell it.

Hiram's business was brisk, and would be until Amos could locate his still. Hiram had been hiding it for years, and so far, its location remained a mystery. We were pretty sure he had help. Of course, Hiram wasn't the only source for alcohol in Winter Break. Booze was sold in Hugoton, so anyone who wasn't willing to risk internal bleeding drove out of town, bought the stuff, and carried it home.

Suddenly Odie's loud horn broke the silence, causing me to jump. I grabbed my Bible and my coat and went outside, wading through the snow to Odie's truck. We bounced and slid on the back roads until we got to the main street, which was in the process of being cleared once again by Milton and his sons. Odie and I waved our thanks as we passed Milton on his tractor with the large scoop attached to the front. He waved back and smiled. When we turned into the church parking lot, Milton's son Pervis had just finished scraping it. Once again, we waved as a way of letting him know how much we appreciated his help. He grinned and drove out of the lot, heading out to the street. He and Milton were probably on their way to their own church, which started later than Faith Community.

We found a parking space and Odie held my arm until we got inside. Then he took his spot at the front door. Odie was an usher and a greeter in the church, and he took his job quite seriously. We'd gotten to church a little early so Odie wouldn't miss welcoming the main stream of worshippers. I slipped into the sanctuary and found a seat. The choir was practicing for the morning service, and I sat back and listened to their wonderful Christmas songs. Many of them would be sung again tonight at dress rehearsal.

While I waited for the service to begin, I thought about what Amos had discovered last night. If Mort's farm was targeted when he was away, just like Newton's and Maynard's, then someone really did have firsthand knowledge of the comings and goings of Winter Break farmers. It was a little scary, but at least no one had been hurt during the robberies. I figured that was something to be thankful for.

As Pastor Taylor stepped up to the podium to begin the service, I caught Sister Crystal staring at me. It gave me the willies.

11

I sang heartily along with the choir's selections, even though I've been told I can't carry a tune in a bucket. Pastor Taylor's sermon was about the real meaning of Christmas. It was nice to be reminded that it's not the *presents* of Christmas we should seek, but the *Presence* of Christmas, Jesus Christ, who gave the best gift ever given. Pastor made a point of mentioning that churches fill up at Christmas and Easter with people who normally never come to church, yet God shows up every day to love us and give us everything we need for life and godliness. Being someone who had always known God existed, I found it hard to understand why anyone would run from Someone who loved them enough to give His life for them. And why hide from a Father who loves you unconditionally—and wants nothing more than to give you abundant life and deliver you from pain and destruction? I thought about Amos, who had never really known the love of an earthly father, yet he ran toward the love of his heavenly Father without hesitation. He'd found everything he was searching for. Then there was Hope, whose father had abandoned her. She had a tougher time trusting Father God because of the mistakes her earthly father had made. At least Aaron and his son still had a chance to heal their relationship. Unfortunately for Hope, it was too late for that. Her earthly father was dead, and she was left trying to trust God, not certain His love would be any different. Of course, that's the devil's number one weapon—lying about who God is. He doesn't want people to see that God is good and that all good things come from Him. I was contemplating that the best way to lose a battle is to not know who your real enemy is, when someone grabbed my arm and jiggled me.

"What?" I said more loudly than I meant to. When I looked around, I realized that people were leaving and church was over. I'd drifted off into my own world again. It wasn't unusual for me, but it was a bit embarrassing. I looked up to see who'd taken hold of my arm. Amos stood next to me, grinning.

"Sorry," he said. "I was really looking for a little more enthusiasm."

"Oh, Amos. You're back!" I jumped up and wrapped my arms around him. "I'm sorry. I was thinking about something and wasn't paying attention. I'd given up on you. I didn't think you'd get here before I left."

He hugged me and laughed. "Lucy and I took Pal back to the house first. Then I picked up my car so I can drive us home."

"How's Pal?" I asked, finally letting go of him.

"The vet said he was doing great. He's going to be just fine. He was acting like his old self when I left him. And Miss Skiffins was quite relieved to see him. She even forgot to drop her 'I couldn't care less' act for a few minutes."

"That's wonderful news," I said, smiling. "Let me get my stuff and we'll get out of here." As I was bending over to gather my purse and my Bible, someone else came up next to us. I straightened up to find Emily and Buddy standing at the end of the pew. Emily was radiant. "Ivy, Mama is going to take Charlie to her house for the afternoon. I thought maybe you and Amos would like to have lunch with us at Ruby's."

"That would be wonderful," I said. "Okay with you, Amos?"

Silly question. Ruby fried up massive quantities of chicken on Sundays. In particular, the men of Winter Break loved fried-chicken Sundays. After Amos happily agreed, Emily and Buddy dashed off in hopes of getting a table before the mad rush of hungry parishioners descended on the restaurant.

Amos and I were headed for the exit when Bev Taylor called out our names. We turned around to see what she wanted, but she only crooked her finger at us and pointed toward the door to a small room in the back of the sanctuary that was used for prayer and counseling. Amos looked at me questioningly, but I could only shake my head. I had no idea what it was about. When we reached the room and stepped inside, we found Bev waiting.

"Sorry to hold you up," she said, closing the door behind us, "but I had something I wanted to tell you in private. Ephraim and I heard that Santa Claus's body is missing? Is that right?"

Amos cleared his throat. "Well, of course, it's not really Santa Claus. . . ."

I slapped him lightly on the arm. "She knows Chuck isn't Santa Claus, Amos."

Bev looked surprised. "His name is Chuck?"

"Actually, it's Charles, but we call him Chuck," I explained. I was beginning to get used to the look of confusion on people's faces when we mentioned the nickname we'd assigned Charles. "Never mind—it's not really important. What did you want to tell us?"

"Yesterday morning, Ephraim came to the church to study for his sermon. It was too busy at our house, and he wanted some peace and quiet. Some of the ladies and I were painting scenery for the Christmas Eve play. You know, a lot of that scenery is pretty old. Anyway, as he was driving around the block so he could park in back of the church, he saw something suspicious at the funeral home."

"Something suspicious?" Amos said. "I don't suppose he saw someone removing a body?" He was joking, of course. It couldn't be that easy.

"As a matter of fact, that might be exactly what he saw."

Amos's mouth dropped open. "Okay, Bev," he said slowly, "give me the details."

Bev lowered her voice even though we were in a windowless room with the door closed. "It was Billy Mumfree. And he had a body bag slung over his shoulder."

You could have knocked me over with a feather. I couldn't think of anything to say. Thankfully, Amos wasn't affected the same way.

"Is Ephraim sure it was Billy?"

She nodded. "Absolutely. He would have told you about this himself, but he had an important meeting with the elders scheduled right after the service. He had no doubt that it was Billy."

"Did Billy see him?" I asked.

"No," she said, shaking her head. "He was too busy trying to put his, um, package in the back of his truck."

"Who else has Ephraim told this to?" Amos's voice was almost a whisper.

"No one except me," she said emphatically. "He was pretty sure you wouldn't want anyone else to know."

"That's great." Amos stared at his shoes for a few moments, thinking. "I would appreciate it if you could keep this to yourselves. Don't even mention it to Elmer. Can you do that?"

Bev grinned. "Ephraim is a pastor and I'm his wife. We know so many secrets we've forgotten half of them. We won't say anything. But promise us one thing, will you?"

Amos nodded. "If I can."

"If it turns out that either Billy or Elmer is involved in anything illegal, let us know so we can be there for them? They *are* members of Faith Community."

"Okay, but I'm sure you know that there are certain procedures. . . ."

"I know, Amos. I'm not asking you to cross the line in any way."

He patted her shoulder. "I'll do what I can, but I'll have to contact the sheriff. After that, it's really out of my hands."

Before Bev opened the door, she shook her head. "You know, I really hope there's some other explanation. Elmer and Billy are both valued church members. I've never seen anything in either one of them that would make me think they were capable of anything this. . .odd."

"Don't worry about it," Amos said. "Right now, we really have no idea what's going on. It doesn't make sense to jump to any conclusions."

She smiled. "Actually, it never makes sense to worry about anything. I've found that it doesn't change a thing. It only delays God's response because we haven't given the situation to Him. Before we leave, let's do that, okay?"

We joined hands and each took turns asking God for His wisdom and direction. We also prayed that whatever was hidden in this situation would be made plain.

We said good-bye to Bev and hurried to Ruby's. On the way over, Amos didn't say much except that he was trying to decide whom to talk to first—Sheriff Hitchens or Billy. Approaching Hitchens about Chuck again was a risky proposition. Amos wanted to follow protocol—but with Hitchens's current state of mind, making the right decision was a little tricky.

"Why don't you just ask Billy what he was doing yesterday afternoon, Amos? You've known him a long time. Why in the world would he want Chuck's body? Maybe there's a simple explanation."

From the way he expelled a blast of air between his teeth, I could tell he didn't agree. "Ivy," he said slowly, "give me one simple explanation for removing a body from a mortuary that isn't supposed to be removed. I can't think of a single reason."

I had to admit that I couldn't come up with anything either. "Hey, maybe he was taking Chuck to the coroner's office."

"Not before Lucy released the body. Besides, Elmer

would have known about it."

We pulled up in front of Ruby's. There was only one parking space left on that side of the street. Big flakes of snow drifted down from the sky and hit the windshield.

"By now, wouldn't Elmer have said something to Billy about Chuck's. . .um, departure?"

"Sure. I saw them both in church this morning."

"Look, Amos." I pointed toward the door to Ruby's. Elmer and Billy were just going inside together.

"Either Billy is hiding what he did from Elmer, or Elmer's in on it with him," Amos said. "I don't want to jump the gun and say something that will spook either one of them."

"But in on what?"

Amos stared out the window for a few moments. Finally, he said, "The only reason I can think of is that they're trying to hide the cause of death—either for themselves or for someone else."

I guffawed. "Oh, come on. You think little Elmer was out trying to shoot Santa Claus off our roof Thursday night? That's ridiculous. Besides, Elmer's the one who told you about the possible gunshot. Why would he incriminate himself?"

Amos scowled at me. "Okay, Miss Smarty-Pants. What's your explanation?"

"I don't have one," I said emphatically. "And that's *Mrs.* Smarty-Pants to you, bub."

Amos didn't say another word. He just opened the car door and got out. I followed after him. Before he opened Ruby's front door, he stopped and waited for me. I knew he wasn't really mad at me. I grabbed his arm before he pushed the door open. "We have to trust that God will show us the truth here. That's what we prayed."

He peered at me, his face tight. "I'm trying. But I have to decide what to do now. Do I do the right thing and call Hitchens, who doesn't act like he wants to hear another word about Chuck, or do I talk to my friends about it first? It's not an easy decision."

I patted his arm. "I know. Let's eat. By the time we're finished, I believe you'll know what to do. Elmer and Billy aren't going anywhere."

When we walked into Ruby's, the smell of freshly fried chicken made my stomach growl. Emily and Buddy had found a table, and they waved us over.

"What took you guys so long?" Buddy said as soon as we sat down. "We had to fight to keep your chairs." He lowered his voice. "Sister Crystal Ball tried to take one, but we told her we were waiting for someone. Believe it or not, she wanted to know who it was. I almost asked her why she didn't already know." He shook his head. "Boy, she's wacky, isn't she?"

"Buddy!" Emily said. "We don't call our brothers and sisters 'wacky.' You stop that."

Buddy winked at us and grinned. "I only meant that in the kindest, most loving way. Besides, you call your sister Caroline wacky all the time."

Emily wrinkled her nose at her husband. "Now you hush. It isn't polite to air your dirty laundry in front of other people. And you, the son of a pastor!"

Amos chuckled. "I can't believe you're surprised, Emily. Buddy hasn't changed much since he was ten years old and told our teacher, Mrs. Mott, that her hair smelled like stinky feet."

Now it was Emily's turn to giggle. "I know exactly what he's like, but I'm hoping if I appear to be appalled, it won't reflect directly on me."

Buddy pretended to look hurt and we all laughed. Just then, Bonnie brought water and coffee to our table, along with a glass of milk for Emily. She didn't ask us for our order. She already knew what we liked to drink, and on Sundays, everyone ordered chicken. Ruby didn't make much else.

"It'll be a few minutes, folks," she said with a smile. "Bert and Ruby are frying up a new batch right now. I'll bring out the biscuits and jelly so you can munch on them while you wait."

No one was disappointed by Bonnie's announcement. Ruby's homemade buttermilk biscuits and strawberry jelly were more than accompaniments to dinner; they were a treat on their own merits. We nodded our agreement, and Amos started pouring coffee from the carafe into everyone's cup except Emily's. I put some cream in mine. Usually I drank my coffee black. But even the cream at Ruby's was better than it was anywhere else. She put a touch of cinnamon in it before she poured it into the small creamer cups that went on the tables. The slight taste of cinnamon did something wonderful to coffee.

"So," Buddy said, "anything new on Santa?"

"Chuck," Emily and I said at the same time.

"Chuck?" Buddy said.

"That's what they call him," Emily said matter-of-factly, as if it made perfect sense.

"O–kay," Buddy said, drawing the word out. "I guess I should have said—anything new on Chuck?"

Amos brought him up to speed, not mentioning that Chuck was actually missing or that he may have been shot. While he told Buddy and Emily about Gina and what we'd found out from her, I saw Emily's eyes fill with tears.

"That might be the saddest thing I ever heard," she said, picking up her napkin and wiping her eyes. "So this man spent his last night on earth trying to make up for his past, hoping to reach out to his child, and he has the wrong house." A tear slipped down her cheek. "So what can we do? How can we help?"

I reached for her hand. "Amos actually found the doll. It's back at the house. We've done just about everything we can think of." I pointed at one of the flyers on the wall near us. "That's Chuck. Sheriff Hitchens says we have to take his picture down. He's turned everything over to the KBI. Looks like we're officially out of it as far as any kind of investigation." I sighed. "We're doing what we can, but we have to be careful. We can't step on anyone's toes."

"But maybe Chuck's daughter is in Winter Break," Emily said. "He just got confused by the address. If we tried to figure out everyone who would be about the right age—"

"Whoa," Buddy said. "You two can't solve all the world's problems. Besides, Emily has to take it easy."

"Sitting around thinking isn't going to cause me any great stress," she replied sharply. "And frankly, I'm getting bored. I'm only pregnant, Buddy. I'm not disabled."

"Thanks," I said, smiling at her. "But I've already run through everyone I can think of. No one seems to fit the bill. Besides, your husband's right. You need to concentrate on yourself now."

Buddy's face lit up. "Hey, did Ivy just say I was right about something?"

I shook my finger at him. "Yes, I did. It was bound to happen eventually. Law of averages and all." Everyone laughed.

While we waited for our biscuits, Amos told Emily and Buddy about Pal. The idea that someone might have purposely poisoned our dog made Buddy angry. He was quite an animal lover. Had been ever since he was a little kid.

"Dewey sells rat poison," he said. "Have you checked with him to see who he sold it to lately?"

"No," Amos said. "We just found out about it yesterday." He told them about Lucy's visit and his night in Hugoton.

"Are you absolutely certain there isn't any rat poison around your house?" Emily asked. "Could there be some stored somewhere that you didn't know about?"

"We thought about that," I said, "but we've been over that place with a fine-tooth comb. Besides, Pal would have had to have eaten the poison sometime in the last week or so. He hasn't been wandering around outside because of the weather." I shook my head. "No, the poison had to have been placed close to the house where he could have found it within a few minutes. That means it almost had to be done on purpose."

Emily reached out and patted my hand. "I hope you're wrong, Ivy. The idea that someone would purposely try to hurt that sweet puppy. . ." Once again her eyes filled with tears.

"Oh, for cryin' out loud," Buddy said. "Being pregnant sure turns you into a crybaby."

But I noticed his own eyes misting up. He loved Pal. When he and Emily visited the house, it didn't take more than a couple of minutes for Buddy to start rolling around on the floor with the exuberant Border collie. I wasn't sure which one of them was the more mature.

Bonnie finally came with our biscuits, and we spent the next few minutes slathering them with butter and the pungent jelly. I ate one, but my upset stomach was back, so I decided to forgo a second one. The stress of the past few days was obviously getting to me.

Amos kept glancing over at Elmer and Billy. They seemed relaxed, although Elmer looked a little distracted. But having a body stolen from your mortuary would certainly cause that kind of reaction. It would be easier if criminals would just slap a note on their foreheads that read I'M GUILTY. It would save a lot of time and frustration. Of course, it would make for pretty short mystery novels.

Emily made quick work of two rather large biscuits. When she noticed I was watching her, she laughed. "I'm eating for two, okay? Being pregnant is the only time in a woman's life she can pig out and get away with it."

Buddy raised an eyebrow. "As long as she doesn't

actually begin to look like a pig."

Emily pushed against him with her shoulder. "You told me you think pigs are cute."

"I told you baby pigs were cute. Now the sows are a whole different deal."

I grinned at him. "I can guarantee you that Emily will never be anything but beautiful. She was always the prettiest girl in town."

Buddy leaned over and kissed his wife's cheek. "I've always thought so. Of course, I'm in love, so who knows? She could be as ugly as a smashed toad and still be beautiful to me."

Emily's fair complexion turned pink. "A smashed toad? You think I look like a smashed toad?"

"N–no. I meant that no matter what you look like. . ."

I couldn't hold back my laughter any longer. "You'd better just back off now, Buddy," I said. "You're digging yourself into a hole you'll never be able to crawl out of."

Now it was Buddy's turn to blush. "Boy, when your wife is pregnant, your mouth can get you into trouble faster than a chicken can pounce on a bug."

Amos and I glanced at each other. We wanted nothing more than to know exactly what it felt like to be expecting. I had to push the thought out of my mind. I hadn't been able to spend much time with Emily lately, and I didn't want to ruin it by getting melancholy.

"So is all your Christmas shopping done?" I asked her, changing the subject.

She nodded. "I started on it months ago when we found out about the baby. I had terrible morning sickness with Charlie, and I didn't want to have to fight that and worry about getting presents."

Buddy stuck out his thumb and crooked it toward his wife. "She didn't want to leave a trail of vomit behind her."

"Buddy!" Emily exclaimed. "We're getting ready to eat. What is wrong with you?"

Buddy's hurt expression made me giggle. "I—I'm sorry," he said. "But it's the truth."

"I've really missed you two," I said. "You're better than TV."

"Well, I'm so happy we keep you entertained," Emily said, smiling. "But I never saw myself as the straight partner in a comedy team. Unfortunately, that seems to be how I ended up."

"You sure didn't think I was too funny yesterday," Buddy said.

Emily rolled her eyes. "He went out to check our fuel tank. With the robberies the other night, we just wanted to make sure we were okay. There wasn't any fuel missing, but Buddy got diesel fuel all over a pair of his good jeans. Once that stuff gets on something, it's almost impossible to get out."

Buddy wrinkled his nose. "Yeah, it stinks pretty good."

"It not only stinks forever; it stains," Emily said. "I finally learned how to get rid of it, but it takes a lot of time and patience. We've had to throw away some of his clothes because I just couldn't get them clean."

Just then Bonnie arrived with a massive platter of fried chicken and a bowl of mashed potatoes. Following along behind her was Bert Bird, her husband and Ruby's son. He set bowls of gravy and corn in front of us.

"Hi, folks," he said cheerfully. "Bonnie will get the coleslaw and then you should be in business." He picked up the carafe on our table and jiggled it. "You're gonna need some more coffee, too." He hollered after Bonnie, who was already going back for our coleslaw, "Hey, Beanie, bring another pot of joe, will you?"

She waved her hand at him to show that she'd heard him.

"Beanie?" I said. "Where did that come from?"

Bert smiled, and his blue eyes sparkled. "Bonnie's sister Mabel's little girl can't say 'Bonnie.' She started calling her 'Aunt Beanie.' I thought it was funny, so I call her that all the time now. She acts like she doesn't like it, but I know she does."

Bert left to go back to the kitchen. Buddy prayed over our meal, and everyone started grabbing chicken. One recipe I couldn't seem to master was fried chicken. The crust almost always fell off when I tried to take the pieces out of the pan. Amos didn't seem to mind, though. Not as long as we could get Ruby's chicken. I put a wing on my plate along with some mashed potatoes and gravy, but I was surprised to find that it didn't appeal to me. In fact, I felt a little nauseated. I nibbled at my food but couldn't do much more than that.

After a few bites, Emily said, "So I hear Zach came by the bookstore the other day."

"Yes. He was looking for a book for Hope."

"I'm concerned about him, Ivy," Emily said. "He's really crazy about her, but she seems to have a problem with men."

"She had a bad childhood. I guess her parents both died young, and she carries the scars."

"We need to trade our scars for the ones Jesus bore for us. Ours weigh us down and His set us free." Buddy kind of mumbled his words before he stuck a forkful of mashed potatoes and gravy in his mouth.

I stared at him with my mouth open. Thankfully, it was empty.

Emily sighed. "And there's the enigma of Buddy. He acts like a squirrel 80 percent of the time, and then he comes up with something like that." She leaned over and put her head on his shoulder. "You're something else, you know that?"

Buddy looked surprised, especially when he noticed the tears in my eyes. "That was beautiful," I said. "Is it something you got from your dad?"

"Nope," he said, starting to realize he was getting attention for something positive. "Came up with it all on my own."

I glanced at Amos, who was staring at his plate like he hadn't heard Buddy's words. But I knew he had. I couldn't help but remember that when Amos proposed to me, he'd declared that he wasn't going to let his past rule his future. He'd made a lot of improvement. In fact, for a while everything seemed fine. But in the past couple of months, he'd gotten more introspective and guarded. It worried me at first, but then my mother told me that a lot of times when God is dealing with someone, they'll seem to get worse right before they get better. It had something to do with facing a problem before you can really deal with it. I'd heard a teacher I really admired say, "Feelings buried alive never die." And she was right. I wondered if those buried feelings were finally clawing their way to the surface.

"I agree with Buddy," Emily said. "I'm just concerned that Hope is too fragile for Zach. I love my brother. I don't want to see him hurt."

I sighed. "I don't know what will happen, but after talking to Zach the other day, I'm pretty sure he has no intention of walking away." I reached over and patted my friend's hand. "And Hope *is* making strides. She's talking to Ephraim. That's a good start."

Emily squeezed Buddy's arm. "Yes, that's a very good start. He did a pretty good job with his son."

Buddy took advantage of our admiring glances to belch. "Oh, sorry," he said, hiding his mouth behind his napkin and burping again. Amos laughed so hard he almost spit out his mashed potatoes.

When things settled down some, Buddy frowned at Amos. "Did you guys have company the other night?"

"Just early Friday morning," Amos said. "And it wasn't really company. Just me, Ivy, the sheriff, Elmer, and a dead body. What kind of *company* are you talking about?"

"There was a pickup parked on the road near your driveway. I passed it on the way home from the church. I was replacing a spot in the carpet that got burned when the candelabra fell over during a wedding a couple of weeks ago." He looked sheepish. "I accidentally fell asleep on the floor and didn't wake up until a little after midnight."

It crossed my mind that some wives would suspect a story like that. But with Buddy, it was totally believable. Suddenly something else occurred to me.

"What night are you talking about?"

"I don't remember. When was that, Em?"

"It was Thursday night," she said. She slapped her dainty hand on the table, causing her husband to jump. "Buddy Taylor! Why in the world would you wait until now to bring this up? Didn't you realize that was the night Santa Claus—excuse me, Chuck fell off their roof?"

"Hey, give me a break," Buddy grumbled. "I had no idea."

"Never mind all that," Amos said quickly. "You say the pickup was parked near our driveway?"

Buddy nodded. "On the road, right next to it. The headlights were off. At first I thought it might have been abandoned there. Then I saw someone inside."

"What color was the pickup?" Amos asked.

Buddy frowned. "Blue and white."

"Did you notice the make and model, Buddy?" I asked.

He shrugged and picked up another piece of chicken. "Sure. It was a Ford F-150."

Emily, who was drinking milk, set her glass down and stared at her husband. "You mean like the one you used to have?"

Buddy shook his head. Then he took a big bite of

chicken, chewed, and swallowed. "It's not *like* the one I used to have. It *is* the one I used to have."

"I don't understand," Amos said, his frustration beginning to show. "You saw your own truck parked outside our place Thursday night?"

"No," Buddy said, using his fingernail to loosen a piece of chicken that was caught in his teeth. "It's not my truck anymore. I sold it a month ago to Delbert Pennypacker."

12

Iknow it sounds suspicious, but just because he was parked on the road near our house doesn't mean he had anything to do with Chuck's death." Amos shook his finger at me. "First of all, we're still not sure if Chuck was shot. And if he was, Delbert Pennybacker couldn't have brought him down with a cannon. He can't shoot. Everyone knows it. Milton used to take him hunting with him and Maynard. Delbert was so bad, they were afraid he was going to kill them. There's no way he could have nailed Chuck with a single bullet."

After a midafternoon nap, Amos and I were rushing around trying to get ready to leave the house. Amos was going to Liberal to meet with Gina, and I was going to the church for dress rehearsal.

"How do you know he wasn't shot more than once?" I asked. "The truth is, we have no idea how many times he may have been hit."

"Hitchens might have missed one bullet hole when he looked at Chuck, but he wouldn't have missed two. He's too experienced. Besides, your theory doesn't make any sense. Delbert would have had to hit his target twice instead of once. That makes it more than impossible."

I mumbled something under my breath about the fact that if he and Hitchens missed one bullet hole, they could have overlooked a second. And on top of that, there wasn't anything that was "more than impossible."

Amos, who was checking Pal's food and water, straightened up and stared at me. "What did you say? Are you mocking me?"

I smiled sweetly at him. "Now why would I do something like that, O mighty lawman?"

He shook his head. "Someone should have warned me about your mouth before I said 'I do.' If I'd only known. . ."

"You not only knew—it's one of the reasons you love me so much." I pursed my lips and blew him a kiss. This time he mumbled something *I* couldn't hear— and he didn't reach out to catch my invisible sign of affection.

He put the bag of dog food in the cabinet and leaned against the counter. "I've decided I should tell Hitchens about Billy before I approach him or Elmer. I tried to call him, but I couldn't get him. Dispatch said he was unavailable right now."

"Then maybe you should call the undersheriff. What's his name?"

"Fred Griggs. I guess I should, but Hitchens won't like it. They don't get along. He's told me more than once not to take anything to Griggs before I talk to him. I hate to irritate him any further."

"Well, wait awhile. Hitchens is usually available, isn't he? Surely he'll check in soon."

"Yeah, you're right. I should be able to reach him before long." He sighed. "I can tell he's getting tired of talking to me. How many times have I called him about this thing *after* he told me to leave it alone?"

"You can't help it if situations keep popping up.

Surely he understands that. He's been in law enforcement long enough to know how it works."

Amos's grunt told me he wasn't convinced of Hitchens's capacity for understanding.

I was rummaging around in a drawer, trying to find the church directory. Most of the families who attended Faith Community were pictured inside. I finally uncovered it beneath some warranty papers for the washer and dryer. I quickly thumbed through the pages. "Here," I said, handing it to him. "Show this to Gina. It's a photo of Delbert. Even if he didn't shoot Chuck, maybe he's the one who drove him here. If she recognizes him and remembers that he was at Boots and Beer Thursday night, I think we'll finally know how Chuck got to our house. Maybe all Delbert did was give him a ride. But isn't it possible that Chuck told Delbert why he was coming to Winter Break? They'd both been drinking, and people seem to get talkative when they're inebriated. Maybe Chuck said something that will finally explain why he thought his daughter lived here."

"Well, anything is possible." Amos took the directory and put it in his inside pocket. "Are you about ready?"

I knelt down and hugged Pal one last time. "I wish we were staying in tonight. I want to spend some time with him."

"For crying out loud, Ivy. You've been treating that dog like a baby ever since he got home. If you don't start acting normal, he's gonna start wondering if something's wrong."

"Nonsense," I said, planting a kiss on top of Pal's head. "I just want him to know how much we love him." He rewarded me with one of his cockeyed smiles, his tongue lolling out the side of his mouth. It was obvious he was happy to be back. It comforted me to see he wasn't traumatized by his experience. I hugged him one last time and straightened up. "I'm just about ready, but I need to take something for my stomach. That greasy fried chicken just isn't sitting well."

"Okay, but I've got to get going if you still want me to make that special stop in Hugoton."

I found some medicine in the bathroom for upset stomach. The pink, chalky pills were rather old, but I chewed a couple anyway. They seemed all right. "Okay, let's go," I said to Amos when I came downstairs.

I turned around to look at Pal before we walked out the door. He'd jumped up on the couch. Miss Skiffins was lying on the arm, staring at him. She turned her head toward me, and I could have sworn she winked. I took it as a sign that everything would be okay. Pal looked perfectly content, and his recovery was nothing short of remarkable. I quietly thanked God once again for taking care of him. Amos and I had prayed and expressed our gratitude together when we'd gotten home from church. I was so grateful that God cared about everything in our lives, including our precious pets.

Amos dropped me off at the church, kissed me good-bye, and left. He planned to pick me up after rehearsal, but I'd made arrangements with Odie to catch a ride home in case he didn't make it back in time.

The first thing I noticed when I walked into the sanctuary was that Zach and Hope were sitting next to each other. I was surprised and happy to hear them laughing together. Maybe things were looking up on the romance scale.

Bonnie Bird was up on a ladder, putting some finishing touches on our Star of Bethlehem. Some sparkly paint and a small spotlight would make it really shine during the performance. Bert was down below, holding the ladder steady. Mavis and Milton Baumgartner were putting the manger in place. Fortunately, baby Jesus was going to be a doll this year. This decision was made after several years of Jesus screaming through the entire production. It really was too much to ask of a baby—to stay under bright lights and endure the singing of the choir while Mama was off to the side watching the whole debacle. There had been some talk of substituting the doll for a real baby at the end, but I couldn't find any way that this wouldn't look like Jesus was being kidnapped while a replacement was smuggled into his place. Neither the screaming nor the kidnapping sat well with my image of the Son of God. So a realistic baby doll would have to do.

I noticed Elmer and Billy sitting off to the side. I smiled at them, and they waved as if they hadn't a care in the world. I'd always had great respect for Elmer, and I'd always liked Billy, too. It was very difficult for me to imagine that either one of them was a nefarious body snatcher.

I felt a tap on my shoulder and turned around to see Barney Shackleford. "Sure looking forward to dinner at your house on Christmas." Barney, who was short and chubby, was dressed in his shepherd's costume. I thought he looked adorable, but I had no plans to tell him that. I learned from Amos that men definitely don't want to be seen as anything close to adorable.

"I'm looking forward to it, too, Barney. There's nothing better than celebrating Christmas with good friends."

He smiled. "You know, Ivy, I never thought I'd be happy again after Dela died, but I am. I really am. I owe it to this church and to the people in this town." He blinked quickly to chase away the tears that tried to form in his eyes. "I feel like I belong here. Dela would be glad to know I'm still here and that everyone is being so nice to me."

I reached out and grabbed his hand. "I believe she *does* know that, Barney. Besides, you're a very easy person to love. You've done so much for Winter Break. Whenever anyone needs help, you're always there." I waved my hand toward the stage. "And we're all grateful you agreed to fill in for Ferd. You didn't have to."

"Well, at the time, I think I was the only one who was big enough to fill his costume. But thanks, anyway." He ran his hands down the front of his robe. "This one was made just for me, so I guess that doesn't hold true anymore. Do you like it?"

I'd been thinking that his tunic looked remarkably white and neat, but it wasn't until his comment that I realized it was new. I glanced toward the stage where several other shepherds were gathered. Hope and Zach had gotten up and were standing in front of the stage.

Their robes were also as white as could be. In fact, they were beautiful. I looked around the room and saw Inez on her knees in front of Pastor Taylor, working on his hem, which looked a little too long. I asked Barney to excuse me, took off my coat, and put it, my purse, and the script down on the front pew. Then I went over to her.

"Hi, Ivy!" she said when she saw me, which probably wasn't a good idea, since she spit out several pins she had in her mouth. She quickly gathered them together.

After making sure she was okay, I asked her about the new robes.

"Oh, do you like them?" She continued to stick pins in Pastor Taylor's costume while she talked to me. "Bertha and I spent all last night and this afternoon sewing them." She looked up at our pastor, who was patiently waiting for her to complete his wardrobe adjustment. "I guess some of our measurements were off a bit, but after a couple of adjustments, we'll be good to go."

Pastor Taylor chuckled. "It's my fault, really. If I'd just managed to be a couple of inches taller, everything would have been perfect." He lightly slapped the sides of his robe. "I must say, this feels much better than the other costume. It was too itchy. This is so soft and comfortable. I really appreciate it, Ivy."

"Well, thanks, but I have no idea how this happened. Someone must have raided their linen closet."

Inez bumped her shoulder against my leg. When

I looked down, I saw her shake her head and hold one finger up to her lips as a sign to keep quiet. Confused, I nodded at her, but I wasn't sure why our new costumes were a secret.

"Inez, I've got to check the script, but would you come and see me when you're done here?"

"Absolutely." She stood to her feet. "Now, Pastor, if you'd slip this off and give it to me, I'll have it sewn up in no time at all."

"I would be happy to do that, but I think I'll remove it in my office and have Bev bring it to you." He flushed a little and laughed. "I have shorts on under my robe, but I just don't feel right about parading around the church like that. Not that I don't have magnificent legs."

"He truly does have great legs." Bev had come up behind him. "He just doesn't want all the women to swoon at the sight of his manly limbs. It's a curse, isn't it, sweetheart?"

"Yes. Yes, it is. But then, you've got some pretty awesome gams yourself there, cutie pie."

Bev giggled and slapped him lightly on the arm. "You need to come with me before you have to repent in front of these wonderful ladies."

They took off for the office, leaving Inez and me behind. When they were out of sight, I gently grabbed Inez by the arm and pulled her a few feet away where no one else could hear us talking.

"So where did the new costumes come from, and why is it such a secret?" I whispered.

She glanced around us to ensure no one was listening.

"We told everyone we were using donated sheets but that the person who donated them wanted to remain anonymous."

"Oh." There were many times when people in the church did something nice for someone else but asked that their names be kept out of it. I understood why, but it certainly didn't satisfy my nosy nature.

"The reason the person who gave us the sheets wanted to keep it secret wasn't because they were modest," she said quietly. "There was another reason."

I stared at her. "What are you talking about? Can you tell me who it was, or would that be betraying a confidence?"

She shook her head. "No, the giver told me that only you, me, and Bertha could know."

"Bertha?" Without meaning to, I raised my voice. A few people standing around the stage glanced toward us.

"Shh." Inez frowned at me. "Yes, Bertha. And I trust her. She really has come around, Ivy. I know she still does some dumb things, but she's trying. She really is. She'll keep our secret."

I held out very little hope of that, but I wasn't going to say that to Inez. If she wanted to believe in Bertha's ability to keep a secret, more power to her. "Okay, so now tell me. Where did the sheets come from, and why can't everyone know?"

Inez took a deep breath. "Elmer gave them to us."

I couldn't keep the exasperation out of my voice. "Why would anyone care if Elmer. . ." And then it hit me. "Are you telling me that those sheets are—are—"

Inez slowly nodded her head, her expression

solemn. "That's exactly what I'm telling you."

"You—you mean—I mean, were they used for. . ." I looked around at our cast, who seemed happy and completely oblivious to the fact that they were standing around in sheets that had once covered dead bodies.

Inez grabbed my arm. "Why, Ivy Parker, they're not used sheets. My goodness. How desperate do you think we are?"

I shook my head in an attempt to get the blood flowing to my brain again. "They're new? Then why can't we tell everyone where they came from?"

She lowered her voice even more. "Because even though they're new, they're morgue sheets. Elmer gets them from a mortuary supplier. I don't believe anyone needs to know that. His supplier sent too many in his last delivery, and Elmer was going to send them back. Instead, he asked me if we could use them for new costumes." She clucked her tongue at me several times. "Used funeral-home sheets. For pity's sake. I wouldn't touch those with a ten-foot pool. Besides, it's probably against the law to reuse stuff like that."

I let out a nervous giggle. "Okay, okay. You're right. So many weird things have happened lately, nothing would surprise me."

Just then Bev came out the side door, holding Pastor's robe.

"Let me know as soon as that robe is ready, Inez," I said. "Since Pastor's in the first scene, we'll wait for you. I really want this to be a real dress rehearsal." I had started to walk away when another thought hit me. I turned back quickly. "Inez, when did you get the sheets?"

She brushed her graying hair back from her face. "Why, yesterday afternoon. Billy Mumfree brought them over." She looked toward Bev, who had stopped to talk with a group of children who were playing angels in the play. I saw Benjie Tuttle in the group.

"I'll tell you something, Ivy," she continued. "When he started up my steps, I sure got a start. Why, he had those sheets inside one of those, what do you call them. . ."

"Body bags," I said quietly.

"Yes. Yes, that's it. They were in a body bag to keep them from getting dirty or wet. But for a minute it looked just like he was carrying a dead body up to my door. I wasn't sure whether I should open up or not." She laughed. "Isn't that silly? Thinking someone like Billy would be toting a body around town in broad daylight?"

I raised an eyebrow. "Yeah, that's silly all right. Thanks, Inez. I have a call to make."

I caught Bev as she made her way to Inez and asked if I could use the phone. "Well, yes, dear," she said. "But why don't you use the phone in the church kitchen. I don't think Ephraim would be comfortable with you in his office right now."

I thanked her and ran to the kitchen. I called dispatch and gave them my phone number. I had to wait a few minutes for Amos to call me back. I quickly told him about my conversation with Inez.

"For crying out loud," he said. "What if I'd actually gotten through to Hitchens? I would have looked like an idiot."

"I know, I know. God was watching out for you. And I'm glad you didn't say anything to Billy or Elmer. They could have cleared things up, but it would have looked like you suspected them."

"Yeah, but we're right back where we started. We still have no idea who took Chuck."

"I'm going to have to tell Bev and Ephraim something. They've got to know that Billy's not a body snatcher. I have a feeling Pastor isn't going to be quite as excited about his new robe."

Amos chuckled. "Well, he does preach a lot of funerals, so he may be a little more used to stuff like this than you think."

"I hope so. See you tonight. Love you, Amos."

"Ditto."

I went back to the sanctuary and grabbed Bev. I took her aside and explained the situation. She started to laugh. "Oh my goodness! Sheets? Now that is really funny."

"It might be funny now, but it wouldn't have been too humorous if Amos had gotten ahold of the sheriff. Hitchens might have arrested Billy on suspicion of stealing a body."

Bev looked at me, her eyes getting wide. As upset as I was that Chuck was still missing and that we had no clues, I realized how ridiculous it was to think Billy Mumfree, a fresh-faced young man who had never been in any trouble, was running around snatching dead bodies. I couldn't keep it in and burst out laughing. Bev and I heehawed until we couldn't breathe. She had tears running down her face, and the cast of our play was staring at both of us like we'd suddenly gone insane. It took a few minutes to get ourselves under control.

Bev took a deep breath. "You know I'm going to have to tell Ephraim, don't you?"

I nodded, still chuckling. "Yes, but tell him for the sake of the rest of the cast to keep the information to himself."

Bev grinned. "I think that might be a good idea."

I walked to the front of the sanctuary and asked for everyone's attention. "Tonight is dress rehearsal. I want to run through the entire play without stopping, no matter what happens. We won't add the sheep until Wednesday night, but just a heads-up. If they try to run off the stage, ignore them. Pervis Baumgartner is going to dress like a shepherd and round them up. Just keep on with your parts as if nothing unusual is happening, okay?" I glanced over at Maynard. His hairpiece seemed to be secure. I wasn't looking forward to an encore performance starring his falling rug.

"Do I look the part?" Hope asked in her soft voice. She was wearing a long black wig, parted in the middle. It framed her sweet face beautifully. Over her hair, Inez had draped white fabric that fell down around her shoulders. She almost glowed. I had a feeling it wasn't so much the part she was playing as it was who was standing next to her. Zach wore a dark blue tunic with a gold outer robe, and a gold headdress held on with a headband. He had a beard pasted onto his chin. I'd never seen Joseph, but if he looked anything like Zach, I could understand why Mary fell in love with him.

"I think you're perfect," I said, smiling. "In fact, you all look incredible." I glanced over at Inez and Bertha, who stood over to the left of the stage. "I think we need to let the women who put these costumes together know how much we appreciate them." The entire cast broke out in applause. Inez smiled, but Bertha seemed almost at a loss to receive the praise. She turned bright red and ran out of the room, Pastor's tunic in her hands.

I went over some points with the cast, and by the time I'd finished, Pastor Taylor emerged in his altered costume. It looked perfect, and I breathed a sigh of relief. Our prophet declaring, "The people who walked in darkness have seen a great light," and falling on his face wasn't the concept I was going for.

"Okay," I said loudly, "everyone take your places. Let's do this."

The lights went down in the sanctuary, and I took a seat on the front row. The lights on the stage came up slowly, and when I pointed toward the side door, the choir members filed in, taking their places on the platform. When they were in place, Aunt Bea took her place at the piano. Gail raised her arms and they began to play and sing "O Little Town of Bethlehem." A small spotlight became focused on the star that hung above the stage, and it began to sparkle. Bonnie had done a wonderful job with it. For some reason, the silly nickname Bert had called her popped into my mind. I wondered if I would always see her as "Beanie" now. When I was little, one of my cousins had called me some strange nickname, too. I couldn't remember it, but it was because she couldn't wrap her tongue around "Ivy."

The music finished and Pastor Taylor came out and began to deliver his lines. While I was listening to him, the idea of nicknames was still rolling through my mind. And I realized something I should have seen earlier. I knew beyond a shadow of a doubt that Chuck's daughter had been standing right in front of me the whole time.

Rehearsal went off without too many problems. Everyone was able to get back on their feet after kneeling, and all the hairpieces stayed in place. When the choir finished the last song, "O Come, All Ye Faithful," I spoke briefly to everyone, encouraging them to go over their lines on their own before Wednesday night and making a couple of other suggestions. Then I waited while people began to leave. But before she was able to get to the back doors, I called one person over to me.

"Sit down, Hope," I said, patting a place on the pew next to me. Zach came up behind us.

"I was going to walk you home," he said uncertainly to her. "Will you be long?"

I pointed to the pew in back of us. "Zach, why don't you wait? I need to talk to Hope, and I think it might be good for you to be here."

He shot me a funny look, but he didn't say anything and sat down. I turned my attention to the puzzled young woman sitting next to me. There were only a few people left in the sanctuary, but they seemed to realize that we needed some time alone, and they left quietly.

"Hope," I said slowly, "everyone in town knows that a man dressed like Santa Claus fell off our roof and died."

She nodded. "A lot of people thought it was pretty

funny. It made me sad."

I grabbed her hand and held it. "I'm not surprised by that. You have a very tender heart, and you've been through a lot. Unfortunately, I might be getting ready to add to your burden."

Just then the sanctuary doors opened and Amos came in. I stopped and waved my hand so he'd see us sitting on the front row. He came down the aisle.

"What's going on?" he asked.

"Just sit down next to Zach, Amos. I believe I've figured out something important."

With a grunt, he settled in behind us. Zach and Amos both looked confused. I was a little befuddled myself, but I hoped in a few minutes things would be much clearer.

"I need to ask you some questions," I said to Hope. "After you answer them, I'll explain why I needed to talk to you."

She nodded, but there was a look in her eyes that concerned me. Was I getting ready to cause her more pain? But something inside me said to go ahead. I glanced back at Zach. His concern was evident, as was his heart. I prayed silently that the next few minutes would change things for the better. Pulling out weeds might hurt, but when they're gone, flowers can finally grow.

I fastened my eyes on hers. "This is going to sound like a really strange question, but when you were a child, did you have a nickname?"

She frowned and leaned back against the padded pew. "Why would you ask me that?"

I squeezed her hand. "Please trust me and answer my question."

"It—it wasn't a nickname anyone else gave me. When I was little, I called myself Ho Ho instead of Hope. It was close to my real name, and it reminded me of Santa Claus. My dad thought it was cute, I guess. He always called me Ho Ho. Eventually it became Ho Ho Heart because our last name was Hartwell."

I looked at Amos. His eyes were wide and his mouth hung open. He started to say something, but I held my finger up to my lips. I knew what he wanted to ask, but I felt we needed to lead into this slowly so as not to overwhelm Hope.

"This might seem like another odd question, but do you remember writing a letter to Santa Claus the Christmas your father left?"

A tear made its way down her cheek. She pulled her hand out of mine and then reached up, removing the linen sheet that covered her head. Then she carefully unpinned the black wig, pulling it off and laying it down beside her. She wiped her face with the back of her hand. Although I was certain the wig was hot and uncomfortable, her actions were obviously a way to delay her answer while she composed herself.

"I—I asked for a Cabbage Patch doll with red hair. It's all I wanted, except for my father's love." She took a deep breath and blew it out slowly. "Silly, huh? Thinking Santa Claus could change his heart." She'd been looking down at her lap, but when she raised her head, the sadness in her face was almost more than I could bear. "I prayed, too. But I guess God and Santa Claus were both busy that year."

I grabbed her hand again. "Hope, why do you

believe your father is dead?"

This time she looked genuinely confused. "Because he is. My grandmother told me he died from drinking."

I let go of her hand long enough to open my purse and remove the flyer I'd shown to Gina. I unfolded it and handed it to her. "Do you recognize this man?"

She stared at it for a few seconds. Suddenly her eyes widened and the color drained from her face. "He's—he's much older, but he looks like—my—my father. Where did you get this?"

Obviously she hadn't been to Ruby's lately. I took the flyer from her and handed it to Amos. This time I grabbed both of her hands and held them tight.

"This is going to be hard for you to hear, Hope, but you have a right to know the truth. Your father isn't—wasn't dead. He's the man who fell off our roof."

She started to pull away from me, shock distorting her features. "What? That—that can't be true!"

Zach reached over the back of the pew and put his hands on her shoulders. That seemed to settle her down a little.

"I should have seen it from the beginning, but you told me your father was dead. That's why I never connected the dots. Your father thought you lived in our house because you stayed with me for a while. Do you have any idea how he would have gotten our address?"

She opened her mouth to protest, but then she stopped. "My cousin Pearl. I wrote to her to let her know about Grandma. Then when I got the job at the library in Winter Break, I sent her your address in case she ever wanted to get in touch with me. I never heard anything back, and I assumed the address I had for her was old. I guess she got my letters and my father contacted her. It's the only way he could have found me." She blinked several times. "But—but why would Grandma tell me my father was dead?"

"Would it have made you feel better to know he was alive but that he didn't want to see you?"

"No." Another tear slid down her cheek. "I guess she thought she was helping me, but I wish she would have told me the truth."

I smiled. "It's hard to tell someone you love something that will hurt them. I'm sure she thought she was doing the right thing."

"But I don't understand. What was my father doing on your roof?"

I felt my own eyes get wet. "Your dad had that letter you wrote to Santa Claus in his pocket. The one you signed 'Ho Ho Heart.' He had a red-haired Cabbage Patch doll with him. In fact, my guess is that you asked for that doll in 1985, because that's how old it is."

She thought for a moment while wiping her tears on the sleeve of her costume. I quickly pulled a tissue out of my purse and handed it to her.

"Yes, I would have been six years old in 1985. That's the year my father left." She stared at me, her eyes red and overflowing. "So you're trying to tell me that my father dressed up like Santa Claus, climbed up on your roof with my letter in his pocket and the doll I asked for when I was six years old, fell off, and died?

Why in the world would he do that? It's insane."

Before I had a chance to say anything, Amos spoke up. "Your father was ill, Hope. He didn't have long to live. He couldn't beat his addiction, but he wanted to do one thing before he died. Of course it was crazy to climb up on a roof in winter, especially in his condition, but he was convinced you lived in our house, and he cared more about trying to mend the past than he did about his own safety."

She shook her head. "The whole thing is so stupid. He threw his life away for nothing."

"Sometimes it's impossible to make up for our mistakes," Amos said, his voice catching. "But when you really love someone, you try. That's the most anyone can do. And your dad tried, in his own way. He gave his life to let you know he loved you and he was sorry."

I knew he was talking about more than Hope's father. Amos was thinking about his own dad.

There was more to say. We would tell her about Gina. Maybe visiting her would help to give Hope an even clearer picture of her father. And there was the possibility of Chuck being shot, but this wasn't the time to go there. And of course there was. . .

"Can I see him?" Hope asked through her tears. "I'd really like to see him."

The thought went through my mind that I'd really like to see him, too. Without thinking it through, I said, "Maybe later, Hope. The coroner needs to complete her work first."

Amos shot me a look and nodded. He obviously felt that she had enough to deal with right now without learning that her father's body was missing.

"What do I do now?" she asked, her voice thin and soft.

"You come with me, that's what." Zach stood up and scooted out of the pew, past Amos. He came around and stood in front of Hope, holding out his hands. "You come with me, and we'll sort through this together. You're not alone, Hope. You have. . ." He cleared his throat and then threw his shoulders back. "There are people in your life who love you. There's nothing we can't get through together."

Zach's expression was set and determined. I glanced at Hope. She stared up at him, an odd look on her face. I held my breath. Then she offered him a small smile and took his hands.

"You're right," she said quietly. "And there are people I love, too. More than you may realize."

Zach's face turned pink. He smiled and pulled her up to him. She wrapped her arms around his neck, and he held her for a few moments. Then they got their things and left the sanctuary, leaving Amos and me alone.

"Well, another fine piece of detective work, Jessica," Amos said, getting up and coming around to sit next to me. "How in the world did you figure it out?"

I sighed. "It was really obvious, Amos. Besides us, the Biddles, and Rosemary Maxwell, the only other person who ever lived in our house was Hope. All the clues pointed to her. I just never put it together because I thought her father was dead. It's like that Sherlock Holmes quote: 'When you have eliminated the impossible, whatever remains, however improbable, must be the truth.' When the clues came together, it was impossible for Ho Ho to be anyone else besides Hope. So what remained was the knowledge that Charles Hartwell couldn't be dead—even though it seemed improbable. It was the only answer left. It had to be the truth."

"Wow." He leaned over and kissed me on the nose. "You really are Sherlock Holmes, aren't you?"

"That would make you. . ."

"I know, Dr. Watson. I give up. I guess if it must be, it must be."

I laughed at him. "So what did you find out in Liberal?"

His expression grew serious. "Delbert was definitely there that night. Gina remembered that he left around the same time Chuck did."

"So now we know how he got here, but we still don't know how he died. Or where he is."

"Exactly."

"Did you run that other errand in Hugoton?"

Amos smiled. "Yes. It's in the trunk. I feel kind of like Santa Claus myself. But if you don't mind, I think I'll stay off the roof."

"Sounds good to me." I reached over and hugged him. "I'm ready to go home."

He stood up and bowed. "Your carriage awaits, m'lady. I think there's a little dog who will be very glad to see us."

"I think you're right." I gathered up my things and followed him out the front doors, turning out the sanctuary lights as I walked past the switches.

I glanced back one more time at the stage, where the star still glittered from the reflection of the few lights that were left on in the room. I had to hope it was a sign. A confirmation that the rest of this Christmas puzzle would soon be solved. Chuck's story wasn't finished, and I was determined that somehow, just like our Christmas play, this tale would come to a satisfying conclusion.

14

When we left for town Monday morning, Pal seemed almost back to normal. We'd been advised to keep him as quiet as possible for the next three weeks. We gave him two pills every day, which he hated. After twenty-one days, the vet planned to x-ray his chest again and do blood work to make certain things were okay. We still hadn't figured out where he'd gotten the poison. Amos and I had done another search of our property for any signs of it, but we weren't able to find the source. Either he had eaten all the evidence or it was lying under a foot of snow. We would have to be vigilant when spring came and watch out for any deadly remainders of the substance that almost took Pal's life.

Amos dropped me off at the bookstore and then drove to his little office down the street. I started a fire and went upstairs to make breakfast. Dewey came in around seven thirty. When he stepped in the door, I noticed that it was starting to snow again. The weather report was calling for light snow today and heavier snow tonight. I was grateful that at least the bulk of it wouldn't come until after the mail truck had made its delivery. Zach was counting on Miss Jellytot making her visit today.

Dewey and I had just about finished eating when Amos came stomping in the front door, trying to knock the snow off his boots before he trailed it through the main room of the bookstore.

"It happened again," he said when he reached the sitting room.

"Hello to you, too," Dewey said. "What happened again?"

"Sorry. Good morning, Dewey."

Amos grabbed a chair and pulled it up to the table. "Another theft of diesel fuel. This time it was just outside Hugoton. Two farmers. Both of the families were at church when it happened." He took a slice of blueberry coffee cake from the platter and poured himself a cup of coffee. "Hitchens had a deputy patrolling the area because he was concerned that this exact thing would happen, but the deputy was somewhere else when the thieves hit. We're trying to watch everything we can, but we just can't cover every single property. It's getting so some farmers won't leave their places unguarded for fear they'll be next. A few of the families I've talked to have even canceled plans to travel over Christmas. I feel like our department is letting them down. No matter how hard we try, we just don't seem to get on top of this thing."

"But you're all doing everything you can," I said. "You can't cover every farm in Kansas twenty-four hours a day."

"I know, but you'd think we'd at least be able to protect the farmers who advise us when they're going to be gone. The thefts yesterday shouldn't have happened."

Dewey shook his head. "But, Amos, there's just too many places for a small department like yours to keep an eye on. You're being unrealistic. And what about the farms that might have been targeted but weren't because a deputy *was* nearby. You really have no idea how many properties you've actually protected, do you?"

"Well, no. I guess not," Amos said grudgingly. He took a bite of his coffee cake and chewed for a few moments. Finally, he rewarded Dewey with a small smile. "You're right. Thanks. I hadn't thought of it that way. Guess this whole thing is really starting to get to me."

"No problem," Dewey said with a smile. "One thing you have lots of time for when you're old and living alone is telling other people what to do."

We spent the rest of our breakfast chatting about the play. Dewey had some funny stories about things that had happened in the past. Like the time when one of the choir members gave birth in the middle of the prophet's last speech or when one of the farmers announced in front of the children that a lamb that had been on stage and petted profusely was going to be the main course for Christmas dinner. The crying, screaming, and carrying on forced the farmer to abandon his plans. The lamb, which was subsequently named Fluffy, lived a long, full life and finally died of old age. I came to the conclusion that I was getting off easy. We had fun and the time flew by. It was almost ten minutes to nine when Dewey finally got up and went across the street—much later than his usual departure time of eight thirty.

I wanted to ask Amos about Delbert, but I knew I should wait until Dewey left. After the door closed behind him, I asked, "Did you tell Hitchens about Delbert?"

"Sure did."

"What did he say?"

Amos stood up and headed toward the front of the store for his coat and boots. I followed him. "He said a few words I can't repeat and told me to keep my eyes focused on the only investigation I'm currently assigned to. I guess he'll just turn that little piece of information over to the KBI if they show any interest in Chuck."

"Oh, Amos. So the KBI might contact Delbert? But he may have simply been giving Chuck a ride. He might not be involved at all." I shook my head. "I hope this doesn't come back to haunt us. I don't want Bertha and Delbert to think we've got it in for them."

Amos pulled on his coat and bent over to put on his boots. "There's nothing I can do about it, Ivy. It's totally out of my hands now. To be honest, I don't think the KBI is very concerned about Chuck. Hitchens says the fact that he's missing just makes it harder for them to investigate. I guess the entire case is on the backburner for now."

"Then that's it?"

He nodded and turned around to hug me. "Sorry, kiddo. Some problems just don't get resolved. We may never know if Chuck was shot or where his body is. This time you may actually have to let something stay a mystery. The most important thing is that you found his daughter and you let her know he loved her. I'm sure that was what Chuck wanted most."

"I know." I kissed him good-bye and he left. Even though I'd agreed with him, I wasn't at peace with the situation. Hope was going to want to know where her father's body was. There was more to Chuck's story. Someone took his remains to hide something. I still wanted to know what it was.

I had another cup of coffee and waited for Isaac to come in. Mondays we always cataloged new books, and today we planned to work all day so we could get completely caught up. Christmas was Thursday, and I wanted to close the store the rest of the week.

Isaac had just walked in the back door when I saw the mail truck pull up across the street. "I'm going to the post office. Be back in a minute," I called out. Isaac raised his hand to let me know he'd heard me. I bundled up and trudged across the street.

Gus Hanover, the carrier who delivered mail to several rural communities, had just opened the door to the post office when he saw me. He held the door open for me, and I scooted inside.

"You must be waiting for something important," he said with a smile. "I've got several boxes on the truck, but I didn't see anything with your name on it. You lookin' for a special shipment?" He closed the door and greeted Alma.

"No, I'm not expecting any books today, but I am looking for an overnight package."

He put his bag down on the floor and started taking things out and handing them to Alma. Most of the items looked like Christmas cards. I began to get a little worried until he pulled out a large cardboard envelope that had EXPRESS MAIL printed on it. Gus handed it to me.

"Is this what you're looking for?"

I read the return address on the label. It was from Noel. "Yes, that's it. Thanks, Gus." After telling Alma I'd be back for the rest of my mail after she had time to sort it, I turned around to leave. I almost collided with Bubba Weber, who was just coming in the door.

"Hi, Ivy," he said with a big smile. "Are you here to see if anyone sent you a Christmas present?"

I stepped back a few steps so Bubba could close the door. He liked to talk. It was never just "Hello" and "Good-bye" with Bubba. I really wanted to get Miss Jellytot back to the bookstore so I wouldn't miss Zach when he came, but Isaac knew where I was. Spending a few minutes talking to Bubba wouldn't hurt me.

"I'm not sure I'll get any presents, Bubba," I said. "My parents are the only people who might mail something to me, but they won't send packages from China."

Bubba's face fell. "Don't they like Christmas?"

I smiled at him and patted his arm. "They love Christmas, but sometimes packages from China get lost. They don't want to take the chance."

He frowned and considered this. "China is a long way away," he said seriously. "That's probably why."

I nodded in agreement. "I'm sure you're right. Are you here to pick up some presents?"

He bobbed his head up and down, and his grin returned. "Yes, oh yes. My cousins said they sent me something, and my aunt Myrtle knits me a new sweater every year. I can hardly wait to put it on. She's a really good knitter."

"I've seen your lovely sweaters. I didn't know your aunt made them."

"I already got one Christmas present."

"And what was that, Bubba?" I asked.

He patted his chest. "My new coat. Do you like it? It even has a compass on the sleeve."

He was wearing a black quilted jacket with a hood. Sure enough, there was an insignia on the sleeve that looked like a compass. The coat looked well made, and I complimented him on it.

"Thanks, Ivy. I think God gave it to me. BeeBomb dug it up next to a tree by my house. It's so nice, but it does smell just a little."

I'd been noticing an odor, but I wouldn't have mentioned it for the world. I didn't want to hurt Bubba's feelings. Actually, this wasn't the first time an unpleasant aroma had emanated from Bubba.

Without any warning he stuck his arm under my nose. "I think someone accidentally got gas on their sleeve and threw it away. I guess it's their loss, huh?"

"It certainly is, Bubba," Alma said. "Why don't you come over here and show me while Gus goes out to his truck to look for your Christmas presents."

I flashed a grateful smile to Alma, who was trying to rescue me from any further conversation about Bubba's new coat. I said good-bye and hurried out the door as quickly as I could without being rude.

As I crossed the street, I noticed a familiar blue and white pickup truck parked in front of the Food-a-Rama. I could see Delbert inside. It wasn't unusual for Bertha or Delbert to go to the store, but Delbert was just sitting there staring at me. It made me a little nervous, and I walked as quickly as I could on the slick street without falling down. I didn't want him to think he was making me nervous.

I opened the door to the bookstore and slammed it behind me, making the bell over the door jangle alarmingly. Isaac was sitting cross-legged on the floor in front of a box of books that we hadn't finished sorting through.

"I didn't realize the wind was so strong," he said with a surprised look on his face.

I took off my knit cap and bent down to unfasten my boots. "It's not the wind. It's me. Delbert's out there watching me. He gives me the willies sometimes."

Isaac chuckled. "Now why in the world would Delbert be watching you, Miss Ivy? I think you're getting a little paranoid."

I placed my boots on the mat next to the door and then pulled my coat off. I was hanging it up when something I'd seen that hadn't registered until that moment popped into my head. I turned around and stared at Isaac. "Oh my. . ." was all I could get out.

Isaac raised one eyebrow and put down the book he had in his hand. "You've got that look again, Miss Ivy. What in the world. . ."

Before I had a chance to respond, the front door was pushed open forcefully, almost knocking me to the floor. I regained my balance and found Delbert standing in front of me. He slammed the door shut behind him. "Get over there and sit down, Ivy," he ordered brusquely. When I didn't move right away, he pushed me. "Now. I mean it." Without taking his eyes from my face, he flipped our OPEN sign to CLOSED and locked the door. After that, he went over to the windows and pulled down the two shades that were up. Then he took a gun out of his pocket and pointed it at me.

Isaac's eyes were huge behind his thick glasses, making him look like a frightened owl. I shook my head slightly as I neared him, trying to warn him to stay quiet. I knew we were in terrible danger, and I had to figure a way out of it. If I couldn't, I wasn't certain either one of us would live to celebrate Christmas.

15

Delbert ordered me to sit on the floor next to Isaac. I complied. I could feel Isaac's body trembling. Then Delbert planted himself at my desk—in my chair. I wasn't happy to see him sitting there, his gun lying on the edge of my desk, pointed toward us. I was also upset when he pulled out his pack of cigarettes, took one out, and lit up. As far as I knew, no one had ever smoked inside Miss Bitty's Bygone Bookstore before. Bitty had never allowed it and neither had I. Delbert took the candy dish I had on the edge of my desk and dumped all the Christmas candy from it into the trash can.

"This will make a nice ashtray," he said, grinning and nodding his head like some kind of insane bobblehead doll. "All the comforts of home. 'Course, things wasn't so nice in prison, Ivy. I thought about you a lot when I wanted a cigarette but wasn't allowed to have one. Or when they served me the kinda slop Bubba wouldn't feed to his pigs."

Delbert had a thin, weasel-like face and large ears that almost came to a point. His teeth were stained dark from tobacco. Any attempt at a smile made him look like he was having gas pains. He looked particularly uncomfortable now.

"Delbert, you went to prison because you were stealing cattle. It had nothing to do with me."

He slammed his fist on my desk, causing the candy

dish to jiggle and almost knocking his cigarette off the side where he'd rested it. "You couldn't keep your big nose outta my business. You got some kinda spooky power that sees when someone's done somethin' wrong. That's why I got locked up. It's your fault from start to finish." He glared at me, his nostrils flaring and his face contorted with anger. "I'm ain't goin' back there, little lady. You can take that to the bank. I hate it there."

"Delbert, I don't have any 'spooky power,'" I said soothingly. "I don't know anything at all about you, and I'm not aware that you've committed any crime. You need to leave before you get yourself into something you can't get out of." I shrugged and tried to look nonchalant. "You came in here to tell me you were upset about being sent to prison for stealing cows. That's understandable. No harm, no foul. Right, Isaac?"

Poor Isaac nodded his head so violently his glasses almost fell off. "Th—that's right. N—no harm, no foul."

Delbert snorted. "You both think I'm stupid?" He pointed a finger at me. "I know for a fact that you got some kinda weird way of solvin' crimes and figgerin' out if someone did somethin' bad. The whole town knows it. I heard lotsa people say it." His hand shook, and I realized he was truly afraid of me. Great. My nosiness had finally gotten me into real trouble.

"I don't think you're stupid. That's why I think you'll leave without this going any further. Because you're smart enough to know that it's the only way we can all get out of here."

Delbert's face twisted with rage. "You and your

little pal ain't goin' nowhere. I told you, I ain't goin' back to prison."

"What are you going to do, shoot us? You'll be put away for life. Surely you can see that."

For just a moment, I almost had him. I saw it in his face. But then anger and fear crowded out what little reason he had.

"No," he snarled. "You ain't gonna use no psy—psy—fancy talk to control my mind. I'm in charge, and you're gonna do what I say." He took a long drag on his cigarette then flicked the ashes off in my candy dish. "I know Amos called Hitchens about the ride I gave that old drunk the other night."

Delbert was on the verge of telling me things he shouldn't. Once he confirmed what I already suspected, he would have no choice but to kill us. And Delbert was just stupid enough to trap all of us into something deadly.

"I—I'm not sure what you're talking about," I said. "But even if you think you have a reason to murder us, you won't get away with it. Someone saw you come in here."

"No, they didn't. I waited until there weren't anyone on the street. The only people who mighta seen me were at the post office, and they were too busy jawin' to notice anything. After I kill you two, I'll just leave by the back door. Ain't no one gonna see me. Ain't no one gonna suspect anything." He flashed us an evil, self-satisfied grin.

"Don't you think it will seem odd that someone broke into the bookstore and shot Isaac and me?" I asked. "Why in the world would anyone do that?"

He shrugged. "You got some money in here, don'tcha? It'll look like a robbery."

Finally, Isaac spoke up. He'd been so quiet, I jumped when I heard his voice.

"We don't keep hardly any cash here. Most of our money comes in checks or electronic transfers. No one would rob this place. It doesn't make sense."

Instead of finding any wisdom in Isaac's words, Delbert just got angrier. He picked up his gun and waved it at us.

"Shut up!" he yelled. "I don't care. Everyone will think it's a robbery. I'll get rid of the gun and that's it. I don't wanna hear nothin' else. You two just shut your mouths. I ain't gonna let no witchy woman put me back in the joint. I ain't gonna do it." His face slid back into a malicious grin. "You like that present I left for your little dog? He should be nice and sick by now. Doubt that he's gonna make it. Just like you, witchy woman." He took another drag from his cigarette, his beady eyes locked on mine. "I had lots of other little surprises for you, too. Things to make your life as bad as you made mine. Jes' didn't have time to do 'em. 'Course, that don't matter now. You ain't gonna be messin' around with me or nobody else."

I knew in that moment that without a miracle, Isaac and I were going to die. Delbert had already tried to kill Pal. His animosity was deadly, and he truly believed I had some kind of special power to see into his soul. Of course, he'd never get away with it. Even if no one saw him come in here, they'd have noticed his truck outside. And with our past history, he'd be the first suspect. Besides, with his cigarettes, he was leaving so much DNA around, the case would be a slam dunk. I could feel resentment rise up inside me because of what he did to Pal, and what he planned to do to Isaac and me, but I knew I couldn't respond to it. I had to stay on my toes. I forced myself to keep quiet.

He took the cigarette out of his mouth, put it between his nicotine-stained fingers, and coughed up some phlegm, which he spit into my trash can. More DNA. Lovely.

"Bertha told me she thinks you got some kinda gift from God or somethin'. But I think you got some kinda spirit livin' inside you. Like from some kind of famous detective or somethin'. Maybe it's that guy, what's his name, Locker Homes."

If it hadn't been a really inappropriate time to giggle, I would have. But the idea of getting a bullet through my head as a result of unfortunate hilarity seemed ridiculous. I shook my head. "I really don't put myself in the same category as—as Locker Homes. I've been lucky a couple of times. That's all." I tried to reposition my legs. One of them was starting to fall asleep. "Come on, Delbert. Let's end this now before someone gets hurt. Isaac and I won't tell anyone."

I could have sworn I heard him growl. My words seemed to have really stoked his fury. He dropped his cigarette into the candy dish and grabbed his gun, jumping to his feet at the same time. "I told you not to say that again!" he screamed. "I'm not the dummy you think I am, and I'm gonna prove it once and for all."

He pointed the gun right at us. All I could do was say, "Jesus." There wasn't enough time for a longer prayer. Suddenly the back door opened and someone shouted at Delbert. At first I didn't think he was going to listen. But after the intruder yelled once again for him to put his gun down, he slowly lowered the pistol. Sheriff Milt Hitchens closed the back door and came into the room, his own gun drawn.

Isaac scrambled to his feet, trying to pull me up with him. "Sheriff Hitchens, how wonderful to see you. You came just in time! This crazy man was going to kill us!" He stared down at me and pulled again on my arm, trying to help me up, a look of confusion on his face.

"Sit down, Isaac," I said in a low voice. "We're not out of trouble."

He looked back and forth between me and Hitchens, obviously bewildered.

Hitchens pointed his gun at Isaac. "Unfortunately for you, she's right," he said. "But I don't want you to sit down. I want you to get up, Ivy. I want you both in the back room, away from the windows."

This time I got to my feet, following my thoroughly frightened assistant to the sitting room, where Hitchens commanded us to sit down on the couch closest to the fireplace. He dropped down in one of the chairs across from us and ordered Delbert to sit at the table where he could see him. Delbert looked like a little boy who'd been spanked. His expression was a combination of antagonism and humiliation. I suspected that he'd liked being in charge.

"She was in the post office with Bubba, Hitchens," Delbert screeched. "She saw the coat."

"Shut up and keep quiet," Hitchens barked at Delbert. Then he leaned back in his chair, a scowl on his face. "Delbert here called me this mornin' to tell me somethin'. Somethin' that concerned me. That Bubba Weber was wearin' an item he shouldna been wearin'. When Delbert wasn't where he was supposed to be"—he shot a look at Delbert that was even colder than Winter Break in December—"I put two and two together and figured he'd come here. He thinks you have some kinda second sight to see his evil deeds, Ivy. He's afraid of you. I told him to knock it off, but I guess he's more scared of you than he is of me." Hitchens shook his head. "If I'd known he was so stupid, I never woulda brought him in on this deal in the first place. But by the time I realized he was terrified of your 'unearthly powers,' it was too late. He was knee-deep in the middle of things."

Isaac, still confused by what was happening to us, said, "What things?" He turned to look at me. "What things, Ivy? What's going on?"

Hitchens smiled and waved his arm at me. "You got it figgered out already, don'tcha? Then be my guest. But just remember that this time, I ain't crouched in the shadows, waitin' to save you."

He was referring to a situation that had happened earlier in the year when I'd gotten a murderer to confess to his crime. Hitchens was hiding around the corner and arrested him before he could kill me. And he was right. This was a lot different. I wasn't sure what to do. Either I had to talk him out of killing us, and that seemed impossible since he and Delbert had already incriminated themselves, or I had to stall for time and hope someone would rescue us. I realized that I had no choice. I had to keep him talking as long as I could.

"It's hard to know where to start."

Hitchens shrugged and grinned. "Don't matter none to me. Just get going. Amos ain't supposed to be back until tonight, but I don't intend to fiddle around here too long. Got important things to do. I gotta work on lookin' sad."

"And why is that?"

He shook his head and tried to look morose. It was ludicrous and reminded me of the Greek mask of tragedy used in the theater. "For when I tell people that Miss Ivy and her faithful servant have been shot and killed by some crazy person. And if I catch the killer in the act, that should wrap everything up nice and neat, don'tcha think?"

A slight, involuntary twitch of Hitchens's eyelids told me who that "crazy person" was going to be. Delbert hadn't figured out yet that he was the loose end that was getting ready to be tied up permanently. Hopefully Hitchens had just given me the key to getting out of here alive. I kept my face expressionless. "You won't get away with it. It's only a matter of time before someone else figures out that you were the one behind the fuel thefts. It had to be you. You're the only one who knew exactly when certain farms would be vulnerable. Farmers told you their schedules because they thought you were protecting them, just like they did yesterday morning. You and Delbert were busy stealing fuel while your targets were in church."

The sheriff grunted his agreement. "Took a little finesse to get information from folks who live out of the county, but most people around here don't question anyone in uniform when they tell them there have been thefts in their area. They're ready to tell you anything." He smiled. "And you're wrong about someone suspecting me. Those farmers trust me completely."

I leaned back into the couch and crossed my legs. I wanted to look comfortable. Maybe Hitchens would relax a little, too. Just enough to make him vulnerable. He'd already lowered the gun to his lap, although he maintained a tight grip on it. "Did you cook up this scheme by yourself? Stealing diesel fuel and reselling it?"

Hitchens snorted. "Well, it sure as heck didn't come from Dumbert over there. I got into a deal with an old friend from Oklahoma. We done a few other transactions before. He runs a trucking company, but fuel prices were about to shut him down. He already had other people tappin' diesel for him, and I told him I could get him some more. Maybe not as much as one guy he has takin' it from gas stations. Man has a big box trailer with large tanks inside. Delbert and I just used transfer tanks on the back of our pickups. We can get four hundred gallons in there easy. Much more than that makes it hard to get your pickup goin'."

"So basically, you found out when certain farmers weren't going to be home, filled up your tanks, and ran the stolen fuel to Oklahoma?"

"Nah. Never had to take it that far. Just down to

Elkhart, right near the border. My friend has a guy who meets us, transfers the fuel, and takes it where it needs to go."

"How much are you making off this, Hitchens? I can't imagine it's enough to risk your job and imprisonment."

His face turned beet-red. "I've already cleared over twenty-five thousand from this little venture."

I glanced over at Delbert, whose head snapped up in surprise. Obviously he had no idea he and his wily partner had made that much. Hitchens was probably giving him crumbs compared to what he was taking in. Good. A point for our side.

Hitchens kept talking, unaware that he'd already said too much. Either his anger had made him careless, or he was counting on Delbert's stupidity. "I been takin' care of this county for over thirty years, and I don't even make enough to have a decent home. Now they're forcin' me to retire, and there's no way I can live on the piddlin' pension they wanna give me. I decided to come up with my own retirement plan and blow this whole state. Got my eye on a nice little cabin in Arkansas where I can fish and do what I wanna do instead of chasing around after the stupid hicks that live in this backwater part of the country."

Milt Hitchens was one of the biggest "hicks" I'd ever met, so I wasn't sure just whom he was referring to. Obviously he saw himself above the people he'd sworn to protect.

"Now jes' when did you tie it all together, Miss Jessica? What was it that set that brain of yours onto my trail?" He tried to look amused, but I knew he was furious—and dangerous.

"You already know the answer to that, don't you?"

He laughed harshly. "I suspect it had somethin' to do with why Dumbert called me this morning."

"You mean because he saw Bubba Weber running around in your jacket? The jacket you tossed away the night you stole fuel from Mort Benniker?"

His face flushed. "My highly intelligent partner over there spilled diesel fuel on my sleeve while we was pumpin' it out. I shouldn't have taken him with me, but since Mort was out of town, we brought both trucks. Turns out that dumb farmer didn't even have a full tank. We barely got four hundred gallons. Don't know why he didn't buy more. Poole and Sons delivered a couple of days before we got there."

"So you tried to steal fuel right after it was delivered?"

"Sure. But not all the time. It would be too obvious. I ain't that dumb."

"You and Delbert didn't always go together, then? The night of play practice, Delbert was in town."

Hitchens was starting to get a little antsy. His knee had started to bounce up and down, and he was shooting looks toward the front door. I wasn't sure how long I could keep him occupied. I prayed with everything in me that God would send help. Fast.

He stared down at the gun in his hand. "Usually one of us acted as lookout while the other one filled their tank. Then we'd switch places if there was time. When we hit a couple of farms the night of your little play practice, Delbert helped himself at Newton Widdle's place after they left for town. Luckily for us, they went out to supper before goin' to the church, so there was plenty of time. Delbert took the stuff back to his place and put it in his own storage tank. Then he took off his transfer tank, drove that ugly wife of his into town, and called me on my walkie-talkie. That's how we kept in touch. He kept an eye on all of you while I took care of business at Maynard Comstock's place."

"Okay, I understand how and why you took all that diesel fuel; now tell me why in the world you thought it was necessary to shoot Charles Hartwell."

He threw back his head and laughed. "You mean Santa Claus? Why did I shoot good ol' Saint Nick?"

I nodded.

He leaned forward in his chair like he was getting ready to tell a funny story. This new topic had regained his attention. That was good, but his cavalier attitude about Charles made my already nauseated stomach do flip-flops.

"Now that's an interesting question. As a matter of fact, I had no intention of shootin' him." He glared at Delbert, who'd been eyeing him suspiciously for the past few minutes. I hoped he was finally starting to realize just how short his future looked. "This chucklehead gave Santa a ride from a bar in Liberal—on the way to Mort Benniker's farm. His tank was on the back of his truck. When he called me to say he'd dropped someone off at your house, I couldn't believe it. Obviously I couldn't take a chance Santa might mention Delbert and his tank to Amos. If Delbert got caught, I was certain he'd give me up to save his own skin. This boy really don't want to go back to the pen."

"So you drove over there and shot Chuck."

He guffawed. "I forgot 'bout you callin' that guy Chuck." He composed himself, and his face hardened again. "Actually, you're wrong there, Miss Jessica. I didn't need no bullet hole in him. I knew that would bring in the coroner and the KBI. I was already in Winter Break, so when Delbert here called and told me what he done, I drove as quick as I could to your place, hopin' to find your visitor passed out on your lawn or somethin' and not already inside your house. Delbert said he was three sheets to the wind. I parked my truck on the road and got as close to the house as I could. If he was still outside, my plan was to make it look like he'd been overcome by the demon rum and fallen asleep in the snow. No one would suspect anything if an old drunk had simply frozen to death."

"So why did you shoot him?"

He scowled. "Stupid fool was sittin' right there on the roof. Thanks to Amos's super-duper yard lights, I could see him clearly. I decided that if I fired a shot close enough, he'd get scared, lose his balance, and turn into a stain on your driveway. He'd already tried standin' up several times but kept slippin'. I knew I only had one chance. I figured you was asleep and wouldn't recognize the sound of a gunshot, but Amos—he'd know exactly what it was." Hitchens shook his head. "He told me he was havin' to wear earplugs at night 'cause you're a snorer. I had to get my shot off before you woke him up and he took those things out. But then somethin' I didn't count on happened. That sappy Santa had some kind of bag at the top of the roof. When he tried to reach for it, it slid off the back. Stupid fool suddenly grabbed the chimney and stood up. I accidentally popped him right in the head, and he slipped down the roof. Got caught on somethin' for a few seconds, but it couldn't hold him and he dropped off. I snuck back to my truck and drove away before you and Amos could come downstairs. Then I waited for your call. After that, I came over and checked out your dead Santa Claus. I could see that I'd shot him in the same place where he'd cracked his skull. I figured you wouldn't know what happened, but I knew the coroner would find the bullet hole. That's when I knew I had to get ahold of that body. I didn't need the Bureau guys sniffin' around."

"And where is Chuck?" It was a question I was afraid to ask.

Another freakish smile. "You could say he's on ice. It ain't hard to keep a stiff stiff in Winter Break. Bury him in a snowbank and you've got lotsa time to make final arrangements. And I intend to do that before I leave town." He frowned and stared at me. "Did you ever figger out what the heck that guy was doin' on your roof? I know he was schnockered, but that was one of the weirdest things I ever seen."

Even though I knew he wouldn't care, I explained the relationship between Hope and Charles. I was right about his lack of compassion.

"Well, I guess stupid is as stupid does. Sounds like

I put Santa out of his misery." He shook his head and chuckled. "Yep, I did the old guy a favor." He shook his finger at me. "Back to the coat, Miss Jessica. How could you have figgered anything out from seein' it? I have to admit, you got me stumped this time."

"Well, first of all, we need to thank Bubba Weber's dog for uncovering that piece of evidence."

Hitchens swore under his breath. "So that's how it ended up on Dubba Bubba, huh? All I know is that Dumbert called me all worked up 'cause he saw Bubba walkin' around town in my jacket." He shot me a disgusted look. "How could you know it was mine? I don't remember wearin' it around you."

"Amos told me your cousin from England gave you a jacket. It wasn't until I got back here and was hanging up my own coat that I realized the insignia on Bubba's sleeve was Stone Island. My father has a Stone Island jacket. They're made in England. It was when I started thinking about the coat and the stench of diesel fuel on the arm that I remembered you had no coat on Thursday night. From there, it was easy to figure out why. Of course, as soon as I connected you in my mind to the fuel thefts, it was easy to put the rest of it together. The truth was in front of us all along. And even before Delbert burst in here and confirmed my suspicions, I figured you had something to do with killing Charles. I knew Delbert had given him a ride to my house from Liberal, and Charles died the same night Mort Benniker's fuel was stolen. It was circumstantial, but the connection between you two was obvious. I didn't know why you killed Charles until you explained it, but I was pretty sure you'd done it."

Hitchens glared at Delbert. "I guess you was right callin' me after all. You stopped Miss Jessica from callin' for reinforcements. For once you wasn't the stupidest hick I've ever known."

It wasn't much of a compliment, but Delbert grinned like it was. If something didn't happen pretty quickly, that was liable to be his last smile on this earth. Hitchens planned to shoot us, blame it on Delbert, and then kill him and claim self-defense. I suspected evidence would show up on Delbert's property, tying him to the fuel thefts. Since Hitchens could easily shut down that investigation by blaming a dead man, no one would ever suspect him. He'd take the money he'd made, retire, and leave town. He'd get away scot-free. I realized that I needed to keep the conversation going, but I was running out of things to talk about. I searched for something else. "So—so you lied to Amos? You never contacted the KBI about Chuck and you were never going to."

His face crinkled in a wolfish grin. "You got that right. They won't be ridin' in on no white horse to save you, if that's what you're thinkin'."

Hitchens's foot stopped tapping and his grip tightened on his gun. It was time to bring Delbert into reality. It was all we had left. "When are you going to tell Delbert that he won't be leaving the bookstore alive?"

Hitchens raised an eyebrow and stared at me. "You got it all figured out, don'tcha? It's time for you to shut up. Permanently." He stood up. "Both of you get up and face me."

"You know, you could have just let Delbert shoot us instead of stopping him when you broke in here. If that's your plan anyway, why didn't you just let him do it then?"

Hitchens laughed and pointed his gun at us. "Wanted time to think it out a little. But it gave me the idea, so I guess it worked out okay anyway."

Isaac and I slowly got to our feet. We were standing right in front of the fireplace, facing Hitchens.

"Delbert, hand me your gun." He swung his gun toward his frightened partner in crime, keeping his eyes on us.

Delbert was stupid, but not so stupid he hadn't finally figured out what the sheriff was up to. "You're gonna shoot them with my gun and then kill me, ain't ya?" he said, his voice high and squeaky. "Then you're gonna blame the stealin' on me, too! Well, I ain't gonna let you do it!"

He raised his own gun toward Hitchens, who turned his attention from us long enough for me to reach up to the mantel and grab Aunt Bitty's urn. At the same time I heard a shot ring out, I hit the sheriff on the head as hard as I could.

16

"So in the end, Aunt Bitty saved the day," Amos joked. He cut another slice of ham and looked around the table at our guests. "Who's ready for seconds?"

"I'd be happy to oblige," Zach said, holding out his plate. I was happy he could join us for an early Christmas dinner. He and Hope were going to his mother's house for another meal in the evening. I was surprised either one of them had gotten any food down. Holding hands and gazing into each other's eyes tended to make using utensils a little difficult. Zach had presented Hope with *Miss Jellytot's Visit* before the Christmas play. He also made it very clear that he was head over heels in love with her. Hope had finally opened her heart and let him in. It was wonderful to see them both so happy.

Barney and Dewey held their plates out, too. Amos carved a few more slices and distributed them.

"Yes, Aunt Bitty sure came through for me," I said with a smile. "I have to say, I was surprised that Hitchens gave me the opportunity to grab her urn."

"Especially since he was there when you conked another murderer on the noggin," Amos said, shaking his head.

"Well, I'm certainly grateful he didn't think about it." I laughed. "You know, even as loving as Bitty was, I'm sure it would have given her distinct pleasure to bop Hitchens on the head and knock him out."

"Too bad for Delbert that Hitchens got that shot off," Dewey said, helping himself to another spoonful of au gratin potatoes.

"It could have been worse," I said. "He only got Delbert in the shoulder. He'll have a lot of time to heal. About ten to twenty years, right, Amos?"

He nodded. "At least."

"So how's Bertha taking all this?" Barney asked.

"I think she's actually relieved to be rid of Delbert," I said. "We're going to get together next week and talk. She had no idea he was working with Hitchens to steal diesel fuel. And although she knew Delbert hated me, she feels terrible thinking that she fueled his paranoia by telling him I had some kind of supernatural powers. Of course, there are other people in Winter Break who helped to perpetuate that story, so it doesn't just rest on Bertha's shoulders."

"So when Delbert found out that you knew he'd given my father a ride that night," Hope said, "it pushed him over the edge and made him think you were going to figure out everything he'd been up to."

"And the fact that he noticed Bubba running around in Hitchens's coat," Isaac said. "When Ivy and Bubba crossed paths in the post office, he figured the jig was up. He went crazy, thinking that his only chance to stay out of prison was to silence Ivy permanently. The truth is, he was right in thinking Ivy had his number. She really did put it together when she realized the coat had to belong to Hitchens."

I nodded. "That and the odor of diesel fuel on the sleeve. Of course, there is one other thing I considered."

"What was that?" Hope asked.

I grinned. "Believe it or not, it was a word from Sister Crystal."

Dewey snorted. "You're kidding."

I shook my head. "No, I'm not. She gave me a quote from Isaiah 51:45: 'My righteousness draws near speedily, my salvation is on the way, and my arm will bring justice to the nations. The islands will look to me and wait in hope for my arm.' "

All I got were blank stares from everyone at the table.

"Well, the spill on Hitchens's coat sleeve, or his *arm*, was instrumental in leading me to the conclusion that he was involved. And that clue did bring justice."

Barney laughed. "That's really reaching, isn't it?"

"The coat was made by Stone *Island*. And Amos remembered that Hitchens mentioned his cousin works for *Nations* Bank in England. You tell me."

No one said a word as they considered this. Was Sister Crystal's word from God? Maybe—maybe not. But in the future, I didn't plan to blow her off so easily.

"So what happens to Hitchens now, Amos?" Dewey asked, changing the subject.

"He's been arrested, but he's been taken to Sedgwick County. Putting him in jail in Hugoton wasn't an option. The KBI didn't want him someplace where he could influence a Stevens County employee to let him out." He snorted. "Not that any of us would. We all suspected Hitchens was playing fast and loose with the law. Making concessions for some people and harassing others. But it was always hard to prove and no one wanted to go up against him. That's why the county decided to retire him."

"Who will fill the sheriff's shoes?" Barney asked.

"Right now, Fred Griggs, the undersheriff, is in charge. The governor will appoint someone after party officials nominate them. I suspect Fred will get the job. He's a good guy. He'd make a great sheriff."

"Hope, I understand you want to hold a memorial service for your father?" Alma said.

Hope smiled. "Yes, I do. After Sheriff Hitchens revealed where Dad was buried, his body was sent to the coroner's office. When it's released, Elmer has offered to provide him with a funeral at no cost."

Elmer nodded. "It's the least I can do."

"I'm sorry we had to turn Opal Nell over to the authorities, Hope," I said. "But it sounds like you'll get her back when they're finished. She doesn't seem to be an important piece of evidence."

Hope almost dropped her fork. "What did you call her?"

"Opal Nell. That's the name on her birth certificate."

"Oh my goodness." Her eyes flushed with tears. "My middle name is Opal. That must have been one of the reasons my father bought that doll. How odd. It not only looks like the doll I asked Santa for, she has my name."

I grinned. "Your middle name is Opal? Hope Opal. H-O, H-O. I get it now."

"Yes, but I don't really want to be called Ho Ho anymore." She gazed into Zach's eyes and smiled.

"I promise I won't call you that," he said. "I love your name. I'm telling everyone that I've found my Hope at last." He leaned over and kissed her cheek.

The looks on their faces told me Inez would be planning for a wedding before long. I intended to ask Hope if Amos and I could step in and fulfill the role of her family—not just for her but also for Charles. One last thing we could do for him.

Isaac cleared his throat. "Since the conversation has taken a romantic turn, I wonder if I could make an announcement?" Alma blushed bright red and looked down at her lap. "While sitting on the floor in the bookstore, wondering if my life was over, I came to a decision. Tragic circumstances from my past have kept me from moving forward with my life, but I've decided that life is too short for living anyplace except in the present." He grabbed Alma's hand and turned to look at her. "I have asked this wonderful woman to marry me, and she has consented. I wanted you all to know."

Whoops and hollers preceded congratulations heaped on the happy couple. I loved Isaac and was thrilled for him. He'd never looked as happy as he did right now. I had a lump in my throat, but I was determined not to cry. I'd been doing a lot of that lately.

"I understand what you're saying about not allowing the past to determine your present," Amos said. "I don't intend to do that anymore either."

"I feel the same," Aaron said, smiling at his son. "I have a lot of years to make up for, and I'm committed to giving it my full attention."

Hope chuckled. "It seems we've all been learning the same thing lately. The past is really nothing more than a memory. We don't have to keep it alive. Looking forward is so much more important than looking back at something that doesn't even exist anymore. And any empty space in your life can be filled by God, who has a wonderful future planned for all of us, if we just allow Him to bring it to pass in our lives."

I knew that God definitely had a plan for my life. One of those plans would be shared privately with my husband after everyone left. He hadn't yet received the best Christmas present he would get this year. With the play the night before and dinner preparations today, I'd decided to wait until things settled down and we had some time to ourselves. Seems my upset stomach had turned out to be something quite different. Good thing I had that extra pregnancy test.

I gazed around the table filled with friends. This certainly was a special Christmas in more ways than one. The play had gone off without a hitch. Even the sheep had cooperated. After it was over, Amos and I drove over to Marion's small house. Amos sneaked up to the front door and placed the bike Benjie wanted so badly on the front steps. Then he'd rung the doorbell and run like a crazy person back to the car, where I sat with the headlights turned off. We drove away as quickly as possible. It was so much fun we decided to make it a Christmas tradition. It might not be a bike next year, but we were determined that every Christmas we would find someone who needed a touch of God's love.

Pal nudged me under the table, and I broke off a piece of my roll and handed it to him. I had the feeling he was making the rounds, but no one seemed to mind.

I sat and listened to my friends laugh and enjoy each other, and I thought about Aunt Bitty. If she hadn't come to Winter Break, this day never would have happened. I wouldn't have ended up here, and Amos and I wouldn't be together. These people wouldn't be celebrating Christmas together. Each life at this table had been affected by Bitty's desire to follow God's will for her life.

"Honey, God has a good plan for everyone," Bitty used to say. "And it's only through giving our lives to Him and finding that plan that we will ever have true happiness. Until we do, we'll only be bumping into walls in the dark. And that's not the way to live."

She was certainly right. I'd found God's blessings in a small town called Winter Break. My prayer was that everyone would find their Winter Break—the place God had prepared especially for them. I've discovered that it's a wonderful spot where our loving Father keeps all our hopes and dreams safe until the day we find our way home.

Jelly Tots

2 cups flour
½ teaspoon baking powder
¼ teaspoon salt
1 cup soft butter
1 egg, separated
½ cup sugar
2 tablespoons water
1 teaspoon vanilla
1¼ cups finely chopped nuts

In medium bowl, combine and sift dry ingredients. In another bowl, cream butter, egg yolk, and sugar for 90 seconds. Add water, vanilla, and half of flour mixture; blend. Add remaining flour mixture and mix well. Form into small balls. Dip into egg white and then into nuts. Place on lightly greased cookie sheet. Bake at 350° for 5 to 6 minutes. Remove from oven and make imprint in each cookie using thumb or thimble. Return to oven and bake 5 to 8 minutes more. Cool. Fill impressions with jam (raspberry and strawberry work well).

Nancy Mehl's novels are all set in her home state of Kansas. "Although some people think of Kansas as nothing more than flat land and cattle, we really are quite interesting!" she says.

Nancy is a mystery buff who loves the genre and is excited to see more cozy mysteries becoming available to readers who share her passion for novels without explicit sex, profanity, and graphic violence. "I love authors like Agatha Christie," she says. "I choose to read novels that follow the true ideals of mystery. I also enjoy characters with depth and humanity. Hopefully readers will find these attributes in my books."

Her newest work, the Ivy Towers Mystery Series, combines two of her favorite things—mystery and snow. "Some winters have been pretty dry in Kansas. I enjoy writing fiction because I can make it snow as much as I want!"

Besides writing, Nancy works for the City of Wichita, assisting low-income seniors and the disabled. She also runs a volunteer group, Wichita Homebound Outreach.

She has been married for thirty-five years to her husband, Norman. Her son, Danny, is a graphic designer who designed several of her earlier book covers.

Visit Nancy's Web site at www.nancymehl.com.

You may correspond with this author by writing:
Nancy Mehl
Author Relations
PO Box 721
Uhrichsville, OH 44683

A Letter to Our Readers

Dear Reader:

In order to help us satisfy your quest for more great mystery stories, we would appreciate it if you would take a few minutes to respond to the following questions. We welcome your comments and read each form and letter we receive. When completed, please return to:

Fiction Editor
Heartsong Presents—MYSTERIES!
PO Box 721
Uhrichsville, Ohio 44683

Did you enjoy reading *There Goes Santa Claus* by Nancy Mehl?

Very much! I would like to see more books like this! The one thing I particularly enjoyed about this story was:

_____
_____
_____

Moderately. I would have enjoyed it more if:

_____
_____
_____

Are you a member of the HP—MYSTERIES! Book Club?
Yes   No

If no, where did you purchase this book?

_____

Please rate the following elements using a scale of 1 (poor) to 10 (superior):

___ Main character/sleuth   ___ Romance elements

___ Inspirational theme   ___ Secondary characters

___ Setting   ___ Mystery plot

How would you rate the cover design on a scale of 1 (poor) to 5 (superior)? _____

What themes/settings would you like to see in future **Heartsong Presents—MYSTERIES!** selections? _____
_____
_____
_____

Please check your age range:
     ○ Under 18   ○ 18–24
     ○ 25–34   ○ 35–45
     ○ 46–55   ○ Over 55

Name: _____

Occupation: _____

Address: _____

E-mail address: _____

Heartsong Presents

Any 8 Titles for $32! A 20% Savings!

Great Mysteries at a Great Price! Purchase Any Title for Only $4.97 Each!

HEARTSONG PRESENTS—MYSTERIES!
TITLES AVAILABLE NOW:

___MYS1 *Death on a Deadline*, C. Lynxwiler, J. Reynolds, S. Gaskin

___MYS2 *Murder in the Milk Case*, C. Speare

___MYS3 *In the Dead of Winter*, N. Mehl

___MYS4 *Everybody Loved Roger Harden*, C. Murphey

___MYS5 *Recipe for Murder*, L. Harris

___MYS6 *Mysterious Incident at Lone Rock*, R. K. Pillai

___MYS7 *Trouble Up Finny's Nose*, D. Mentink

___MYS8 *Homicide at Blue Heron Lake*, S. P. Davis & M. E. Davis

___MYS9 *Another Stab at Life*, A. Higman

___MYS10 *Gunfight at Grace Gulch*, D. Franklin

___MYS11 *A Suspicion of Strawberries*, L. Sowell

___MYS12 *Murder on the Ol' Bunions*, S. D. Moore

___MYS13 *Bye Bye Bertie*, N. Mehl

___MYS14 *Band Room Bash*, C. Speare

___MYS15 *Pedigreed Bloodlines*, S. Robbins

___MYS16 *Where the Truth Lies*, E. Ludwig & J. Mowery

___MYS17 *Fudge-Laced Felonies*, C. Hickey

___MYS18 *Miss Aggie's Gone Missing*, F. Devine

___MYS19 *Everybody Wanted Room 623*, C. Murphey

___MYS20 *George Washington Stepped Here*, K. D. Hays

___MYS21 *For Whom the Wedding Bell Tolls*, N. Mehl

___MYS22 *Drop Dead Diva*, C. Lynxwiler, J. Reynolds, S. Gaskin

___MYS23 *Fog Over Finny's Nose*, D. Mentink

___MYS24 *Baker's Fatal Dozen*, L. Harris

___MYS25 *Treasure at Blue Heron Lake*, S.P. Davis & M.E. Davis

___MYS26 *Everybody Called Her a Saint*, C. Murphey

___MYS27 *The Wiles of Watermelon*, L. Sowell

___MYS28 *Dog Gone!*, E. Key

___MYS29 *Down Home and Deadly*, C. Lynxwiler, J. Reynolds, S. Gaskin

___MYS30 *There Goes Santa Claus*, N. Mehl

___MYS31 *Misfortune Cookies*, L. Kozar

___MYS32 *Of Mice. . .and Murder*, M. Conneal y

(If ordering from this page, please remember to include it with the order form.)

MYSTERIES!

Heartsong Presents—MYSTERIES! provide romance and faith interwoven among the pages of these fun whodunits. Written by the talented and brightest authors in this genre, such as Christine Lynxwiler, Cecil Murphey, Nancy Mehl, Dana Mentink, Candice Speare, and many others, these cozy tales are sure to challenge your mind, warm your heart, touch your spirit—and put your sleuthing skills to the test.

Not all titles may be available at time of order.
If outside the U.S., please call
740-922-7280 for shipping charges.

COZY IN KANSAS

THREE ROMANCE MYSTERIES

NANCY MEHL

Mystery, love, and inspiration in a small town bookstore. College student Ivy Towers has definite plans for her future. But when her great-aunt Betty is found dead inside her rare bookstore, Ivy must travel back to a place and a past she thought she'd left behind. She discovers that Bitty's supposed fall from her library ladder seems quite suspicious. Ivy's decision to poke her nose into things changes her destiny and propels her into uncovering carefully hidden secrets buried deep below the surface in the small town of Winter Break, Kansas. Along the way, she will discover that love can be found where you least expect it—and in the most mysterious of circumstances.

ISBN 978-1-60260-228-1
$7.97

Available wherever books are sold.

ALIBIS IN ARKANSAS

THREE ROMANCE MYSTERIES

CHRISTINE LYNXWILER
JAN REYNOLDS
SANDY GASKIN

Two sisters find mystery and love in small-town Arkansas. No matter where southern sisters Jenna and Carly go, murder turns up like a bad penny. When the local newspaper editor is killed and Carly's son is a suspect, Jenna decides to go undercover to get the scoop on the murder. A vacation in Branson, Missouri, sounds like fun, but Jenna and Carly are surprised to find that the glittering lights and twanging tunes make a perfect backdrop for. . .murder! Back home in Lakeview, Carly's new diner is really cooking. But last time she looked, murder was *not* on the menu.

ISBN 978-1-60260-229-8
$7.97

Heavens Reflections

Peta Condon

*Scripture quotations are from

Jerusalem Bible   marked TJB

Complete Jewish Bible   marked CJB

The Passion Translation   marked TPT

New International version marked NIV

*Arts and graphics by Isobel Elsey

* Photographs by Peta Condon except
From stock.adobe.com by:
Chiketin – pages 36, 38, 39 & 40
Alexander Potapov – page 44
jamenpercy - page 56
Vovik_mar – page 60
Leonid Tit – page 73
Brozova – page 76

Published Seraph Creative

Copyright 2020

ISNB 978-1-922428-16-5

Peta Condon

Contents

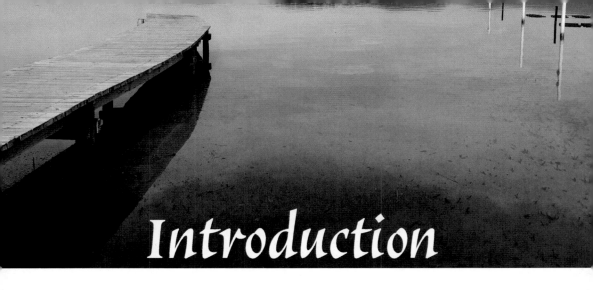

Introduction

Fresh waters are pouring forth in this new era, bringing forth a glorious awakening to the reality of the truth of our oneness in Christ and with all of creation. Living in and abiding from heavenly realms, walking the eternal dimensions. Awakened to our divine nature and union with Yahweh, emanating His kingdom wherever He leads.

The manifest revealed sons of God are arising in this new era, walking in relationship with Yahweh and not religious systems; hearing the call to the ancient pathways and carriers and releasers of the greater glory and restoration. Participating in the fullness of our inheritance and our new creation reality. Kings and priests of the Most High God, living the ascended life and presenting Yahweh to all of creation. Living gateways and heavens reflections.

"So wake up, you living gateways!

Lift up your heads, you ageless doors of destiny!

Welcome the King of Glory, for he is about to come through you"

Ps 24:7 (TPT)

Creation itself carries a sacred sound, a resonance, and prophesies and reflects the wonder and awe of Yahweh and the realms of heaven. The eternal Word is reflected in every plant, animal and in all of humanity. Creation awaits for the sons to walk fully in the truth of who we are in Christ, to be set free.

My heart on putting together a compilation of reflections, ponderings, pictures and writings is to invite the reader to engage more deeply the truth of union, oneness and relationship with The Divine and all of creation. To journey into the fullness of the heart of Yahweh, becoming as He is and fully awakened to who we are, releasers of the Kingdom government of love and peace into all the cosmos.

Take this journey with me through my writings; taking time to reflect, be still and engage.

Peta Condon

Relationship

"Its all about relationship"

We are in a period of transition into a whole new era, a reformation and an awakening to the reality to the truth of who we truly are in Christ. There is a passionate people arising across the globe knowing its all about RELATIONSHIP and not religious systems, rules and traditions. A generation walking, living and flowing in the dance of life, participating in and embraced in the divine dance that is the Holy Trinity, a divine movement of love. Living out of relationship of ONENESS with Yahweh, one another and all of creation.

A moving, flowing, dynamic loving – a flowing in and releasing out.

"for in Him we live, and move, and exist".

Acts 17:28 (CJB)

Awakened to the awareness and knowing that we are continuously, seamlessly joined in oneness. Conscious that we are eternally present in Christ and He in us. Resting and rejoicing in the very truth that we are created inside the infinite love of the Trinity. Awakened to relationship, connection and ones true and full identity. Awakened to the knowing and experience that we are saturated with God, living in and from our union with the Divine. Allowing the flow of that union to move in us, with us and through us; the eternal life giving waters to the world and cosmos. We exist in relationship. A communion with the triune God. A realisation that you and the divine are one. The loving infinite power is in the divine dance of relationship which we are already included in and invited to participate in. We dance the dance!

Every person is created by God as unique and irreplaceable; one to whom God has transferred and communicated His divine image and likeness (essence) in relationship and oneness with Him. The image of God is at the core of our very being.

"Let us make humankind in our image, in the likeness of ourselves".

Gen 1:26 (CJB)

Our genesis is in the One from whom all things have come. Our deepest identity is "love", the image of God constituting the very nature of the core of our being. Christ came to reveal and awaken us back to this reality of whom we truly are and to the relationship that is central and deep within all things. Reconnected in the knowing of the glory, wonder, awe and beauty of our deepest identity.

TAKE a MOMENT to be SILENT
and REFLECT upon...

* the foundational nature of reality is relational, a constant connection and interplay with one another.

* all the power is at work in the Trinity in the loving relationship between them, and this infinite love is the divine dance itself.

* we, as members of His mystical body, partake in the divine nature of the Trinity.

* transformed people transforming the world and cosmos around us.

Oneness

"The heart of the Divine"

The glorious journey of our faith is a path of walking into the reality and the knowing that you and the Divine are one. Being transformed and letting go of any false beliefs of separation from God. Our union with God is already given to us. A moving from any mere belief or belonging systems to an actual inner experience of the Divine Presence, a true enlightenment and a consciousness of a total communion and oneness. A transformation and journey to a place of a describing of "there being no other"; not denying the distinction between us and God, who is infinite; but denying any separation.

The oneness from which we come, that we already have and the oneness that all long to experience is an invitation for all to fellowship at the banquet of divine love. One of the greatest dis-eases facing all of humanity is a profound sense of disconnection from God, our true self, others, the world and all of creation. Christ comes to awaken us and call us back to our true identity and the reality of our oneness, to the relationship that is deep with all of creation and the cosmos. A revolution is occurring in the midst of this changing era where there is an increasing awareness to the oneness of all the earth and an increasing consciousness that all of life is interwoven and therefore one part affects all.

"and one God, the Father of all, who rules over all, works through all and is in all"

Eph 4:6 (CJB)

All of creation being interrelated, coming out of the very "essence" and heart of Gods being, holds deep within it a harmony and a tune that is the song of our beginnings, a sound of oneness and interdependence that is at the very core and heart of all life. Every atom vibrating, resounding with the Eternal Presence, carrying within the sound of the sacred. Christ comes to reveal the memory of our deepest identity that we are made in the image of God and reconnecting us to the reality that humanity and all of creation emerge from the Heart of God .

The Age of reason or simply the Enlightenment of the C18th brought many great and ongoing changes in philosophy, politics, communications and science, yet it led people away from oneness and the interrelatedness of humanity and creation. The reformation of this new era is an awakening at the core of our being that the human family is one, that Christ may be seen and experienced in all of creation. This is an era of great transformation, and an invitation to walk awakened to the connection and oneness with The Divine and all of creation. Every place is an opportunity to find God and experience Him.

I invite us all to take a silent moment to reflect more deeply on the sacredness of all of humanity and creation.

* *That the human family is ONE, yet dynamic and diverse.*

* *May the eyes of our hearts be open to see the Christ in all of creation, its oneness and interrelatedness.*

* *That life is interwoven and that what we do and be to a part, we do and be to the whole.*

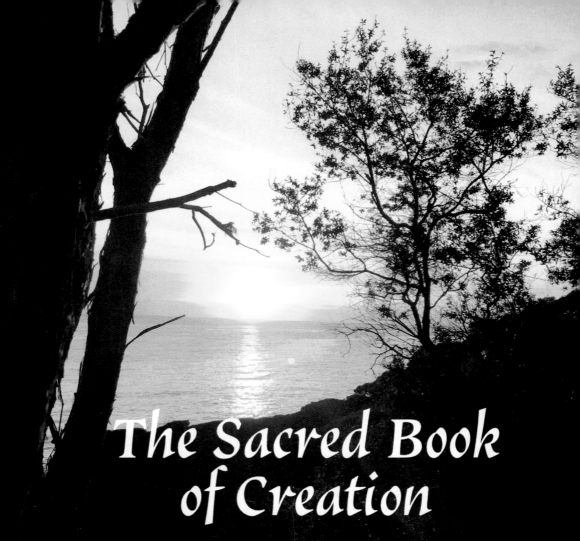

The Sacred Book
of Creation

> *"For ever since the creation of the universe his invisible qualities—both his eternal power and his divine nature—have been clearly seen, because they can be understood from what he has made"*
>
> *Rms 1:20 (CJB)*

There are two books written through which God speaks and reveals Himself to us, the book of scripture and the book of the vast universe of creation. All of the natural created world of the elements, all flora and fauna echo back the Divine voice that created them, continuously speaking and revealing to us the divine design and a revealing of Yahweh's heart. Creation is a living sacred text that we are invited to read and engage, a universal language through which God has spoken across all ages. The whole of the universe revealing and displaying a facet of the divine, a reflection and expression of God.

In the beginning, God created and called it good. The immense diversity, beauty, creativity, goodness, glory, light and love of God displayed in and through all of creation. We can hear within nature and all of creation the sound of the heartbeat of God. All created life, coming from and out of the womb of Gods being, carries within it the sounds of the sacred. We are not saying that nature is identical with divinity, but we are invited to view the sacred within all of life and be attentive to sound within that remembers its divine origin. Over the years especially in Western civilisation we have been educated out of hearing the sacred sounds in all of creation; yet creation is a place to perceive the eternal Word reflected in every plant, insect, birds, animals and humanity and awaits our engagement.

All of creation is holy, a living energy, forever expanding, intertwined and divinely interconnected throughout the whole cosmos; the seen and unseen related. Our infinite God is still actively involved in creating, continuing to bring forth divine purpose and redemption through Christ; and the sons of God are invited and predestined to partner in the eternal purpose of restoration. In Romans 8:19-24 Paul writes of the eager yearning in creation to be freed from its bondage to decay and its waiting for the revealing of the sons of God.

Yahweh has given dominion (custodianship) to humankind (Gen 1:26). Mankind being made in the image and likeness of God, who is love. May the heart of our spirituality carry a deep love for creation, and that we are part of bringing the redeeming work of Christ to a cosmos that God has said is good.

Take a moment to reflect and engage

* The cosmos is a living sacred text that we can learn to read and interpret.

* Listen for the sacred not away from life but deep within all that has life, expecting to meet God in all of creation.

* Rest awhile, listen to the birdsong or engage a glorious facet of the Divine in the still or mighty waves of the ocean. Allow the engagement to draw you through a portal into the heart of Yahweh's world.

* Part of this era of great change and awakening is the growing consciousness of our oneness with Yahweh and all of creation. How will we respond and disciple this knowing.

THE SONS of GOD and CREATION

"The creation waits eagerly for the sons of God to be revealed"

Rms 8:19 (CJB)

Christ came that we may be reconnected to the heart of Yahweh, to walk as Yeshua walked on earth and to have total access to the realms of God, with everything in His world available to me now. For those who believe and belong to Him are born from above and have been seated in heavenly places. The gates and door to the heavenly dimension have been open for all humanity, the veil has been torn.

The sons of God are awakening to the truth and essence of our original design, taking our place as sons of Yahweh and stepping into our true destiny and authority. As one mystical body, kings and priests of the most high God, presenting Christ in His fullness to all the cosmos, nations and creation; bringing heaven to earth. Sons (men and women) coming into agreement with heavens purposes, only doing what they see the Father doing. Tabernacles of the most High God, walking in fullness in this new era, responding to the call to come up here to the heavenly dimensions, taking our positions, living the reality of an ascended and transcendent life. Citizens of heaven, the unseen realm.

Christ's redeeming work includes all of creation. Yahweh has ordained the body of Christ, the ekklesia, to take their position to rule and reign, to bring together the divine and natural world. The sons of God, gates and doors (Ps 24), carriers and releasers of the overshadowing government of love and the light of His being. The kingdom of God displayed and released through us from our relationship and union with Yahweh. A lifestyle of living as a gateway, not one of endless works and efforts; abiding in rest and covenant, in relationship and union with Yahweh.

Abide and Be

then

We Become and Do

Sons burning with the fire of Yahweh, living in the transforming love of Yahweh and releasers of the power of that love upon the earth. Living in awe and wonder of Yahweh and becoming the sign and a wonder, a living epistle to the world around. Yahweh's heart is that we experience the fullness of His love for us and for all of creation, to walk in every spiritual blessing and engage all that has been opened for us through Christ. Relationship with all of Yahweh's world including the angelic, the seven spirits of the Lord, the cloud of witnesses and men in white linen, the living letters, partakers of and entering into and engaging His realms and mysteries. Standing in the counsel of The lord to be builders, releasers and restorers of Yahweh's design for all of creation.

Yahweh's purpose and plan is that the supernatural kingdom of God and His government be manifested upon the earth through His sons, who are submitted to His Kingship and Lordship. We are His voice, His breath, His frequency to frame and co-create, becoming part of the heavenly resonance that responds to the groan of creation.

Take a moment to reflect upon and respond

* to the call to come up higher, seeing humanity and all creation through Yahweh's heart.

* to live in the fullness and out of the truth that I am born from above, a citizen of heaven.

* to say yes to access of all of Yahweh's world now; the door is open.

Creation awaits for the sons of God to walk fully in the truth of who we are in Christ!

Yahweh's Restorative Love for creation

All of creation is a reflection of the outpouring of Yahweh and His love and His eternal desire is for relationship, connection and communion. The outflowing of the Divine Presence into a physical world, is a displaying and revealing of His goodness and glory. All creatures and matter carrying a divine energy, a reflection, a vibration and voice of the Divine. His breath and His DNA is in all of creation, all things created through Christ and for Him (Col 1:16).

Yahweh within all things yet also transcending all things - "There is only Christ. He is everything and He is in everything"

Col 3:11 (TJB)

Yahweh's heart is one of restoration of relationship, the finished work of the cross making a way for our reconnection and knowledge of our oneness with Yahweh and all of creation. This is Good news! The government of the Kingdom of God is one of love, an energetic powerful flow. Love entails relationship; relationship with Yahweh and His seen and unseen world. Yahweh's love is inclusive of all that He has created.

As we transition through and are in the midst of this new age, humanity is awakening to the oneness and interconnectiveness of all of creation. To care for and outwork our concerns and heart for the healing and restoration of all of creation, it entails relationship coming forth from the essence of love .

Restoration of Relationship!

Sons of God journeying in rest and in the reality and fullness of their identity, knowing the love and restoration of Yahweh are in turn the releasers of healing, alignment and restoration to creation. Sons have an impact and an influence on creation. Our presence, what emanates from our heart, our words, our sounds and frequencies, the breath of Yahweh released through us, our overshadowing government are and will be key in freeing creation from the bondage of decay. Sons understanding and positioning in our authority calling forth the original intent, design and purpose of all of creation. Sons as carriers of His light, power and love, entrusted to care for and bless the land and all of creation.

There is a sound, a tune, a hymn that fills the whole of creation. It is the reality of the experience of the Divine Presence. It is there whether we hear it or not, whether we stop to perceive its frequency and vibration. A communion of oneness and relationship with The Divine and the whole of creation and a communion with the Divine through the whole of creation. May we be fully awakened to the knowing of the Divine Presence at the heart of all creation. Fully awakened to a new birthing of an ancient sound of love and Yahweh's desire for relationship and the flow of oneness of and in all.

Take a moment for reflection

* What could I do to take time out to ponder and see the inherent beauty and goodness in all of creation.

* What would I perceive differently by embracing Christ's redeeming work for all of creation.

* What would relationship and restorative love look like in my journey with Yahweh.

ENCOUNTERS
and PORTALS

* ENGAGING THE DIVINE PRESENCE and
HEAVENLY REFLECTIONS within CREATION.

* CREATION AWAITS and RESPONDS to the
DIVINE PRESENCE within THE SONS of GOD.

Allow a picture, writing or
Encounter to be a gateway
into the wonder and depth of
Yahweh's Heart and World.

SILENCE

for to me the summit of worship is silent prayer

Sitting in silence upon a high majestic rock ledge that overlooks the sapphire blue ocean and the gentle waves that roll in upon the shore.

I recollect on the Presence of Christ within as I focus on His breath, breathing in and releasing out.

The gentle sound of the waters cause me to enter into a place of encountering the glorious waters of heaven and the flowing river of life.

Nourished, refreshed, and drawn deeper and deeper within, lost in union and meeting with my Beloved

The silence communicates its way of knowing, bringing me into the mysteries of Yahweh.

I listen with my heart and am drawn into realms and dimensions of my Fathers heavenly world.

The "space" of the natural world leading me to the very depth of my being with Him.

I have no agenda but just to "be", no goal or request, only to perceive His heart, hear His whispers and be abandoned to the oneness of our mystical union.

This place of stillness, trust, bliss, peace, union and love is itself the wonder and purpose of the journey, leaving all else behind.

Yet at times in the stillness I am led to a releasing and a flowing out that emanates the Kingdom and Presence within.

I actively chose to flow with that leading that comes from Yahweh.

From that silence I become the prayer, the gate through which His purposes are released.

A frequency, a word or decree, a sound, a tune, a quiet kingly roar, the fire of His love, His breath, and His light or translocated to a place of His desire and purpose.

All for the sake of His Kingdom alone.

Silence where we are taken by love to love Himself.
Affirmed of the oneness that belongs to all of life .

SILENT SERMONS

All of nature carries within a message that reflects the Divine creator

Nature has been revealing the glory and goodness of Yahweh from the beginning of created time.

There are many wondrous revealings in all of nature, in every creature and element within the cosmos.

Awakened to perceive the Divine Presence in all humanity, a flower, a blade of grass, a mountain or any one of His creatures – one's heart is open to receive Yahweh's transformational message of love and revelation.

All of the cosmos is overflowing with heaven and every bush aflame with God.

Sitting beneath a huge overshadowing tree full of dancing leaves and birdsong pouring forth from its canopy, I hear His voice re the healing of the nations and the praise of all of creation.

I engage the mighty powerful waves upon the seashore and it leads me to deeply ponder, in awe and wonder, the majesty and transcendence of Yahweh.

I watch an eagle soaring overhead in sheer delight riding the thermals and I am drawn higher and higher into heavenly dimensions and into the reality of the Divine dance.

Creation is sacred and there is wisdom pouring forth if we have both natural and spiritual eyes to see.

The tide ebbs out revealing, yet it always turns to flow back in – there is always a Divine flowing in and releasing out.

The larger set of waves rolling towards the shore come in three's – Divine wholeness, completion and perfection. A highlighting!!!!!!

A wallaby stops to engage a "son", there is no fear only presence

Look to perceive the beauty, look again to see the interrelationship of all of creation, yet look again to perceive and discern Yahweh's message in the now moment of time.

SOARING HIGHER
The way of the eagle
One of the four faces of God

Having a natural affinity with eagles, as my name means goldeneagle,
I have encountered and engaged many wondrous experiences with these
magnificent creatures.

Bodysurfing within a school of whiting, an eagle began to circle overhead.
The exhileration, oneness, awe and wonder I felt as I let out a cry of
recognition towards this majestic creature.

I could sense its "acknowledgment" as it released a sound and dropped its
talons to swoop on the nearby prey.

I felt a part of the experience, a vibration and frequency resonating in my very
being as the eagle dived with the clear sapphire waters dancing around me and
the waves surging forward.

Then a partner joined and then there were three eagles together delighting in
the movement and the thermals of the breeze that was blowing.

They soared up higher, searching for every new dimension and thermal,
dancing and frolicking in delight before the "sun".

NEVER disturbed by or RETALIATING to the boisterous, shrieking birds
below.

NO reaction, no displeasure to the tormentors, gossips or negativity
displayed. Just flying and soaring higher.

Singleminded in purpose in catching their prey.

Then returning to the REST, JOY and Fun and the DANCE with YAHWEH.

Creatures of the light.

Living life from the higher dimensions.

The call and reality for our lives.

THE WAY
of an EAGLE
CHRISTIAN

More than conquerors.
Free as the wind.

I climbed a glorious mountain in Wales to find a place of quiet and pondering as a deep longing for my homeland of Australia overwhelmed me.

I lay upon the grasses near the summit where I had encountered and engaged eagles before.

I called to the eagles and leaned into my union with Yahweh.

One appeared and circled overhead calling in return; I was swept up in bliss and the wonder to heavenly realms, engaging wisdom and receiving the reassurance of my King of kings Yahweh. My heart settled knowing where I was meant to be.

MORE than CONQUERORS in CHRIST JESUS.

Freedom is a call and a release that often arises deep within my spirit.

As I stand upon the physical mountain tops or when I soar in the spirit over the land and nations.

Also it comes upon me as a call to young eagle christians to soar to the mighty heights in Christ Jesus, to take their place to arise and see through eagle eyes from higher dimensions.

Walking on the Isle of Mull in Scotland, I watched as an eagle called to the others to soar high.

They responded soaring to such a height that they were no longer visible with the naked eye.

Eagles gracefully riding the thermals to a majestic and a different height and view.

SOARING aloft to the open skies.

COME up HIGHER and be FREE.

Sons of God SEEING as an eagle through the eyes of YAHWEH.

THE HEART of an EAGLE

Sitting beneath a huge eagle's nest on a river bank I watched as a huge male eagle left the nest.
He returned not long after presenting to his mate a flowering twig as a gift of love. A majestic, powerful and courageous creature displaying great tenderness and faithfulness.

I have watched in awe the eagle's courtship flight high above the earth, a truly beautiful sight as they soar high together, somersaulting like dancers often with wondrous love calls that seem to echo across the skies.
Eagles mate for life displaying great joy, delighting in one another on life's journey. A reflection for us in our divine dance of union with Yahweh.

Watching from a kayak as two parent eagles lead their young to the oyster reef for feeding.
The parents ascend to the highest point in the trees and watch protectively their young. Patiently perched high in authority and rest, as their young explore the feast available.
Suddenly one parent, single in purpose and having remarkable eyesight takes flight high above the lake and swoops upon a prey of fish. Acute vision from the highest place and returning to that position where it roosts and feeds.

The eagle a creature of great power, authority, courage and strength. Yet displaying and reflecting the qualities of rest, patience, being protective singleness of purpose and faithfulness.

Yahweh likens our call, path and heart to that of an eagle.
Come JOURNEY as an EAGLE, living our life to the fullness in Christ.

DIVINE FLOW

Bodysurfing the perfect yet gentle rolling waves I found myself amongst a massive school of salmon. It was an astounding sensation as I began to swim in unison with their movement and direction. As one with creation and her gentle leadings and flow.

It was not long before a magnificent pod of dolphins arrived for a feast of feeding. The dolphins were so near that I could almost touch them and experience their great delight.

The wonder as I watched some dolphins break away to catch the waves in sheer precision. I did the same and found myself eye to eye with a dolphin as we caught the same wave.

As I broke left in the wave the dolphin made the same turn, moving with the break and flow.

Sheer delight, exhilaration and joy that we both seemingly experienced.

We both returned to the deeper waters where the salmon feast continued.

The dolphins continued to feast yet also play and interact with myself in glorious harmony.

The engagement touched me at the core of my being and opened a realm of awe and wonder in the magnificence of a journey in the flow with The Divine. The oneness and connectiveness of creation engaging my inner being and expanding the knowing of the Divine love and ease of flow with Him.

Harmony, flow, feasting, sheer joy and bliss as we move in our union with Yahweh.

All of creation is a connection and revelation place of The Divine.

I look out from my oneness in Him to see oneness in all things.

RELEASE OUT
divine care for all of creation

Strolling along a water canal in Wales I was lost in awe and wonder of Our creator and the beauty of all the ducks, flowing waters and spingtime flowering water lilies. I looked ahead 50 meters or so becoming aware of many ducks vying for their perfect mate.

My heart began to release out care and protection towards the females.

With that one female took flight and came and sat at my feet quacking, looking for and receiving my love and care as I bent down beside her.

We stayed like that for quite some time with many passersby commenting on the experience being so beautiful and unique.

The next day I purposed to stroll along the same path and look for this precious creature. The next minute I saw and heard this female mullard duck take flight along the water toward me and come again to my feet.

I recognised her and this beautiful female duck recognised me.

This scene continued for some days to come .

I allowed and purposed to release from my heart the Presence and all that I carry in Christ as a son.

The Presence of the Spirit of God within us affects creations response to us.

Creation yearns and is waiting for the revealing of the sons of God. (Rms 8)

Our priestly role brings together the divine and natural world.

ENGAGING
THE WATERS

Sitting still and in quiet upon the rocks overlooking the ocean my heart turned towards Yahweh, I begin to worship, engage and sound out His name Yod-Heh-Vav-Heh (YHVH).
The waves rise up in sets of three joining with me in the praise and worship of Yahweh.
Let all the earth praise Yahweh (Ps 148:7).
I sense also the waters obeying the Presence within me and responding to my engagement.

Various dimensions of heaven continue to be accessed and activated as I sound out the name of YHVH. I continue to engage from the heights of the heavens moving between various realms that open.
A great rest and peace is in and upon my whole being.
I sense the sea and waters that are within every heavenly dimension as I move between them.
I find my soul and the waters of my physical body aligning to the frequency of the realms of heaven and Yahweh's Presence.

At times I know to release out what I perceive from these realms into the cosmos, over nations, towards creation and those that are in my heart.
At other times I know to continue to stay in deep rest and allow the resonance of His Presence and heaven to pervade my whole being.

All the time in adoration and awe and wonder of Yahweh and all of His world.

The physical waters of creation a place of engagement that activate personal and universal transformation.

LIVING WATERS
source of life

Great rest and peace embrace me as I sit engaging
the waters of the seas or the gentle flowing rivers.
There is a connection with the sounds and
vibrations deep within the waters that brings life
and a flow of rest within.
As an arcing of the life of the Divine within and the
life force that is within the waters.

I frolic and duck-dive through the waters and the
waves, immersed in the energies within the waters.
Embracing and experiencing all the new life that
is flowing in and around me both physically and
spiritually.
Totally drawn into and engaging with the heavenly
waters that are pouring forth in the next age that
we are transitioning into.

A new age is dawning that God has written within
the stars and the heavens, a cosmic gate has
opened. The majestic stars and constellations
pointing to the heavenly living waters that renew
and transform.

Regenerating, renewing and resetting
spiritual life and practice.
Moving from the age of Pisces, represented
by the fishes, to the age of Aquarius represented
by a man, a water bearer pouring water forth
from a vessel.

The water bearer is sometimes portrayed with wings, pointing to a heavenly, immortal and perfected man.

Water itself reminds us of the Holy Spirit who is called a river of living water.

Engage the living waters pouring forth, living from and in the spirit as spiritual life and its administration is moving forward into a next age.

TRIBES of ISRAEL
vision within a rock formation.

Travelling in glorious Israel with friends five years ago I had a remarkable encounter within the Negev desert. We had journeyed to this area to engage near where the desert fathers may have dwelt. We ascended the physical walls of the heart shaped crater to sit and be still in our alone space and to engage Yahweh's Presence and His realms and dimensions. The heart shape of the crater itself an expression of His love for this beautiful nation.

I was gazing out and all of a sudden I became aware of what appeared as twelve human figures depicted in the rock formations opposite from where I sat. I was in the spirit and enquired of The Lord whether He was desiring to show me something significant.

Yahweh spoke into my heart that I was observing a representation of the 12 tribes of Israel.

Immediately I recalled Rev 21 where the 12 tribe names are written upon the 12 gates of the City of God.

I asked if there was more to understand at this time, and I was instructed to search out the greater mystery as I went from there.

I began to search the scriptures while re-engaging the encounter and looking beyond the natural to the deeper revelation, I saw that these are gates to some of the heavenly dimensions opened through Christ for us to move through and explore.

It was here too where I went down into the craters waters as baptised into Yahweh's heart.

My encouragement to all is to:
Re-engage our encounters and explore more deeply the world of Yahweh opened for us.

Search out as kings the mysteries for the greater revealing.

Activate the wondrous revelations for our and our world's transformation.

Engagements & Activations

OUR GOD
is a consuming fire
(Hebrews 12:29)

In this new era of time Yahweh is looking for those He may fully rest and habitat within, a dwelling place. Those that walk in the fullness of who they are as mature sons in their union in Christ. Transitioning from anointing to glory, having stepped beyond the torn veil and caught up to God and His throne. An overcoming body reformed to the administration and realities of The Most Holy Place, a company of priests and kings of the order of Melchizedek, ruling and reigning with Christ Jesus and entangled in the fiery passionate love of the trinity.

The sound and voice that has been released upon the earth in this era, has the vibration and resonance of awakening and reformation. It is a sound that is shaking and changing everything. It carries a frequency and a call to the mystical body of Christ to sit at Christ Jesus feet, to come under the government of God, consumed with The Fathers love and heart, only releasing what The Father ordains.

This light of reformation is and will be carried by those who have willingly stood before the sea of glass saying yes to total transparency.

During one of my engagements over ten years ago in the realms of heaven, I found myself in this place. An overwhelming encounter that seemed to last only a short period time yet was hours in earthly dimension of time. I had not looked for the engagement but had been in worship with another with our hearts as priests turned to The Lord crying:

Holy Holy Holy
is the Lord God, the Almighty.

Standing in this place was a engagement with Yeshua, the cloud of witnesses and the angelic beings; various questions were asked of me in my heart that would lead me forward and higher along the path that is before us. Transparency and vulnerability enfolded me. Two angels were assigned to me at this time that would accompany me on my journey.

Yahweh is looking for those He can trust, those that have emerged out of the ashes of the sanctification process of Yahweh where those things that are not of Him have been shaken, burnt in the fire of His all consuming love leading us forth towards perfection. Living in the abandoned place of awe and holiness, the reverential fear of the Lord. Those that have said yes to the fiery coal to their lips carried by the seraphim from the altar, able to eat the scroll given – able to say use me, flow through me, I am yours fully entwined in relationship, totally surrendered to your ways and purposes. Hearts full of worship that minister first unto Yahweh, having moved away from all systems and religion to relationship, kingdom and glory.

Fire transforms, changes the structure or pattern in order that a reframed form comes forth. Fire cleanses, burns out the debris, allows the light to shine through, the soil nourished and growth coming forth that is stronger and healthier. Fire burns, ignites, tames and transforms.

Yahweh's all consuming love and fire transforms.

I write these words only months after devasting fires impacted the south east coast of Australia including the region in which I live. It was a period of time in which I witnessed much suffering; yet I can already see within the land restoration, regeneration and a recreating and a redesign. My own personal journey during the time bought refining, a deeper place of rest in Christ and an outworking of increased authority as a son of God. The most amazing passionate and all consuming love of God includes death and resurrection with the cycle of life always including death, new life, renewal and restoration.

I had opportunity to leave the region for safer areas inland as I, too was evacuated three times yet I knew that it was the Fathers heart that I stay. In obedience and faith I did, knowing there is always a counting of the cost to walk in higher authority. Holding in my heart and overshadowing the region in my authority as a son of God and to be here with my community, I knew to be Yahweh's purposes and heart. Yes I could have done that in the spirit but Yahweh asked me to stay and trust the journey, staying in the fires physically and spiritually.

Ruling and reigning as a son of God and taking and remaining in my position seated in heavenly places in Christ Jesus, connected in the spirit with others was part of my journey during this season of fire. There were varying administrations from heaven to release, always seeking to perceive Yahweh's heart and ways. Always ungirding every release is and was the government of love of Yahweh and my love for my region, her peoples and my nation.

Some of the various activations, administrations and outworkings
were :-

* to set a boundary line in which the physical fire could come
  no closer.

* roaring as a king in the face of a fire as I engaged in the four
  faces of Yahweh. This roar was accompanied by a oracle
  decree that came to pass.

* in the spirit with others breathing forth the breathe of God
  to abate the fires.

* engaging the elements such as the winds and the rains, all
  with significant change.

* engaging with the angelic assigned in that time.

* living from and in the spirit turning in and out to release as

I share and record the above humbly but in a place of knowing who we are in Christ and how Christ came to show us who we are.

I desire that we would arise as mature sons in this hour, the TIME is now as we reframe the future ahead in this changing world and new era.

Mature sons fully aligned to Yahweh's heart, submitting fully to His all loving all consuming fire.

Will we say yes to His all loving all consuming fire transforming us.

Will we say yes to the hour we have entered into, the new era we are transitioning to.

Will we walk as mature sons in the heavenlies and upon the earth,

ANCIENT PATHS

within a new era

> *"Yahweh says this:*
> *Put yourselves on the ways of long ago*
> *enquire about the ancient paths.*
> *which was the good way?*
> *Take it then, and you shall find rest"*
> *Jeremiah 6:16 (TJB)*

There is a sound being released in this time that is calling us forth to engage and walk these ancient paths. Drawing us to seek and search out, stand and look beyond and walk in a way that leads to deep rest. These are the ways of truth and mercy, justice, righteousness, holiness, oneness, the everlasting way, the way of the tree of life, light and love. The ancient ones walked these ways and through eternal dimensions, knowing heaven as their abode and source. Accompanied on the journey with the seven spirits of The Lord and the angelic, engaging wisdom, courage and humility. The way is narrow and sometimes rugged yet surrounded by glorious green pastures and blessings, it leads to life and the place of deep rest and peace. These paths are an ancient way yet forever new, when one feels that they have come to the destination, the sound calls and the way draws and leads forth again. The next age that we have entered into calls us to these ancient paths where the good way is; it is a way that is least trodden yet leads to the heart of the Father. Our source and rest and joy is in the heart of our King, our creator , our Father , Yahweh. Abiding, enfolded, entangled in the source of all life Himself.

A path into the heart of the Father

The foundation of the ancient ways lead us forth into our future, our destinies engaged from and in the heart of The Father and from a place of rest. As we engage in the restoration of the ancient paths new mantles are released, the angelic assigned and our personal being resonates with our call in deepening awareness of our oneness with Him and with others and creation. Restored and redeemed to the reality of the truth of who we truly are. Taking our position on the ancient path that is enthroned at The Father's right hand. Engaging the houses of heaven as the doors open to receive revelation to walk in authority as mature sons upon the earth and in the cosmos.

Creation will begin to respond as we align to our sonship and heavenly authority

Connected and positioned in spiritual families, walking as a living dynamic organism, the body of Christ. It is not about denominationalism or organisation, nor structures or programs but about relationship. Relationship with Yahweh to know Him and to experience the multifaceted mysteries awaiting to be encountered. Relationship, with those we are being called to walk with, carrying the vibration of the Fathers heart. Relationships that have been forged in the fires of sanctification, the fire of divine love. Where honor has been established and a true valuing of one another. Overcomers, called out unto the Lord, a remnant separated out to be a seed deposit to the nations. Positioned to be gateways of heaven to earth.

Will we say yes to relationship and our Fathers business, the ancient and good way

My heritage is Irish and I love when I walk on the land there; there is a sense of coming home in many respects and I experience the sound and frequency of the land and the walk of the Celtic saints who have gone before. I have had many encounters on the land in Ireland that have led to me engaging in the spirit with the saints of old. I see, hear, feel their walk upon the ancient paths and have been deeply impacted how they walked and tasted of the power of the age to come. Last time I was in Ireland I revisited places that both Columba and Patrick walked and I had powerful encounters where I was caught up to perceive their watching and cheering us on in this era to the greater glory. Witnesses in the great cloud on every side of us, not able to reach perfection except with us. (Hebs 11,12)

My own voice and resonance is one as if sent from this very land of Ireland, a land of ancients and Celtic saints.

Allow oneself to perceive the richness and resonance of our heritage.

Every nation has a sound and a destiny. Every land a purpose. The earth itself a rhythm and a cry. I love Australia, the nation and land of my birth and as I walk the land and also overshadow it in the spirit, I always have cause to feel deeply its call and sound. To look beyond, to heavens blueprint and mandate. To hear the call of the land of this glorious country and the heart cry of our first nations people and those born or migrated here after settlement. Our land is an ancient land with a deep unique sound. As the voices arise of those that abide on the ancient path of dwelling in the heart of the Father and resonating with His love for the nation and her peoples, there are sounds, frequencies and purpose and destiny to be released and called forth. Many voices rich in diversity and oneness, flowing in the spirit, functioning in the Kingdom government of love, bringing restoration to the land.

*May we see the richness in all
our peoples in our lands.*

*May we see in the spirit the
destiny, beauty, sound and
uniqueness of our lands.*

*May we join with others
in the spirit to call forth
from Yahweh's heart our
land's original purpose and
restoration.*

TRANSFORMATIONAL
not TRANSACTIONAL

The journey of our faith is one of transformation, moving one deeper and deeper into the reality of our communion with Yahweh, one another and all of creation. Maturing and transformational faith invite us to participate fully in the divine dance of the trinity, knowing that it is in the relationship of the three persons of the trinity where the flow and power exist, that God is the dance itself. It moves us away from either/or thinking and leads us to feast upon the tree of life and live in the experience of the depth of Yahweh's love. He is love and the source from which we come and in whose image we are created. Our deepest identity is love. This journey of personal enlightenment, communion with The Divine and all of Gods creation is not a set of religious transactions and moral behaviours nor just a reading of scriptural verses to gain more knowledge. It is an encounter and engagement with the living Lord, abiding in His love and living as love, which is a powerful light to transform all of creation and the cosmos around us.

Let us truly be Heavens reflections.
Awakened to "I am love".

Mature faith is simply a matter of becoming who we already are, living in the flow, life-based and love-centred more than intellectual beliefs or knowledge centred. Its about who I am, its all about the journey not an end destination. It's about the flow of the trinity towards, in and through me to all around. The kingdom of God emanating from me from my union with God, which has been freely given. The deepest mysteries and truths cannot be obtained via pure head belief, but through experience, engagement, encounter and a different way of processing which is the contemplative practice. These engagements involve the whole essence of our being, our heart, mind and body leading us to deep transformation and truth.

"since it is in Him that we live,
and move and exist" Acts 17:28

Awareness of The Christ mystery and a knowing in one's heart of the truth of Christ in and through all things in creation totally rewires us at a cellular level and allows one to see in a totally new way. Our faith journey is experienced along a totally different path and moves us away from just conforming to a doctrine or dogma, theory or a pursuit of and desire for more knowledge. Relationship is the core of reality, and we experience the cosmos at this relational level, when we are mirroring and reflecting our Trinitarian God.

Contemplative practices are life transforming and a glorious way that allows and assists us to see through a totally different frame. A processing of reality that was a common practice for early Christianity and for the mystics of old. These practices are not dry rituals but a dynamic and heart awakening experience to the Presence within and the action of God's presence in our lives. It opens a new way of knowing as the contemplative mind sees things and reality in its wholeness not just parts. The prayers of stillness and silence, centering prayers, walking meditations, ecstatic dance, chanting, YHVH prayer through each breath, scripture meditation are some of the forms that are ways to engage the contemplative life. Contemplation is an awareness of fully being with God, an opening of our heart, mind and body to God who is beyond any thoughts or words. The inner stillness through engagement also shows us who we are, not only as a son of God flowing in our union with The Divine but also a revealing of who have uniquely been made to be, our beautiful heavenly blueprint with our heart desires and yearnings.

Transformed people transform the world around them and beyond as we engage, overshadow regions, our nation and lands and nations. What pours forth from our hearts in love touches, changes and restores. The path of transformation at times can feel rocky, challenging, dismantling and even chaotic but walking with and in the Divine love is a journey that leads through to resurrection life. I myself as a trailblazer and an edge-dweller by nature still can find change challenging at times but when one's heart and mind is stilled by Yahweh's divine love and rest, this path often least travelled leads through to glorious freedom and peace and fullness. Silence and contemplative practice in whatever way is right for us leads us along a path that shows us there is no separation from secular and sacred, awakens us to our true identity, and a discovery that we let go of any need to judge, allows us see and know our reality as one with The Divine.

> *"Our unveiled gaze receives and reflects the brightness of God until we are gradually turned into the image that we reflect".*
> *2Cor3:18 (TJB)*

> *We become what we behold.*

This is the era and time of awakening to transfiguration. Transformational faith journeying in our oneness and union with Christ. The Kingdom era of restoration, transitioning and knowing the times and seasons as the cosmic celestial clock moves towards and under the influence of the mazzaroth house of Aquarius. A celebration of The Father's plan and calender. The water bearer pouring fresh living waters out of heaven; this water bearer is often portrayed with wings depicting the heavenly and immortal perfected man. Transfigured to great majestic beauty and light, elevated and ruling and reigning from heavenly dimensions. At the transfiguration Jesus' change in appearance gave an glimpse of who He truly is and also what we can fully share in. By becoming man, Christ reconciled humanity to God and revealed and awakened the reality of who we truly are and what we participate in, The Divine nature.

TRANSFORMATIONAL faith journey,
a path that is not about external requirements
and transactions but a total actual change
of heart and mind, an interior change
and a living from the inside out.

Ponder and position oneself to live in awe and
wonder and entirely within His Presence.

We live in the times of transfiguration
and the transcendent lifestyle.

NEW
BEGINNINGS
A NEW
BIRTHING

There is a most amazing transformational awakening and re-reformation along with a birthing coming forth in this time of the Kingdom era, and it has the sound and frequency of new beginnings and restoration. A new birthing occurring within christendom,our own personal lives, relationships, creation, communities and nations . A call has gone out to cross over, move forward with hearts and minds fixed on things above in this God appointed time and season. Our Divine Lord with His heart of redemption and restoration, calling forth the sons to walk fully in their Kingdom authority and identity, manifesting and bringing heaven to earth.

Just as a child comes forth from a mothers womb after the waters are broken and released, new life bursts forth affecting all around and there begins an exciting new journey. We are entering into such times as we move forward under and in the plan of Our heavenly Father; the seasons and times are written in the heavens , the prophetic star signs known in scripture as the Mazzaroth (Job 38:32), the 12 houses or constellations. As reflected and displayed in the heavenlies we are transitioning from the age of Pisces (the fish) to the age of Aquarius (water bearer).

Fresh waters pouring forth affecting everyone and everything.

With this transition comes a shift and a change, a new expression of Christ's mystical body with a new outworking and expression of spirituality. This expression is looking to become visible within us and amongst us today . Spiritual expansion and rebirth, built upon relationship, our oneness with Yahweh and creation and upon the ancient foundations and pathways.

A birthing of mature revealed sonship upon the earth, living from heavenly realms, engaging the greater outworkings of the Kingdom of God, administrating and creating what they perceive from The Fathers heart, releasing His oracles and words framing a new order. The illuminated constellation opposite Aquarius is Leo, the lion, the king. Our Lord is King and He is King of kings.

God has the most amazing plan; will we listen to the sound, abide in the reality of our union with Him and be co creators as He leads, walking and functioning in our heavenly priestly and kingly roles.

This is the time of oneness, networking, connections, participation, science and faith working together bringing forth new innovations and technologies. New medical ways and methods of healing that will benefit and bless humanity. New words and language that will frame and unlock what is to come. An arcing with others in the spirit, connected in heaven to frame and bring forth the new. Families both natural and spiritual, unity and connection are at the heart and core of this reforming and awakening journey. The breaking down, shaking, and shattering of dogmas and wrong foundations as ancient foundations are renewed and restored. Fresh living waters gushing forth.

Let us align to the relational connections Yahweh is revealing to us individually and corporately in this time.

Awakened to seeing the sacred unity of all of life and all things coming forth from the heart of God's being. All of creation is holy with a living energy that comes forth from the very depths of God himself. A harmony, a flow, resonance between Christ and all of the cosmos. A time of increased Christ consciousness in and through all things. Every place an opportunity to find and experience God. Christ comes to remind us of the memory of who we are, to wake us up, to see the relationship deep within all things and to perceive the sound of the "Beginning " that is carried within all. As we perceive more deeply and are awakened, and entwine in the dance of life with the Trinity, a new lifegiving and expanded love flows through us to our communities and nations. The deeper waters of knowing our oneness with Christ and a drawing closer in our entanglement with The Divine, draws us nearer to the heart of one another. At the core of every soul is the longing for union, a natural God given yearning. John, the beloved, not only saw from the heights and heavens perspective symbolised as an eagle but he leant upon the chest of Yeshua and heard his heartbeat. A birthing or rebirthing happening in the hearts of humanity today, a spirituality emerging where oneness and connection are part of its foundation.

May we be those that look into the hearts of one another, perceive the deep cry for love, union and oneness and respond as Yahweh leads.

May we look with the eyes of our heart and look and engage beyond.

Perceive and be releasers of light, love and hope and Christ to our families and nations.

As with any new birth, we need to feed, protect and nuture those revelations and knowings that we are receiving. I sit and re-engage the new things I perceive ,pondering them in my heart as Mary did. I allow the dreams, visions, encounters and revelations to flow and re-flow in and through my heart in meditation, knowing that Yahweh will reveal and a deeper knowing will come, as He has promised to teach us all things. I engage the spirit of truth and search out the deeper mystery in relationship with Yahweh, with His word being an anchor for my spirit and soul. I invite heaven to have fellowship with me in my ponderings, and I'm content to know that Yahweh has a perfect path, destiny and timing for me that was established from the beginning of time, a not desiring of another's journey. I explore with those I am in relationship with, those I trust in the spirit, knowing too that they will see from another dimension and a greater picture is formed and wisdom and understanding gained.

In all new things and revelations I engage
wisdom and the counsel of God in rest.

Always seeking His heart and His ways.

Nuturing all that He is bringing
till there's a knowing within.

The TIME is here.

New beginnings, a new birthing.

The manifest sons of God arising.

Oneness and connection in our hearts.

Called to shift and shape not
in haste but as Yahweh leads.

Build and restore in love and light.

Bring to creation what we have received .

Called to create from the heart of Yahweh.

Creations awaits for the sons to be revealed.

SONS ARISE
Now is the time, creation awaits

WE are living in unprecedented times as we look around with our natural eyes and see the shakings and great change across the whole of our world. Yet at the same instance we know that we are in a kairos moment of time as we transition into the next age of the Kingdom. Prepared and called forth for such a time as this, sons not tethered to the chaos around, living the transcendent lifestyle, our souls awakened to our deiform in communion and union with The Most High God. Allowing the eternal flow to move through us, with us and in us. The salt of the earth, arising letting our light shine forth, carriers of His government of peace and love, bringing forth Kingdom reformation upon the earth and in all the cosmos. Overcomers manifesting upon the earth what we see in the heavenly realms.

> ## *"Of the greatness of his government and peace there will be no end". Is 9:7 NIV*

The dynamic administrations of governing, ruling and reigning from the realms of heaven through our oneness with the Trinity are for our engagement and deepening revelation, abiding as heaven dwellers. Encountering the mysteries and hidden truths is by the light of experience not by just reading or having information of what another has engaged. We receive progressive revelation as we continue to engage Yahweh's world and as we walk the ancient paths through eternal dimensions as the ancients such as Enoch and Noah walked. Engaging and walking with wisdom, aligning to all of Yahweh's ways and His heart, having responded to the call and sound to cross over beyond the veil, take up our full inheritance and embrace our heavenly position, to come up higher. With this new order and new era, creation will begin to shift and restore as the revealed sons walk in the fullness of their new creation reality, emanating all that we are. Ruling and reigning is not about dominating but the bringing of His love, life, peace and Yahweh's design and framing up what is to be. Creation recognises the source of Kingdom government.

> *"The whole of creation is eagerly waiting for God to reveal His sons".* Rms 8.19 (TJB)

Governing and releasing from that place of REST. Come up here and sit down, sonship coming from relationship and intimacy, knowing our identity, and entering rest. Sons of light transitioning from anointing to glory. Walking in meekness and true humility, prepared to entwine in the reality of their oneness and union with Yahweh, engage heaven, truly transition from the old to the new with no foot in the old camp. Called out to bear the image of Christ in all the earth and cosmos; overcomers, separated out as a seed to and for the nations having let go of all Babylonian thinking. A gateway of heaven to earth, oracle voices from Yahweh's heart to creation.

"TRULY HEAVENS REFLECTIONS"

We are the shields of the earth. Arcing with others in the spirit as light to be protectors and providers, caring and loving others and creation. One spirit with The lord, capacity to be where He is and others in the mystical body of Christ. Meeting in the spirit, beyond the dimension of internet and phone, with others in heavenly dimensions in our oneness leads to a very powerful engagement, exploration and outworking of exploring Yahweh's heart, His ways and His release for kingdom purposes. In my journey in this hour the meeting and connecting with others in Christ in heavenly dimensions often from other parts of the globe has a rest, a purity, an engagement that is bringing Kingdom fruit; we are positioned, standing and moving in Persona Christi in our full authority as sons. Conscious communion with the divine and others, desiring what Yahweh desires, resting in what He ordains, becoming the prayer and a release from a flow that is not necessarily words. A frequency, a breath, His fire, light, a lightning rod as His power moves through, a sound, a resonance vibrating with what the Godhead is doing.

Translocation and transportation our inheritance to outwork heavens purposes.

Some 12 years ago I had an encounter as I spent time away in the glorious snowy mountains of my country. During the night I was awakened to see written across the skies outside 5 Hebrew letters and at the time I did not fully understand their meaning or why this had occurred. Revelation unfolded to me as I have re-engaged and desired to know the meaning and purpose of such an encounter for myself and the body of Christ and His kingdom. The 22 living letters of the hebrew alphabet, the alef-beis, are a continuing source of creation and also there for our reflection and inspiration with such deep meaning and mystery contained within each letter. They are foundations of our earthly and spiritual existence, as God utilised these letters to form heaven and earth. Many scholars and mystics extol these living letters as the manifestation, a code or blueprint for the cosmos. Each letter just like every person, has an unique purpose in the divine plan. Created by Yahweh, each letter is alive and has a "voice" so that as we engage with them they have mysteries and truths to be revealed.

Mysteries to be searched out by us as priests and kings, revealing and reflecting Yahweh's world.

A few years ago while I was travelling and sharing into some hubs in UK, a powerful word was ushered into my spirit like a lightening bolt. It was an answer for me to give and release at particular times. "I'm here about my Fathers business" and it is so powerful and relevant in this hour. I cannot help but emphasise how the journey before us is about the Fathers business, fully based around relationship and not task. Yes everyone's journey is different and at a different pace but it is all before us as we continue to step forward in the spirits leading; always willing to let go of what we walked in before and what was good to embrace what Yahweh is doing now. I have felt and heard the glorious blessing of my Father to me ... "this is one of my beloved sons".

Yes it is time for the sons to arise,

Walking in the fullness of the reality of who we are, Creation waits !!!!!!!

Take some time to ponder and reflect and activate what Yahweh is speaking to your heart or showing you in His heavenly dimensions.

Align and reset to the sound coming forth from Yahweh's heart.

The time is NOW!

Final
thoughts

RESET and
RESONATE
with the life and light
and love of The Kingdom

As I draw near to the conclusion of sharing my writings I come back around to where we started—it is all about relationship, our union and oneness with Yahweh and with all of creation. All Kingdom government comes out of relationship, intimacy, rest, and Yahweh's Lordship and Kingship in my world whether it be family, community and regions, nations and the cosmos. Relationship in our union with Yahweh, walking as a revealed and manifest son upon the earth, going about our Fathers business, living the transcendent lifestyle. Living entwined in the Divine nature, a pillar in the sanctuary of our God (Rev 3:12), no more in and out. Living from rest, having left aside first principles (Hebs 6) and a coming up to perfection. Jesus Christ as our pattern, the first born of many sons (Rms 8:29). Caught up to see what the Father is doing, co-working and co-creating with Him as He builds a whole new heaven and earth.

We are created to be a reflection of His glory!

Journeying as transfigured sons!

There is a heavenly sound and song that resonates and aligns bringing earths' beat and rhythm back to its design. As we get in tune like a tuning fork with YHVH, we release the sound and frequency that is governmental and the earth agrees and resonates. We as sons are the restoration of all things. We have been "educated out", particularly in Western culture, of hearing and listening to the sacred sounds of creation, yet it carries within itself that sacred sound and resonance. Creatures know the rhythm of the earth, they have not forgotten of which they are part. To hear the heartbeat and energies of all of creation that come from and are filled with God, radically changes how we view and interrelate with one another and all of the cosmos. We are free to move in relationship. We are free to turn into creations sound, align ourselves to the sounds we hear coming forth in heaven, tune to our sound and release.

When I sit in that silent position in heavenly realms, in heart to heart communication,

I engage the name of YHWH and the physical world responds. The waves dance up, the winds

arise and the song of nature engages me.

There is a faithful hidden generation coming forth, walking as sons with overshadowing power, full of and emanating love, light beings co creating and restoring with Yahweh. Walking with a pure heart and in true humility, knowing who we are and going about our Fathers business. Knowing that what we think and carry in our hearts has a voice and creates; understanding that His breath, His word, His frequency and sound impacts all of creation. A holy generation, separated out unto God, our hearts totally aligned with Yahweh's heart, no agenda of our own, having responded to the banquet of Divine love and where "being" is more important than doing. To know Him and Him alone.

Priests presenting Yahweh to creation.

Emanating light to all around.

Bringing together the divine and created world.

Reflecting heaven upon earth.

Living from the source of the tree of life, engaging our relationship, the dance and flow. Dining and feasting and drawing life from the inside out. Our hearts, mind and body open to God's living Presence. Having moved away from mere belief or a knowing about and belonging systems to an actual living dynamic inner experience . Freedom to walk in the fullness of our identity and inheritance, having being invited into the reality of our oneness with Him. He is the way, the truth and the life. Celebrating life and full of joy, a gift and engagement that comes from knowing God and outflows into every area of our lives and the world around. Creation awaits for the sons to arise, we are the travelling ark of the covenant and His tabernacle.

Creation displays and is
Heavens reflections.

May we perceive Christ in all
of creation.

May we constantly behold
Him becoming a living
radiant reflection of heaven
upon earth.

Peta Condon born and raised in beautiful
Sydney Australia , now living on the glorious
South coast of NSW.

Passionate to see others walk in the fullness
and freedom of their unique design and
oneness with Yahweh and all of creation. One
of her profound loves of life is engaging and
enjoying nature in all its forms.

Seraph Creative

Heaven's Heart for Earth

Seraph Creative is a collective of artists, writers, theologians &
illustrators who desire to see the body of Christ grow into full
maturity, walking in their inheritance as Sons Of God on the
Earth.

Sign up to our newsletter to know about the release of the next
book in the series, as well as other exciting releases.

Visit our website :
www.seraphcreative.org

Made in the USA
Monee, IL
21 April 2021